Times of Used to Be

Denvil Mullins

Cover Art and Design by David Dixon

The Overmountain Press
JOHNSON CITY, TENNESSEE

*To Connie, Wesley, Denny, and Stephanie,
my family,
for their love and support*

Introduction

Humor, according to Webster's dictionary, is something that is—or is designated to be—comical or amusing.

This book of short stories is an attempt to go back in time to an era when the people in Southwest Virginia were trying to dig out from the aftermath of the Great Depression. Times were hard during that era, but life was more satisfying and healthier than it is today. The people of Wise, Dickenson, and Russell Counties, to name a few, took time from their daily grind in their efforts to dig out a living in the coal mines and their steep hillside farms to visit one another. Or sometimes they sat around on a Sunday afternoon—after church—to spin a few yarns and laugh. Going to the store for a week's supply of groceries was often turned into a family outing. The entire day could be spent talking with friends, trading knives, and trading horses and mules. There was no rush of traffic or maddening crowds to get lost in; no shopping centers, only the general store; no drug dealers to contend with. They were just an easygoing, laid-back people taking time to enjoy life.

Southwest Virginia has produced a number of successful authors and storytellers. The area is well-known for its mother lode of material to write about—from history to humor. Humor is the subject of my endeavor. I hope that everyone who reads this book gets at least one chuckle. To make someone laugh makes my day. If I were deprived of the right to laugh and cause others to laugh, I would surely shrivel up and die.

Not all people have the opportunity to express themselves through the medium of the press. I feel very fortunate for this chance to reach out to the reader with this book about a wonderful people and a memorable time. Growing up in a large family has left me with a million memories that I hope to write about and share with others.

I grew up in a home with loving parents and a houseful of brothers and sisters, enjoying the good times and conquering the hard times, forming a family bond that even time cannot break. That is a great blessing. I suppose that one of my greatest blessings is the ability to look at the funny side of life, write about it, and share it with others.

Table of Contents

Glossary

This is a list of words that I have used in my book of short stories. I hope they will give you a better understanding of the book when you read it.

again', prep—against
banty, noun—small breed of chicken
barred-rock, noun—a speckled chicken
bench-legged feist, noun—a small dog with bowed front legs
blowing-viper, noun—hog-nosed snake
brud, noun—brother
chickey-diddle, noun—a baby chicken
crack-a-loo, noun—a game of pitching coins at a crack in the floor
dander, noun—dandruff
dauncy, adj—sickly; puny
domer, noun—a speckled chicken
domernecker, noun—a speckled rooster
drap, noun—a drop
feznit, noun—a pheasant
fit, verb—fought; battled
founder, verb—to upset the stomach by eating too much
froe, noun—a tool for riving wood roofing shakes
gimp, verb—to limp around showing pain
gnyammed, verb—chewed food noisily with the mouth open
haint, noun—a haunt or ghost
head chuckings, noun—the act of rubbing the head with the knuckles
medder, noun—meadow
nary, adj—none; not one; not any
'nozers, noun—bulldozers
ort, verb—ought
Paw, noun—grandpa
playing, verb—square dancing
quiled, verb—coiled
ragged out, verb—worn out; tired

salit, noun—salad greens

scrouge, verb—to crowd; sqeeze; press

scrouge, noun—room (I use it as a noun at times)

shag, verb—to move deliberately

shagging around with, verb—hanging out with

slurp, verb—to suck food into the mouth with a noisy gurgling sound

sluve, verb—to laze around; to be sloven

spar-bird, noun—sparrow

stob, verb—to stab

stob, noun—a wooden stake for pitching horseshoes

stropping, verb—a spanking with a razor strop

well-off, adj—odd acting; crazy

The One-Round Mule

Olden Seedy rode Old Packer, his high-stepping mule, down the rutted, muddy road. The constant flow of traffic up and down the narrow road that ran almost parallel with the rushing little stream known as Less-Than-Perfect Creek was almost impassible.

Old Packer had been on the "Happy Hollow Ranch" much too long to suit Olden. That is what Olden called his farm, his small lump of acreage on the side of Much-of-a-Mountain, a range of sharp-pointed peaks that stretched so high toward the sun that there was a small crack at its base, giving evidence that the mountain range had strained its moorings from its anchor on the sandstone base which covered the thick vein of fossil fuel—coal.

Olden Seedy was a horse trader from "way back." He enjoyed the art of trade so well that he often lost his underdrawers in the deals. He did not want anyone to think that he would not trade for a horse. If the nag could breathe, that was good enough for Olden, for he would get it to walk—somehow. If he could get it up off its haunches and encourage it to take a few steps, that was sufficient enough to say that it would put out its last ounce of energy to work.

With several of his trades, the last ounce of energy was just that. The next step for Olden had been, in each case like that, to dig a hole and roll the expired nag into it.

Old Packer ranked much higher than the aforementioned condition. He was a very young mule, maybe twenty years old. Mules are hard to put into an age category, since they are so cantankerous about being ordered around.

A mule is one animal that cannot be trusted. Most of the time it will work like a little "mule angel," just waiting for the first sign that its master has grown lax and trusts it, and then, Wham!—a size two or three mule shoe upside the head. A kicking mule can rake up a big pile of dander and make the owner aware of the fact that he still cannot trust his mule.

"Step lively, Ol' Packer," Olden coaxed his already struggling mule.

"All the good trades will already be made before you get me to the trade grounds."

Old Packer continued his constant pace along the muddy road, slipping occasionally as his well-worn calks failed to grip the clay roadbed. The old gray mule never said a word as he gained his composure after almost falling head-first into the mud. If only he could talk he would give that fussy load on his back a word or two to mull over. His mule vocabulary was as good as his owner's, maybe better, but all that he could do was yodel a discouraging bray to the world as he slopped along in the mud, and that he did.

"Cut out that devilish yodeling, Ol' Packer," Olden Seedy said, ramming his heels into the sides of the braying mule.

The mule ceased his yammering with a snort, slinging mule slobber and snot all over the road.

"They ain't no good-looking she-mules to be found along this forlorn strip of woods," Olden said. "Get your mind off romance and back on business."

Cars and trucks passed the rider as he made his way to the mouth of Less-Than-Perfect Creek, the little stream running through Happy Hollow.

The people who lived in Happy Hollow were so happy that they had to write away for a dose of sadness, just to break the monotony of laughing all the time. Olden would have written letters every day, but he knew the mail was so slow that he would be out of the mood to be sad before the letter could reach its destination, wherever that was.

"Hey there, March," Olden yelled as an old, dilapidated truck passed the equestrian and pulled onto the hardtop road which made travel much faster for the automobiles, but not a whit faster for fleet-footed Old Packer.

Old Packer was just as fast in the mud. He had one pace, and it never changed. It was the same the year-round.

"Do you know who that was, Ol' Packer?" Olden asked his plodding mule. But before he received an answer from his transportation, he continued his conversation. "That was March Cornfield, the windiest human being that ever paced this green earth. I've seen him blow up an onion-sack and bust it. You know him. You probably didn't get a good look at him with your blinders riding so close to your eyes. He's the feller that come to buy my bull, Ol' Bawler. I had him help me put that shoe back on that you lost off your hind foot. Now, is it coming back to you? Well, you'll probably 'member it by the time we get to the trade grounds."

There was no answer from the mule, except a long bray of disgust that echoed about the steep, rocky slopes. The clickity-click of shod hooves carried through the stillness as Old Packer stepped onto the paved road.

"I really hate to trade you, Ol' Packer, but I need a little boot to carry me over till next payday, and if things work out just right, I might just trade back for you," Olden explained to his mule.

Several cars passed, the drivers blowing their horns as they recognized Olden Seedy riding happily along the highway.

"Are you going to burn somebody today?" one fellow called in a friendly, laughing manner.

"No, boy!" Olden responded. "This is the best mule that ever filled a collar." His message never reached the driver of the departing automobile. "You don't know the difference between a good mule and a Jersey cow!" he shouted.

* * * *

A bustling sound came from a crowd in a huge bottom along Bass Creek River as Olden reined his sweating mule through the open gate which gave access to the meadow.

Old Packer brayed long and loud as he picked up his pace from a creep to a crawl with the anticipation of meeting some animals with whom he could carry on a sensible conversation. On the way to the trade grounds, he could not get Olden Seedy to understand his efforts to chat. He had been ignored completely, except for the few times that his master had yelled at him for just trying to make small talk.

"You're too late for the festivities, Olden," Lake Poole called, a big grin splitting his homely face as he greeted his life-long friend.

"My goodness, if it ain't a sight!" Olden rejoined as he greeted the man. "I wouldn't have thought of you for a fifty-dollar bill, and here I have to look you right in your ugly face. How are you doing?"

"I don't believe that you've seen yourself in a looking glass lately," Lake Poole replied, laughing loudly. "If you had, you wouldn't be so ready to blackguard me. I'm doing tol'able. How are you?"

"Fair, I guess." Olden said as he slid from the saddle, gingerly touching the ground due to the stiffness and tingling in his legs. He straightened up slowly and shook hands with the group of men.

"We have a big crowd today, but no traders, 'cept Col Modut standing over there by his rack of ribs," Lake Poole said, pointing to an emaciated fellow in faded but clean overalls. "He's been wanting to swap that mule for a big pony. He wants something that don't eat too much, and from the looks of that skeletal figure by his side, it ain't been eating too much, either. Your mule ain't too big. He'll probably trade for it. Trade with him, Olden. You have lots of corn left over from the winter, and there's plenty pasture on Less-Than-Perfect Creek."

"I don't know," Olden said as he tethered his mule to a fence post. "I hate to part with Ol' Packer. He's a good working mule. I don't think I could find one as good, even if I traded every day. I just came in to see what mules are selling for."

"Nobody's trading or selling today," Lake informed his friend and confidant.

"It's just ten o'clock," Olden said, looking at his watch. "Some of the swappers ain't even got out of the bed yet."

"I don't think there'll be any more traders today," Col Modut said, ambling over to greet his friend.

"I told my wife, Punkin, that the horse-trading business was gradually fading away, and I think that it has *already* faded away," Olden stated, shaking hands with Col Modut, greeting him with a strong grip.

"I guess we're the only traders here today," Col said, motioning for Olden to take a look at his mount tied to the fence, where it chewed contentedly on the scrubby sassafras sprouts in the fencerow.

"What kind of trade do you have stored under that battered straw hat?" Olden asked placidly. "I hope you don't have any cheating thoughts running through your mind."

"I would never cheat a friend as dear to me as you are, Olden," Col vowed, untying the lead-rope from the fence and turning the mule around for a thorough inspection. He knew that Olden would give the bony mule an absolute scrutiny. He handed the bridle reins to his friend and said, "Take a jaunt down to the other end of the field and back. See just what a good brute you can trade for."

"That won't be necessary," Olden said as he opened the mule's green-colored mouth to check his age. "Old as the hills!" he exclaimed, letting the mule's mouth plop back together. Green mule slobber sprayed from the floppy lips, striking Olden's chest, discoloring the front of his faded chambray shirt.

"He ain't much over twenty," Col stated.

"I would say he's *very much* over twenty," Olden replied.

"He ain't any older than that antique that you rode in on. I heard his bones creaking as he came over that rise," Col said, pointing toward a little knoll beyond the fence.

Everyone turned toward the crest where Col pointed his grubby finger.

"That's just a little far-fetched, old pal," Olden replied. "Well, let's talk a little trade. Your mule is on the gaunt side, maybe from hard riding and no feed and water this morning, but he's still on the thin side, though. Tell me the truth. Is he a good worker?"

"I tell you for an honest-to-goodness fact, he's a one-round mule," Col said, seizing the moment to put that disclosure into the trade talks.

"I know better than that," Olden chuckled. "You can see that he's just skin and bones, plus a little fat here and there, mostly around the knees. But that don't matter a whit to me. I can fatten him up in a few weeks. He'll look like a barrel busting at its hoops when you lay eyes on him again."

"I doubt that, but if you don't want to trade with me, that's all right," Col said as he bantered Olden into a trading fever. "I want you to know that he's a one-round mule."

"I can look at him and tell that you have already told one big whopper about your asset," Olden declared, leading the mule around the meadow, checking for limps and swollen joints. Finding none, he felt that there was an animal that could be fed and straightened out. "How much boot will you hand out in a swap?" he asked, then waited for an answer.

Col gripped his protruding chin with his left hand and mused and mulled over the question.

"Are you going to wait till dark before you give me an answer, Col?" Olden queried impatiently.

"Man, give me some time," Col stated, still gripping his chin in his left hand as he walked over to Old Packer. He rubbed his right hand down the mule's back, stopping occasionally to rub a fly-bite on the tough skin, checking to see if it was a fly larva imbedded in the mule. He knew that Old Packer was a much better mule than his Old Barney, but he couldn't let Olden Seedy see his eyes bulging at the specimen of mule he was caressing. The animal had well-formed legs and shoulders, without any scars to indicate past accidents. "Is he a good worker?" he finally asked, breaking the silence.

"I ain't had him long enough to know just how good he is. But my boy, Dee-Bo, says that he's the best brute that I've ever traded for," Olden reported. "You know how young boys are. They'll fall in love with any horse or mule that they can handle easy-like without any danger of getting kicked to the spring and back. I hated to take him away from Dee-Bo this morning. He wanted to plow the corn out and get it hoed, but I told him that I had to come to trade day. I've never missed a trade day in over forty years. I believe he was crying when I rode out of sight. He had his head in his hands, and his body was shaking like a heaving dog. I hated to leave him crying like that, but I couldn't help it. Maybe he'll like your mule just as well."

"I ain't particularly fond of your mule," Col said as he prepared for a long and drawn-out set-to of bargaining.

"What do you mean by 'not fond' of him? Anybody would be fond of that animal, if he could just stay with him long enough to learn his temperament," Olden responded, getting into his trading spirit. "My boy, Dee-Bo, has been farming with him, and he's just twelve, going on thirteen. Now, if a kid can handle a mule like mine, you would have to be willing to do some swapping with lots of boot."

"I'm not planning on giving boot, Olden Seedy," Col asserted, continuing his perusal of the sleek body of Old Packer.

Olden had done very little looking at the specimen of mule at the end of the lead-rope clutched securely in his big hand. He held that rope as if he knew there would be a swap made, and he was ready to lead his prize away. He could almost tell that he would be getting a bargain in the rack of ribs standing patiently at the end of the lead-rope.

A couple of weeks of grazing the nourishing orchard grass and plenty of corn and sweet feed would put the pounds on that skeleton. A real mule would be reborn in that bag of bones. But Olden was more interested in the boot money than the mule.

"This mule is in fair shape, so I guess I'll take around fifty dollars and trade with you, Olden," Col said as he slowly raised to a standing position after a complete inspection of the mule's feet.

"Fifty dollars to boot on that bag of bones!" Olden exclaimed. You're gonna have to give me boot, man."

"Well, just trying," Col laughed, seeing the surprise on Olden's face. "Give me credit for trying. I really don't want to trade my mule. I just rode down here to see what was trading."

"I don't have to trade mine, and that's a certainty, but for the sake of trading, I'm prepared to take some boot and trade with you," Olden offered, scuffing his foot in the meadow grass.

"Just how much to boot are you asking for this broke-down fleabag?" Col asked, continuing to check the mule's physical condition.

"I'll take a hundred dollars and trade with you," Olden bartered.

"Take off one of the zeros and it's a deal," Col Modut offered, reaching for his wallet. The leather billfold, worn and out of shape, strained against two rubber bands used to hold it together, preventing its contents from falling out.

"My mule is worth more than that bone yard and ten measly dollars!" Olden exclaimed, looking at his friend, surprised.

"I can't see that much to boot in a mule trade. Don't kid yourself, Olden," Col returned, rejecting the offer. He continued to rub his hands over the sleek body of Old Packer.

"Ol' Packer is worth a good hundred and fifty dollars as he stands," Olden Seedy remarked. "I'm allowing you fifty dollars for that skeleton covered with a thin layer of hair. You couldn't make good leather out of a hide that thin."

"I'll give you ten dollars and trade with you," Col proposed. "If you don't want to trade on those terms, I'm not interested." He reached for the lead-rope clutched tightly in Olden Seedy's strong hand.

"How about fifty?" Olden asked hopefully.

"Ten," was Col's stern reply.

"How about twenty-five?" Olden anted, continuing to lower the boot necessary to make a good swap.

"Ten," Col said, sticking to his offer. He pulled at the lead-rope, still clutched tightly in Olden's hand. "Let me have my mule so I can be going on down the road toward home. I see that you don't really want to trade."

"Won't you consider more to boot than a mere ten dollars? My mule is worth more than that," Olden lamented.

"Ten is my final offer," Col replied, lifting his left foot to the stirrup in an effort to mount the mule. He held the bulging wallet in his left hand. He felt sure that Olden would give in and take his final offer.

"I'll take it," Olden finally agreed, looking at the stuffed wallet. He knew that Col Modut had enough money to dicker long and hard over the boot that he would be willing to pay.

"You sure drive a hard trading bargain," Col laughed, chiding Olden Seedy.

"You're the one that drives the hard bargain," Olden grumbled.

"Remember that he's a one-round mule," Col advised his trading adversary for the hundredth time, smiling sheepishly at Olden, happy knowing that he had bested Olden in a trade.

"He's more like one *scrawny* mule," Olden snapped.

The transaction was climaxed with the swapping of lead-ropes, and the two men mounted their newly acquired assets, if one could call the rack of ribs that Olden had traded for an asset.

* * * *

"How do you like him?" Olden asked his son, Dee-Bo, as the boy hitched the trace chains to the singletree on the one-horse John Deere turning plow.

"I don't think much of the bony thing," Dee-Bo replied in disgust as he lifted the lines and clucked to his power source. "He's nothing to compare to Ol' Packer. That was the best mule that we have ever had. I was getting used to working him, and he's the only one that I have had long enough to get used to. Why is it that you allus trade the best animals and come home with trash like this? If the wind blows real hard, it'll blow this poor excuse for a mule away, and me with it if I get caught up in these check lines. What's his name?"

"His name's Ol' Barney, and don't worry about this mule, boy. I believe he's going to be the best working mule that I've ever traded for." Olden assured his son.

"I sure hope so," Dee-Bo quipped. "I would like for you to trade for a mule that I could keep for more than a day or two. I don't like to have to try to break a new one to work ever' week."

Old Barney began his trek to the opposite end of the big field. His body bunched into a knot as he strained against his collar, causing the plow to cut into the soft ground, covered with fallen cornstalks from the previous year's crop. The dirt was rolled over by the plowshare, forming a dark furrow that followed the mule through the field.

Dee-Bo humped along at an unsteady pace, trying his best to keep up with the straining mule. He was small and had to try to manhandle the plow.

At the opposite end of the field, Old Barney turned and started back, with Dee-Bo grunting and humping to keep up. On the return trip the mule stepped up his gait, yanking the plow out of the ground, and was almost at a run when he reached the end of the furrow. He did not stop when Dee-Bo gave him the command.

"Whoa, Ol' Barney!" Dee-Bo shouted as he pulled back on the check lines and dug his feet into the soft dirt in the plowed furrow. "Whoa, you hard-headed mule!"

Old Barney headed for the barn, with plow, boy, and Olden Seedy in hot pursuit. The closer he got to the barn, the faster he went. The little boy hanging onto the plow handles was almost at a flag-waving position—his feet straight out in the air. The mule finally stopped as he entered the hallway of the barn.

Dee-Bo's feet hit the ground with a thud. "Dad, that is the stubbornest mule that I have ever seen," the boy replied. "Help me get him back to the field."

After another round through the field, the mule headed for the barn once more, and try as they might, the two workers were unable to stop him.

"One-round mule," Olden said as he slowly realized what Col Modut had tried to tell him before the culmination of the trade. "Son, I cheated myself on that swap. I should have seen that there was something wrong about that trade. After one round through the field, he's ready to go to the barn. Col Modut was trying to tell me that Ol' Barney would do that. I'll have to swap him off, Dee-Bo."

"I gladly agree with you, Dad," Dee-Bo sighed, relieved to know that he would not have to contend with that cantankerous mule. "You'll have to swap him off."

"Come on, one-round mule," Olden Seedy said, unhitching Old Barney from the idle plow. "Looks like me and you'll have to go on another trading spree."

A Peach Orchard and Thirty-Five Cents

Dock Peeves turned the bottle, which was either half-full or half-empty, around and around on the oilcloth-covered table. He squinted at the liquid as it sloshed about in its glass confinement. Air bubbles formed in the peach brandy and floated to the top where they burst. The bottle and its contents remained still for a moment. Dock tried to focus on the contents of the bottle. From his view of the brandy, he had double the amount he had at his last inspection. He blinked his eyes to be sure that he was looking at it correctly. "I thought I had drunk more than that," he mumbled to himself as he made a thorough scrutiny of the bottle.

The dilated pupils were dark blots in a sea of red blood vessels running through the whites of his watery eyes.

"Ain't it a caution how some people make it through this troubled world?" he said, slurring his drunken words. "Some people have a great lot in life while I have to scratch for a living."

"That bottle is holding you back, Dock," Pet, his kind and faithful wife, said as she cleared the breakfast dishes from the table. "I know for a fact that your rheumatiz is bothering you something awful, and you need the brandy to help limber you up, but you look like you're already about ragged out."

"I'm not ragged out—just relaxed," Dock replied as he continued to slosh the liquid around in the bottle and watch it come to a heady-bead.

"I think you should get out and find some work 'stead of trying to make it on this lump of dirt stuck in the hillside," Pet complained, nagging her spouse. "Look at Ed Tydings—he has that good job working for the state highway. Why don't you get out and hire on with him. You two could make a good team together."

"Pet, I'm going to amount to something without having to do a lot of hard work," Dock rejoined, still sloshing the brandy in the bottle. He uncorked the decanter and drank a swig from it, making the neck of the bottle gurgle as the liquid went from the container to his mouth. He smacked his lips to get the extent of the flavor, while he made a grimacing face due to the burning sensation from the strong beverage flowing to his stomach.

"If you can't stand the taste of it, why don't you throw it out and drink something that tastes good?" Pet suggested. "I think a man is dumb to drink stuff that hurts going down, and hurts coming back up as he upchucks his gizzard out. It just doesn't make good sense to me for you to punish yourself just to feel good."

"It ain't the taste that a man looks for," Dock responded as he popped the cork back into the bottle and began to slosh it around once more. "It's the good feelings he gets."

"Grunting, puking, and gaging sure sound like a lot of good feelings to me," Pet replied sarcastically. "You manage to get a swig of liquor or brandy whether or not you get something for the table."

"We have never starved, and our presence here is evidence of the fact," Dock grumbled, vigorously sloshing the brandy. His coordination was slowly deserting him. The next slosh he made, with a gyrating motion of his arm, sent the bottle for a spin across the floor. It struck the cast-iron range in the corner of the room with enough momentum to crush the glass container to smithereens, permitting the fluid to flow over the floor. It gave off a strong, eye-smarting essence. "Bust take it!" Dock shouted, trying to stand, hoping to be able to save some of the brandy. "I lost the last drap I had. Now, I'll have to do without, 'cause I don't have enough dollars and cents to buy more."

"Good!" Pet beamed with delight, looking at the spreading liquid. A smile replaced a frown that had been on her face most of the morning. "I don't know how many dollars you have, but I do know that you don't have any sense. I'll mop it up. You get to bed and try to sleep off the effects of your foolishness. Maybe you'll wake up with a different outlook on your plight and learn a lesson from this."

"I'm going to amount to something," Dock mumbled drunkenly, searching for a way to the bedroom by leaning against the wall and feeling his way along. "I'm going to buy me a peach orchard and make my own brandy and sell it."

"The way you've been guzzling it this morning, I doubt if you'll ever let any age enough to sell," Pet replied, putting emphasis into the mopping instead of her words. Her arms worked like pistons in the revved-up engine of a race car.

Dock fell across the bed with a grunting sigh, trying to position himself comfortably on the extra-high four-poster bed. As he grunted and clawed for the covers, he lost complete control and fell head-first on the floor behind the bed. His feet stood straight up in the air as the weight of his body slowly pressed against his lowered head, resting on the hard floor. "Bust take it all to blusterations!" he shouted, trying unsuccessfully to push his weight back upon the bed. That was a wasted effort due to his alcohol-relaxed muscles. "Come here and help me, Pet," he screamed at the top of his lungs.

The little lady worked diligently and laboriously as she helped her wobbly husband back to a normal position. "Now, take your clothes off and settle in and get some rest. You ought to feel better directly, and then I want you to go to the store and get this list of groceries for me," she said, vigorously waving a penciled list before his befuddled eyes.

"Let me count my finances before we make a commitment that big," Dock intoned, taking a very thin, well-worn wallet from his hip pocket.

"Commitment or no commitment, we have to have these items for survival, or scratch with the chickens," Pet replied haughtily.

Dock opened the wallet as carefully as he would open a box with a rattlesnake in it. He fingered the money, hunching forward and then swerving backward as he tried to focus on the moving bills. After several attempts to count the money, he stopped and looked at his wife. "Pet, Hon, when did they start making 'leven-doller bills?" he asked. "I have one of the suckers right here, sure as snuff." He began to count once more—very slowly. "Aw shucks! I've counted this wad of bills a dozen times or more and I get a different number ever' time. Would you help me count it, Pet?" He continued to peer into the thin billfold.

"Here, let me have it," Pet inflected, jerking the wallet from her husband's trembling hand. "You drunk nut! You don't have but two dollars in here. How could you count up to fourteen dollars? Lie back down and sleep this fit off. You can go to the store later on if you feel like it. We can make out till then. Now get back to bed."

"Don't bother me, woman. I'm going 'cause I'm plum' out of brandy," Dock spat, trying to rise to a sitting position on the soft bed.

"You don't need that brandy, Dock," Pet snapped, trying to help sober her spouse. "If you're set on going to the store, be sure to get some coffee, lard, salt, and vinegar. I'm going to have to kraut the cabbages and pickle the cucumbers that are going to waste, 'cause of not having any salt and vinegar."

"If I get all that list of stuff, I won't have anything left over for luxuries," Dock protested. "You took all my money, 'cept two one-dollar bills. I know I had more than that. I counted around an even fourteen or fifteen dollars awhile ago. I saw several big bills in there. I know that you've never took from me, and I hope you don't have any ideas of starting now, 'cause I don't have much to spare for groceries."

"If you're set on going to the store today, get on out down the road, and hustle along, for it'll be almost completely dark before you can make it to Big Onion Gap and back," Pet growled, realizing there was no use to arguing with Dock when he was drinking. She tried to help the heavy man rise from his prone position on the side of the bed.

"Give me my britches and shoes, woman," Dock ordered, searching the room for his boots and trousers.

"You've got them on, you drunk nut," Pet retorted, shaking her head in disgust. "You're worse than a child. You can't dress yourself. You can't even walk. You can't think nary bit over the level of a child's mentality. I don't see why I stay with you. It has to be pity 'cause I'm so disgusted with you that I wonder if it was love that plopped us in this situation or total pity. Sometimes I feel like up and leaving you, but if I did, you would probably just shrivel up and blow away. When the brandy dried up in you, you would be like a fishworm in the hot sun. The Lord might frown upon me if I left you in such a helpless state. Lord forgive me for thinking such thoughts."

"Get my shoes and pants so I can get to the store and get the groceries for you," Dock muttered, still searching the room for the elusive clothing.

"You've got them on, Dock," Pet replied, shaking her head.

"Oh, yeah," Dock babbled drunkenly, rubbing his rough hands over his pants and shirt. "Bust take it if I don't!"

"I'll be back in just a jiffy, Dock," Pet said, leaving the room. As she went through the door, Dock fell backward, landing on the bed, sound asleep.

Dock awoke with no idea of the time or how long he had been out of the race with the world. He wasn't very sleepy, but he had a headache that could stifle a stubborn mule. "Hush your grouching, woman. Can't you see that your loud voice is hurting my sensitive head?" he yelled. "Get my shoes and britches and let me get on to the store at Big Onion Gap." When he got no response from his beloved wife, he realized that he must have been dreaming of her continuous nagging.

"Where is that shopping list that's big enough to choke a starving goat?" he asked as he entered the kitchen, where the little woman was in a race with the dust. She was trying to annihilate it before it even had a chance to land on the shining appliances.

"Here it is," Pet said, taking the list from her apron pocket. She handed it to Dock and watched as he crumpled it up and crammed it into his pocket. She was sure that would be the last time her husband would see the neatly-penciled shopping list. "Don't forget my things," she called after the departing man.

The words fell on deaf ears, for there was no reply from Dock as he stumbled through the gate onto the highway and started in the direction of Big Onion Gap.

Several cars passed as Dock plodded along the dusty road—not looking up to see who was at the controls of the vehicles as they raced along, stirring up a blinding dust. He merely stuck up his left thumb, without even turning in the road to see who had passed him by.

Sometime later, and several miles farther down the pike, a rattletrap car braked to a stop, its worn shoes rubbing against the brake drums, crying out in its pain and effort to stop the big eight-cylinder-powered car.

"Hey, Pops! Where are you going in such a dither?" a voice called from the interior of the rusted-out sedan. "Looks like you moved your left foot there about ten minutes ago. Don't get in such a hurry. We might not be able to keep pace with you, with you going that fast."

"Go on about your business, you smart aleck," Dock spoke, without turning around to look at the stopped car. He did not recognize the voice, and he wasn't interested in getting acquainted with it.

"Hey, I'm not trying to be a smart aleck, man," the voice said as it responded to Dock's reply. "I'm S. A. Storey from over in Coal Bank Holler. I'm on my way up to Big Onion Gap. I was just wondering if you wanted a ride over there with me and my buddy, Lyle Ott. You look like you're about tuckered out, and it's a far piece over to Big Onion Gap. Hop in and let me make things easier for you."

The stranger opened the rear door to allow Dock to get in. "Hop in and rest your tired feet while I wheel you over the road. I didn't catch your name during all that conversation you were bellering out as you humped along in all the dust."

"I'm Dock Peeves from up Milk Gap Holler. I'm real pleased to know you, and pleased that you stopped for me to ride with you," Dock informed his new acquaintance, settling back on the soft, greasy seat.

The odor of oil, grease, cigarette smoke, and gasoline filled the rear half of the car. The air from the open windows wasn't enough to rid the compartment of the unpleasant stench.

"You look like you're about ragged out this evening, Mr. Peeves," S. A. Storey said, peering at his passenger.

"I don't feel so good right now," Dock complained, rubbing his face with his big hands. "You'll have to forgive me for being so short with you. I had a rough morning."

"That's okay. Just try to make yourself real comfortable in that pile of softness," S. A. Storey invited, giving Dock a complete scrutiny. He winked at Lyle Ott. "Where are you going?" he inquired.

"I'm going up to Big Onion Gap to get me something to sort of settle my nerves, Dock replied, rubbing his face and eyes with shaking hands. "My wife gave me a store list for some groceries and faddle like that, but I don't think I'm going to spend my money to buy her wants 'stead of my needs."

"That's just like a woman, wanting things when she knows good and well that a man has to have his needs first," S. A. Storey agreed with Dock, warming up to the conversation. "I guess you told her straight out that you would decide whether or not her wants would outweigh your needs, didn't you?"

"I hope I did. I really don't know," Dock said as he looked ahead, after a good facial massage. "She was clucking around about something as I left. I told her, 'All right!' to whatever she said. I didn't understand her. I didn't want to argue with her, with me feeling so bad and all."

"I'd say that she got the gist of your message and tucked her tail and ran back into the house," Lyle Ott chuckled, daring to enter the conversation.

"I guess," Dock replied. He continued rub his haggard face.

"Do you work at a public job or just make a scratch living on your farm around here somewhere," S. A. Storey asked as he began an at-random inquiry, trying to ascertain an inkling of the man's monetary worth, since it was Monday and the man wasn't working that day.

"I live on a small farm up in Milk Gap Holler, just to have a quiet neighborhood," Dock responded, looking up from the intent act of rubbing his face. His rough hands in contact with a light stubble of beard sounded like sandpaper on a rough board. "I have a peach orchard up on Blue Domer Creek. They should be getting to a ripe turn in a few days. I want them to be real ripe before I start to harvest them. I'm going to make them into peach brandy. Did you ever try a swig of fresh peach brandy? Nothing can compare to it!"

"How big of an orchard do you have, man?" Lyle Ott asked, his interest rising several notches.

"I've got fifty acres of prime trees, loaded to the breaking point," Dock lied as he bragged of his imaginary asset. "I'm going to stop at the store and get something to revive me a little, then I'm going on up to check on the crop. After I see how things are up there on Blue Domer Creek, I'm going over to Coaley Creek to buy a crop from Dash Cornfield. He has about fifty acres, give or take a tree or two. I should have a full force of pickers and makers on the payroll by the middle of next week. I have most of my work force picked out—the same folks who helped me last year. Dash Cornfield's boys are good workers—don't drink—and I can depend on them."

"Me and Lyle Ott might be interested in helping you. We're out of work right now," S. A. Storey said as he became more interested in the gentleman in the backseat of the car. "We're between jobs right now, and peach picking ain't out of our vocation very much. We're miners by trade, but we can trade the mines for peaches, can't we, my friend?"

"Sure," Lyle Ott agreed. "Work is work, and I'm not too good to stoop to peach picking. I can use the money, and I won't be too choosy how I get it."

"We'll stop with you at the store," S. A. Storey offered, goosing the accelerator on the old car to send it on a frog-hopping lurch over the rough road. "You shouldn't ought to walk all the way over to Coaley Creek. We'll go with you and look over the work that we'll have to do. We can be better prepared to grab and grunt head-on with that peach crop."

"You fellers won't have to do that," Dock said. "Just taking me to the store is enough for you to do all at once, since you don't know me very well. Now, if I was a close-stuck friend to you, I could understand you wanting to take me over there. That's a far piece out of your way, and the price of gas is a long way above cheap."

"That's no bother to us. We'll get money for gas when we pick your peaches. That ain't what matters the most, though. With you carrying money to pay for that crop of peaches, we don't want you to fall into the wrong hands," S. A. Storey spoke, pretending concern. "Are you going to pay cash for the peaches, or run your brandy and then pay off for the peaches?"

"I'm carrying all the cash I have. It'll be sufficient to pay my way through to the end of the run," Dock bragged. The man was telling the truth about carrying all the money he had. He was only two dollars from being broke, though.

"We'll go with you to protect our interest in this," S. A. Storey volunteered, winking at Lyle Ott. "We want to work. My kids can use some new clothes, and I owe payments on this car."

When the trio reached Big Onion Gap, S. A. Storey drove the sedan up as close to the store porch as he could without banging the bumper against the building.

Dock Peeves got out of the car and lumbered awkwardly toward the door. Inside, he asked for a plug of tobacco and a pint of brandy, hoping the clerk had some on hand. He said that Pet needed the brandy to make some cough syrup.

The clerk, Luke Watters, left the building by way of a rear door to get the bootleg brandy from a secret hiding place behind the store. He said when he returned, "That will be a dollar and sixty-five cents. Cash or charge?"

"I've got cash, my friend," Dock replied proudly.

"Get a pay day?" Luke asked as he placed the plug of tobacco in the bag with the bottle.

"I guess so," Dock said, smiling timidly.

Luke Watters counted out thirty-five cents in change and handed it to his customer. "Have a good one," he said as he watched Dock amble toward the door.

"I was just talking to Luke Watters, and he says that Dash Cornfield just went by on his way to Bass Creek," Dock informed his new-made friends. "I guess I'll head back to the house. I can see him later."

"Jump in. We'll take you home," S. A Storey offered. He eyed the bag clutched tightly in Dock's hand. "Got anything to drink in that paper poke?" he asked, his mouth watering with the anticipation of having a snort.

"A pint of peach brandy," Dock replied. His face lit up with a thistle-eating grin as he realized a way out of his dilemma. "If you boys can find a secluded spot, we can share this brandy."

Dock hoped there would be enough brandy to get the two fellows high enough to forget his bragging about going to buy a peach orchard. He did not want them to find out that he had no peach crop to harvest.

S. A. Storey drove the big sedan into the woods by way of a logging road. He got out of the car, opened the door for Dock, and motioned for the older man to get out.

As Dock rose to his feet, his new friend pointed to a flat rock beside the road and said, "Have a seat Mr. Peeves. Let's have a drink and some good conversation. We can work out an agreement to our working conditions and daily wages. We're willing to work for less than we ordinarily get when we are on the payroll at the mines, but we'll have to get enough pay to make our efforts worthwhile. You can understand that, I'm sure."

"Sure, I can see your point," Dock agreed. He stood up, letting the cramps slowly leave his body. All at once the sun went down for him as Lyle Ott hit him on the head with a hefty piece of galvanized pipe.

"We should go ahead and kill him. You should have hit him just a little bit harder. It would have got him out of his misery," S. A. Storey said as he looked at the prone body lying on the ground. He searched the man's pockets and found an empty billfold, a crumpled up grocery list, a Case pocketknife with one handle missing, and thirty-five cents.

A trickle of blood ran from a cut on the back of the unconscious man's head.

"He lied to us about having enough money to buy a peach crop," Lyle Ott complained as he saw the coins in his friend's hand. "A peach orchard and thirty-five cents. I don't believe it! A man who'd lie like that don't deserve to live."

Dock Peeves heard those last words as he regained consciousness. He lay on the ground in a lifeless heap, hoping that his two assailants would think that he had shipped out when the galvanized pipe connected with the back of his head.

"What will we do with him?" Lyle Ott asked, checking for a pulse on the silent body. "I believe he's still alive. Let's get out of here and be on our way."

"I think we ought to kill him for lying to us," S. A. Storey threatened, nudging the still body with his foot.

Dock was afraid to even breathe. He prayed silently as he feared the dreaded end.

"Let's take the brandy and leave him here," S. A. Storey said, rising and opening the car door. "He'll be all right, but I still say that you should have hit him just a little harder for lying. He'll never report this to the authorities. He would be too embarrassed to let people know that he's a broke blowhard."

"How about the thirty-five cents?" Lyle Ott asked.

"We'll take it. It's enough to buy a couple gallons of gas. Let's go," S. A. Story suggested, dropping the money into his shirt pocket. He got into the car, waited for his friend to get in, and drove away, leaving Dock Peeves lying where he had fallen when Lyle Ott thwacked him on the head.

* * * *

"I tell you, Pet," Dock explained to his excited wife, "I was afraid they would finish the job. I 'peared like I was a dead duck. That was all that saved me. I'm gonna go down to the highway office and apply for some type of work tomorrow. Did you say that's where Ed Tydings is working? If I hadn't 'peared to be dead, I would have been a goner."

"Why did you tell them that you were a rich orchard owner?" Pet asked as she cleaned the lump on Dock's head.

"I don't know, Pet. I guess that I just wanted to make people think I am worth something," Dock whined. "But you can rest assured that my days in a peach orchard are over, since I no longer need the brandy."

"What did they look like, and what kind of car were they driving?" Pet asked her husband. "We could get the law to chase them down and prosecute them, and that way you could get even with them and get your thirty-five cents back."

"I don't ever want to see them again, Hon. I went through a miracle-cure—a drying-out process," Dock groaned. "I almost met my Maker," he continued. "And I was still in the throes of a hangover. You can rest assured that my days of imagining great wealth from a peach orchard are over."

Dock grimaced as the caring hands of his wife rubbed over the sensitive lump on his head.

Shoot Again, Judge L.

"Is Tester Seedy in here?" Dump Cornfield asked as he looked at the crowd in the old 1937 DeSoto. "I can't take any more kids along to watch after and wipe their proboscises."

"You'd better stop that talking ugly!" Gillis stormed at Dump in his little-boy authority.

"I didn't say anything ugly, Gillis," Dump laughed boisterously. "I was talking about kids' noses, not anything distasteful."

"Oh, I thought you were talking ugly," Gillis replied, settling himself on the seat once more.

"You should have brought your dictionary along, Gillis," Bart said as he ribbed his little brother. "Then you'd know what us big guys are talking about."

"I don't have a dictionary," Gillis quipped. "Even if I did have one, I couldn't look a word up in it. I can't spell a word that big."

"Since Seldom Seedy ain't going along to help with the little fellers, I can't afford to take on more responsibilities than I already have with that bunch of babies in the backseat," Dump said. "I wouldn't have the time to swim, fish, or anything else that's a lot of fun."

"Tester went to get his camping gear," Gillis Cornfield reported as he peered through the dusty rear window. He was sitting next to the door.

"Yeah, he'll be back, directly," Teed stated, looking over Gillis' bony shoulder from his vantage point in the center of the seat. Teed had not wanted to sit in the middle, since he was prone to car sickness. Car sickness was a handicap for him. He had ridden next to the window several times without getting sick, but from his inside position he was afraid that he would be puking like a dry-heaving dog pretty soon.

Gillis did not care one way or the other, because he could slip off the outside edge of the seat very easily. That could be done with a mere motion of a hand lifting a door handle, and Teed could hold his upchucking momentarily. Either that or choke, and he was sure that Teed would use his Adam's apple like a check valve and hold the puking till he got out of the car.

"We're going, fellers," Dump decided, shifting the car into low gear and goosing the accelerator, encouraging the old machine to lurch forward over the rocky road like a horse in its efforts to unseat a rider.

"I saw Tester coming through the gate just then with his duffel bag," Teed reported, craning his neck to watch the disappointed Tester hotfoot it along the rough road in his effort to overtake the speeding car.

With a final effort Tester threw his duffel bag into the bushes beside the road and dug deeper into his reserves of speed as he sprinted after the vanishing car. If he had been a little faster, and the car had been a little slower, he could have overcome and would have had the chance to camp out with his dearest friends.

"Dump, if you'll slow down a little, Tester will be able to catch you by the time we get to the Joe-Lot," Teed said as he grunted for the charging Tester Seedy. "He'll never catch you with the speed that you're maintaining. I believe I saw him falter a little, like he's tiring. He shouldn't be tired this quick, should he? We've just gone a little over half a mile. He should do a lot better than that. Are you going to slow down at all? Tester just stopped running. Now he's getting ready to throw rocks at the car. You'd better speed up a whole lot before he chucks a boulder at us. But, if you'd slow down and stop for him, he wouldn't try to break the glass out of the winders."

Teed called the action from the backseat like a sports announcer at a car race. He wished the little fellow could garner more speed and catch up to the moving car. He really liked the kid and couldn't help but wonder why his older brother wanted to run off and leave his friend in the laurel thicket bordering the narrow road.

Tester was a good kid to pal around with, especially on a camping trip, even though he never packed any food in his duffel bag. He always sponged off the Cornfields, whose packs bulged with tasty foods. Maybe that was why Tester had put forth such an effort in his chase after the exiting automobile.

Dump sported a broad smile as he guided the car, searching for the smoothest and softest rocks in the rough road. "My intentions were to leave him behind," he said. "That kid is a pesky little scutter. He eats like one of those sumo rasslers you see in the movies. He wastes more food than he eats. We can do without him this trip. If Seldom had come along to watch him, then I wouldn't mind. You little fellers are enough worries for me. You're all the burden that I need to have this camping trip down on Bass Creek River."

"I could have watched him," Esker Seedy announced, rising from the foot-space between the front and rear seats. "He wouldn't have been any more trouble than me."

"What are you doing in here?" Dump asked, turning to face the buck-toothed Esker Seedy on the backseat, surprised with the boy's sudden appearance.

The air whistled through Esker's buckteeth as he breathed in and out.

"I thought he was Jake's bag of camping gear," Judge L. stated, giv-ing the boy a good thump on the shoulder as a form of pleasant greeting.

"Whew! That was some thump that you placed on my shoulder, Judge L.," Esker moaned, humping and gimping from the solid knuckle-thump on the bony part of his shoulder.

"That was a good frog-popper lick. I pride myself for having a good middle knuckle that produces a frog about every time I slug somebody with it," Judge L. laughed, giving Esker a smug look, shaking his knuckle under the boy's nose.

The old sedan bounced over the road. The weight of the boys caused the springs to collapse as the weak shock absorbers gave way. The car rose up and came back down with a jolting, tooth-grinding thud. No one gave the straining springs and shocks a second thought. The Cornfields had never owned a car, nor had they loaded one down as heavily as they did that one.

Dump, Clem, Bart, and Jake sat in the front seat. Bart sat with his legs astraddle the gearshift situated in the center of the floor. Clem sat next to Bart, while Jake sat in Clem's lap to give Dump room to steer the car.

Teed, Gillis, Cousin Jubal, and Judge L. were in the back, along with part of the camping gear, and there was the unexpected Esker Seedy, making a full load.

"Did you bring anything to eat?" Dump asked the grinning Esker. "If you didn't, then you'll have to catch your own food by fishing; that is if you brought fishing hooks and lines, and that I doubt."

"He can eat some of my grub, Dump, and he can sleep under my quilt—that is if he didn't bring his bedding with him," Teed offered.

"I didn't bring nothing," Esker announced, grinning at everyone. "You all come by so sudden-like that I didn't have time to pack up any grub and quilts."

"Thanks a lot, Teed. You sure make things easy for me," Dump said in a semi-sarcastic tone. "I should put you out right here, Esker, but since your father is such a good old feller, I'll let you stay with us. I wouldn't want Talmage mad at me. If Talmage got mad at me, Dad would get mad at Talmage for getting mad at me. That would cause a lot of trouble. I guess I'll just let things go as they are, but, Esker, you're going to have to help around camp. You can't come with us and just sluve around and expect to be fed and cared for. You'll have to hump around and help."

"Me and Teed and Gillis and Cousin Jubal will be like little beavers, won't we, boys?" Esker announced, his buck-toothed grin covering his entire face.

"Speak for yourself, Esker," Cousin Jubal said as he scrunched down to find a more comfortable position on the crowded seat.

With all the jostling about, caused by the bouncing car, it was hard to maintain a stationary position. As soon as one boy bounced up off the seat, someone grabbed that place. There was a continuous change of little butts on the crowded rear seat.

"Gosh-a-mighty, Jubal, you didn't have to go and poke me that hard!" Esker cried, facing the jubilant Jubal, who snickered at the discomforted boy sitting next to him.

"If you had stayed at home where you belong, then you wouldn't be hurting right now," Cousin Jubal laughed.

"What did he do to you?" Bart asked, turning to check the action in the backseat. He was holding to the knob on the top of the gear shifter, and as Dump hit a big rock in the road, Bart tried to prepare for a jolt by holding tight to the shifter knob. He received no answer from Esker Seedy.

The scream of gears was a good indication that Bart had lost his balance. In trying to cushion the blow from the descent from the top of the car back to the seat, he pushed the selector from low gear to reverse, stopping the chugging car with a scream of gears and a retort from Dump.

"Bust take it, Bart!" Dump screamed as he ripped his face from its stuck position on the dash. "You could cause us to get killed!"

"Not if we stop real sudden in the middle of the road, we won't," Bart laughed, noticing a trickle of blood oozing from Dump's swollen lip.

Dump had received a quick thump in the mouth as he had slid over the steering wheel, striking the hard dash. He was hit on a quick-swell-up spot on the center of his upper lip, and with the swelled-up lip he began to slur his words. That caused the crowded car to reverberate with laughter. Since he was a jolly-good guy, Dump began to laugh, too. It was that slurred chuckle that caused the joviality to grow in magnitude.

Soon everyone was happy again, and Clem started an up-tempo ditty. He was joined by the entire crowd, with the noise growing in volume. If a person had not known better, he would have thought there was probably a tune lurking about somewhere in the car, but right at the moment it was doing a good job of eluding the singers.

Esker Seedy was forgotten by the occupants of the front seat, but not by the denizens in the back. There was still a shuffle and a struggle for positions as the kids fought amongst themselves.

Gillis held to the armrest on the back door. No one was going to evict him from his squatter's position. "Dump, why don't you stop the car and put Esker out. There's no use for us to suffer back here just to let him go along and have fun. You could put Cousin Jubal out, too. All they're doing is taking up some much-needed space and causing havoc each time you run over the biggest rocks in the road."

"You're the littlest one in the bunch, so we might heave you out the winder," Esker Seedy said. A buck-toothed grin resembling kernels of yellow corn covered his homely face.

"No, you won't! I have squatter's rights," Gillis replied, facing Esker, giving him a frown. "I was there at the organization of this trip. I'm staying."

"We're all staying," Dump said, interrupting the spat between the boys in the backseat, pleased with the haughtiness of the little fellow clinging to the armrest. "We'll be there in just a few minutes. It's just around this bend, but we have about two miles to walk. You fellers will use up your short fuses before we reach the camp. You'll be too tired to argue and pop off on one another."

Dump steered the old car into the woods beside the road. The bushes closed in on it, concealing the car from anyone who might pass by. "This is a good place to park," he said. He turned off the ignition and pocketed the key. "We won't even have to lock it. The locks are all broken anyhow, but no one will bother it. We won't be leaving anything in it worth stealing. I don't even have a spare tire or a jack."

"Come on, Teed!" Esker Seedy shouted, bounding into the woods in search of a path that would lead the campers to the river and their planned campsite at the big cliff near the edge of Bass Creek River.

"Come back here, you two! We won't have any shirkers," Dump said as he prepared to chase the two rambunctious boys to bring them back to help tote the camping paraphernalia. "I told you, Esker Seedy, that you were going to help instead of sluve around the camp, gorging yourself with goodies while the rest of us do the work. And, Teed, you know better than to act like that. You know that you have to help out. What got into you to cause you to act like that? Everyone has to carry a load of camping stuff."

"The influence led him down the wrong path," Clem jested, placing a huge sack of potatoes on Esker's bony shoulder, a load that was just a little too heavy for the scrawny kid.

"Stand up and carry that like a man," Jake directed, helping to settle the sack of spuds on the bent-over kid. "That's pretty heavy on him, Dump," he continued, turning to his older brother. "Should we half that sack of taters and let Teed lug some of them?"

"Nah, Esker's big and stout. Just look at those muscles bulging in his arms and shoulders," Dump pointed out, smiling contentedly.

"I think what's bulging is some of his bones, ready to shoot out of his body as soon as they find a weak place in his hide," Bart guffawed at the staggering boy. "Straighten up there, Esker. Show that sack of taters that you're the big boss." he said, shoving Esker toward the narrow path that led to the river.

"I'm doing the best I can," Esker grunted, stumbling about, trying to keep his balance on the rough ground. "I believe that Teed could help out some."

"Sure, I'll help you," Teed offered, reaching for an end of the sack. "Here, Esker, scrunch it off your shoulder. We'll pack it 'tween us."

"Good!" Esker sighed, preparing to remove the sack of potatoes from his shoulder so Teed could help carry it.

"No! No doings, boys," Dump interfered. "Esker is going to shag that whole sack along. If he can't take them all at once, he can carry them one at a time, even if it takes him all night to get them to the river. Anyway, Teed has plenty to weigh him down a bit."

"Gosh, Dump," Esker whined, "if I'd known that I was gonna have to tote a ton of taters, I wouldn't have snuck into your old car. I thought a camping trip was for fun, and here I have to work."

"You know the way home," Dump told the disgruntled boy, pointing a finger in the direction they had come.

"Yeah," Cousin Jubal agreed, sniffing loudly.

"Don't get too bold, Cousin Jubal," Dump warned. "I can point a finger in that direction for you, too."

Cousin Jubal just grinned and sniffed as he hefted a bag of food and bedding to his shoulder and staggered awkwardly down the path toward the river.

"Here, Gillis, you can take this bundle of quilts," Judge L. said, tossing a bale of comforters to the little fellow.

The camping gear smashed into Gillis' face with enough force to bowl the tyke over into a patch of stinging nettles.

"Oh, gosh to it all!" Gillis screamed, rubbing his cotton-white head with both hands. "What did you put in that roll of bedding, Judge L.? Whatever it was sure put a knot on my head big enough for a goat to suck!"

"I put my bolt-action, one-shot, altered rifle in that bedroll to insure its safekeeping, just in case we might meet up with a band of marauding Indians tonight," Judge L. stated. A broad grin threatened to rip his jaws out by the roots.

"They ain't any Indians in this neck of the woods!" Esker exclaimed. "Are they any Indians around in these woods here, Dump?"

"Not many, I guess," Dump answered, a smile playing around the corners of his mouth. "I've heard that there are a few ghosts that admit they're descendants of real Indians. They can't scare people as much as the real Indians of yesteryear, but they can moan and groan really good— almost like an Indian raid on the settlers. Maybe tonight we'll be able to hear a bunch go by, yelling and shooting their arrows through the bushes by the river. We might even hear some of them cross the stream right where we're going to camp. I hear that they used to cross around there as they went in search of scalps and cows and ammunition for their guns. I've heard that Col Cornfield, one of our Indian-hunter ancestors, used to sell their own arrowheads back to them—the ones he pulled out of his door after a raid. He was a shrewd trader. He made good money, too."

"I didn't know that Indians had money," Cousin Jubal said, continuing his obnoxious sniffing. He hurried to catch up with Dump.

"Yeah, *those* Indians did," Dump declared to the curious lad humping along, trying desperately to keep up, hoping to hear the Indian tale. "They had their own money factory. They usually ran it around the clock. That was an industrious bunch of Indians."

"Come on, Gillis!" Cousin Jubal yelled over his shoulder. "Load up and hurry so you can listen to the good Indian stories."

"I'm humping along the best I can," Gillis said, grunting under the bulky load of quilts.

The stories kept the boys interested, causing them to forget about their heavy loads.

The silence was suddenly broken by the excited call from Teed Cornfield as he bent over an object beside the path. "Hey, Esker Seedy, have you ever seen a naked turtle?" he asked. "There's one running around loose somewhere. He must have sent his suit out to have it cleaned, and the cleaner people must have lost it when they tried to deliver it back to him. Look at this," he beamed, pointing to the empty turtle shell.

Esker kicked the turtle shell, knocking it from its resting place in the leaves. "It's as empty as a hainted house," he said.

"I've seen lots of them," Cousin Jubal admitted, kicking the shell a good thump, causing it to disintegrate. The outer layer broke into pieces in the shape of the design on the top. The bottom broke into smithereens. The shell had been in its undisturbed position for many years, just waiting for Cousin Jubal to come along and kick it.

"What will the turtle do when it comes back and finds Cousin Jubal's toe marks all over its suit?" Gillis wanted to know.

"He'll have to go to the closet and search through his wardrobe for a new tuxedo," Bart said, ushering the boys toward the river. "Hurry up. We've got a lot of work to do before dark."

"I thought we were coming to have fun," Esker wailed, with a hint of remorse for choosing to sneak into the car without asking permission to go along.

"The work won't hurt you," Clem contended, straightening the potato sack on Esker's shoulder.

"I sure would like to set this spud sack down for a good rest, fellers," Esker groaned.

"We're about there," Dump announced. "If you get that sack off your back, you won't be able to put it back up by yourself."

"That would be all right with me," Esker grunted. "I hope I never see another tater as long as I live."

"Just wait till you smell them frying with a big onion in them; you'll rear back, stuff your gut full, and ask for another helping," Dump insisted.

"I don't know about that," Esker replied.

"I hear the ripples!" Judge L. sang out, picking up the pace, trying to pass the rest of the hikers.

Everyone hurried along the path, hoping for a chance to rid himself of the burden that held his feet to the ground. At last they arrived at their planned destination.

Dump, Clem, and Bart started an unorganized procedure of setting up camp.

"You little fellers go with Jake and Judge L. to get plenty of firewood to last all night," Dump ordered. "Bart, you can organize the food, while Clem and I dig several foxholes to block out the chilly night winds."

Soon there was a huge pile of dry wood stacked as neatly as the six boys could possibly throw it in a hurry, but that did not matter much. The limbs were small and would burn rapidly. The big pile would not last long enough for it to be in the way.

Four foxholes dotted the campsite like empty graves, and Dump mentioned that to the smaller boys. "Maybe some of those Indian ghosts will be wandering about the woods tonight," he said. "I bet they might be tired and stop off here to rest like travelers do at hotels as they go about the country on their vacations. You tykes will have to bed down early and fight the Indian ghosts out of your foxholes. I doubt if a ghost will disturb you boys if you are sound asleep when he sneaks up and scrouges in between Esker and Teed."

"Esker and Teed will be in Dump's foxhole," Esker said, moving over beside Dump for protection against the eerie woods and its hidden ghosts.

"Yeah, we'll give it a lot of scrouge with Gillis," Teed agreed with Esker, looking over at his silent brother.

"I'll be in the same hole as Dump and you boys," Gillis averred. "That ghost will have all the room he needs."

Clem started a fire between two smoke-blackened rocks. Soon it was crackling happily as it sent smoke, sparks, and flames toward the heavens. The poplar limbs popped loudly as the hot flames consumed them.

Bart began peeling potatoes, taken from the sack that had been Esker's burden. "Get some water from the river, Esker," he ordered, giving the boy a camping chore.

Everyone was busy at an inherited job, and soon supper was on the plates. Everyone slurped and "gnyammed" as he enjoyed the frugal meal.

Dump, Clem, and Bart kept the rest of the campers hopping about with chores as they tidied up the campsite after the meal.

Everyone had been so engrossed in the meal preparation and camp organization that not one fishing line had been wet in the river. The good food had taken everyone's mind off fishing.

"Is anyone going to do any fishing tonight?" Dump asked the lounging campers.

"Not me," Clem grunted, lying back on a pile of leaves to rest.

Everyone agreed that the meal was too good to ruin by using it up before it could be enjoyed to the fullest.

A silent darkness settled over the camp, and soon a beautiful moon ascended the horizon. Only a muffled grunt or a loud belch could be heard as the campers lay about in contented ease.

"That moon reminds me of a book I read one time," Dump began, breaking the silence. "Years ago when I was in school, my teacher, Miss Craft, assigned me a book to read. I had to make a report on it and get up in front of the class and tell the story. It started out about a beautiful moon, like that one up there." He pointed to the moon, causing everyone to look up. "Indians have totems, usually some type of animal, that is carved on a pole and painted odd colors. They think it is holy and pray to it. Different tribes have different totems. This Indian boy had the fox as his totem. He had to go out and stay near a fox pack for a long time."

The boys crowded up as close to Dump as they could. They felt that if they were really close, Dump wouldn't have to repeat any missed words. Actually, they were a little on the scared side, but they would never admit it, even if they should collapse from the fright of the story in the quiet surroundings where possibly there were many Indian ghosts lurking, just waiting for the right moment to pounce upon the unsuspecting campers.

"Go ahead with the tale, Dump," Bart said as he encouraged his brother to relate more of the story. He had heard the narrative many times—each time they had camped out with a bunch of smaller boys who had never heard it.

Judge L. was fumbling around in his bedroll, searching for an elusive object. "Go ahead and tell it if you're going to," he said.

"Well, that Indian boy followed the foxes and watched them as they killed their food," Dump continued. "Sometimes it was a duck, sometimes a groundhog or a rabbit. He was learning everything that the foxes

— 29 —

knew so that he could hunt like a fox when he grew into a strong warrior. He ate all the scraps left at the kills. He had lots of food that way and grew fat and sassy. It was a great life, he knew. He didn't want it to end 'cause he was having life real easy. The foxes seemed to know that he was depending on them for food, so they left the biggest and choicest parts of the guts for him."

"I sure wouldn't eat guts," Cousin Jubal uttered, his usual loud sniff accompanying the words.

"If you didn't have anything else, you would eat anything," Jake exclaimed. "You say that now 'cause you ain't been that hungry. And you are about as full of taters and stuff as a big tick on a bull's belly."

"Go on with the story, Dump," Clem encouraged.

"Well, one night some foxhunters came into the young Indian's range. He was asleep at the time and didn't know that anyone was around. The foxes were just returning from a lope through the woods, just to keep in running shape. They had eaten all they wanted of a big gander they had killed."

"Did they leave the guts for the Indian kid?" Gillis queried.

"Yeah, they sure did," Dump announced. "He had gorged himself to the bursting point. He almost blew up a time or two. Now, those hunters had snuck up pretty close to the fox pack, and one of the foxes smelled the hunters and told the others. Soon the woods began to clamor with a bunch of barking foxes. About that time, a foxhunter shot his rifle at one of the foxes."

Bang! Judge L. fired his gun into the night. Teed and Esker were so startled that they began to grab each other around the neck, trying to hold on to something. They gripped each other so hard that they turned blue in the face, causing them to fall on their backs where they lay almost petrified, not from the choking, but from the scare they had received when Judge L. fired the gun.

"Shoot again, Judge L.," Clem laughed. He rolled on the ground and guffawed at the panic the two boys had shown.

After a few minutes of searching in the darkness, the homemade gun spat into the night. No one was scared that time.

"What fell on me?" Judge L. asked, fumbling in the semi-darkness for the object that landed near his leg. He groped about until he found it. "It's just Clem's hat."

"I had my hat hanging on a stick that I drove into the ground," Clem said, hurrying over to inspect his hat. "I bought that straw hat just yesterday. I hope you didn't molest it much, Judge L."

"He didn't molest it; he shot it," Bart laughed, taking the hat from his brother's hand. "Dead center, too." He pushed his index finger through a hole in the crown of the disfigured hat. "Here's another hole in the brim. It's a good thing you had it hanging on a stick instead of on your head when you told Judge L. to shoot again."

"You've never read a book like that before," Esker Seedy said, brushing leaves from his clothes. "You, Clem, Bart, Jake, and Judge L. planned that just to scare me, Teed, Gillis, and Cousin Jubal."

"I wouldn't do a thing like that," Dump laughed. He was joined by the laughter of the other campers, while buck-toothed Esker just sat before them and grinned.

A Cob for the Boss

"Crow and strut, you big coward!" Dalker Skinner stormed as he threw a clod of dirt at a Rhode Island Red rooster that was showing his stuff while giving the hens a lot of attention.

The red rooster chased a young barred rock rooster, Dalker's favorite, through the plowed earth in the big garden situated just above the house.

"You can have your fun right now, but wait till my rooster gets a little courage. He's still young, but your days are numbered, old boy. The time is slowly growing short for you to strut out loud. When that domernecker gets his spurs set in your head, you'll wish for a hiding place, and if you come out alive, you'll just whisper your struttin' around."

The rooster paid no attention to the words of warning from the angered man. He was unlearned in the human vocabulary. If the man wanted to carry on a conversation with a chicken, he would have to come to grips with the fowl vocabulary. The chicken just rooster-talked as he tried to keep his flock of cacklers in line. He scratched in the soft dirt, searching for the juiciest worms, bugs, and grubs in the garden. When he found a big grub, he called out to a pretty hen, using his rooster lingo to toll her near.

Dalker stomped on toward the house, his head bowed in its normal walking position. He talked and grumbled to himself, probably about getting even with that red rooster. His hands were used liberally as he put emphasis on his chosen names for the strutting chicken. It was the man's nature to talk to himself whenever he puttered about the farm, but at that moment he was talking and hand-waving with a new and avid gesture. "I'll fix that bossy chickey-diddle, just watch and see," he said to no one as he shuffled along the dusty path. "If it wasn't Zonie's rooster," he mumbled, referring to his wife, "I would wring its neck and have some chicken and dumplin's for Sunday's after-meetin' dinner. That's exactly what I would do. I may do it anyhow. She probably wouldn't even notice that the bust-taked thing was gone—that is if she didn't have to scald and pluck it. I can't take a chance like that. I'll think of a good way to destroy him."

"Who're you chatting with, Dalker?" Zonie asked as she emerged from the dairy. She held a can of cherries and a lapful of potatoes. She carried the potatoes in her apron, which was her nature. She gripped the bottom of the apron, forming a bag to carry things in. "I don't see nary a soul for you to chat with. Are you talking to yourself? You seem to do a lot of that here lately."

"Bust take it!" Dalker growled. "I guess I was, Hon. I was just cloddin' that red rooster away from my young domernecker. I want to have a good bloodline, and that young rooster is the one that I want to keep to enrich the laying flock. He's kept scared out of the hens' range, though. He'll never do us any good if he's kept run out into the brambles all the time. We need to get rid of that red rooster, and soon!"

"That's my rooster, Dalker, and we're going to keep him," Zonie replied, giving her husband a good frown to emphasize her seriousness about the matter.

"I don't see any need to keep that red rooster," Dalker declared, walking on past his wife, en route to the corn crib.

"I'll have some dinner ready directly, Dalker," Zonie called after her departing husband. "Don't stray off too far to be out of hearing, 'cause everything is ready, almost."

"I'll be down at the corncrib shellin' a turn of corn for the gristmill," he replied, without turning back to face his wife.

"That rooster's got your hackles raised, hasn't it, Dalker?" Zonie laughed jubilantly as she chided her pouting spouse. "Don't let a little thing like a chicken get your goat. I'm going to keep my red rooster, no matter how you feel about it. Don't be so childish and think that you have to have your way all the time. That could stunt your aging process." She shook her head and went into the house to finish preparing their midday meal.

"I want my domernecker rooster to be boss, and I'll see that he is boss, one way or t'other," Dalker muttered to himself as he shucked the big ears of white corn. He tossed them into a box that had two compartments. One compartment had a crank-type corn sheller bolted to the side. Just as soon as he finished filling the box, he would commence to shell the corn for his proposed trip to the gristmill at the mouth of Jestus Branch.

Several ears had rolled off the rop of the filled box. Dalker paid no heed to the full bin. He continued to shuck the corn and grumble to himself—about that bossy red rooster, of course. He just could not get that chicken off his mind.

Surely Zonie would give in after she had a few good laughs about Dalker's wish to get rid of the red rooster. She was just that way. She liked to laugh at people and pull pranks on them, especially her stubborn husband.

Dalker Skinner was not a cantankerous person—just easy to become abashed by other people's teasing him.

An ear of corn fell from the overflowing box, striking Dalker on the little finger on his right hand as he reached for another spike to shuck. "Plague gone it all to thunderations!" he exclaimed, rubbing the bruised pinkie.

Dalker stood up, still grumbling about that rooster, and now he had a sore finger to add to his miseries. He stretched to get the cramps out of his legs. After his good stretch, he began to shell the corn, one ear at a time. He dropped an ear into the top of the sheller and turned the crank. He watched the grains fall into the big empty box. The falling kernels made a clacking sound as they fell to the bottom of the box and bounced against the sides. He fed another ear into the top of the sheller and watched the sharp, pointed teeth on the round plate bolted to the handle turn inside the housing. The teeth gripped the ear of corn and pulled it down the sheller's throat, tearing the grains from the cob. The corn fell to the bottom of the box while the cob was spit out through an opening in the side of the sheller. He fed another ear into the sheller and methodically turned the crank. His work was interrupted when Zonie called him to lunch.

"Come on and eat a snack of dinner, Dalker," Zonie called from the kitchen door, where she stood fanning her face with her apron. The big wood-burning range filled the room with an oppressive heat. There was little ventilation in the tightly built structure.

"Coming!" Dalker yelled as he rose and headed toward the house and the waiting table of food. He washed his rough hands in the washbasin, wiped them on a not-so-dry towel, and sat down to commence to eat the tasty meal.

Zonie looked across the table at her husband occasionally. A mischievous smile lightened her happy face. She spoke not a word as she enjoyed herself. She took great pleasure in watching her man pout silently. "He'll come around to his senses by bedtime," she thought.

"He's always very friendly then."

Dalker filled his plate with green beans, chunks of cooked potatoes, and fried cabbage. He stirred everything together as he concocted a plate of goulash he called gouge. He poured a generous helping of sorghum molasses over the olio. Again he wielded his fork, giving the recipe another stirring before he sampled his fare by gulping down a huge mouthful. Before he could follow suit with another gluttonous bite, a knock came at the open door.

"See who that is, Hon," Dalker said, breaking the silence. "It might be one of the young 'uns come to visit." He continued to eat as Zonie rose and went to greet their company.

"Come on in, Colby," Zonie invited, greeting Dalker's nephew. "What brings you out in the sun on a hot day like this? I figured you might be tucked away in some cool place, letting your wife carry food and drink to you while you lazed around all day."

"No, Zonie, I can't hide in a cool place right now, 'cause my wife, Myrt, is big right now, and I have to do all the housework, milking, feeding, and garden work, plus all the farming, too," Colby complained. "I don't have time for anything. I'm getting behind on my resting. I've been 'specting this for a whole week now. She's been sorta puny here of late."

"Wash up and pull up a chair and have a bite with us," Dalker invited, without looking up from his plate. "You're welcome to eat with us."

"No, I ate a bite earlier," Colby Skinner replied, declining the invitation. He stood before his uncle and aunt, shifting his weight from one foot to the other as he impatiently waited for the couple to finish their frugal meal.

"Sit down before you wear the soles off your shoes, Colby," Zonie said, watching the nervous young man pace back and forth. "You act like the law is after you or something. Get a hold of yourself. What's wrong with you?"

"Myrt's time has come, or that is what she told me," Colby wailed, wringing his hands. He took a handkerchief from his pocket, wiped the perspiration from his forehead, then sat down in a chair that was offered. Almost immediately he rose from his sitting position to start pacing around the room once more.

"Have you come to get me to deliver your baby, Colby?" Zonied asked, smiling at the fidgety young man.

"Yeah, I did, but I couldn't get it straight in my head 'cause I'm so flustered with the hot weather and all, and her being in such pain and all," Colby stammered, searching for words. "We waited till we were sure that the baby was ready to come."

"How long did you wait before you came for me?" Zonie asked the confused man.

"We waited till she couldn't lie down, or stand up, either, without hurting so bad it would take her breath," Colby stated. "I told her to carry up some water and start heating it, 'cause I knew that you would tell me to start boiling water as soon as you got there. I wanted her to have it all het up and all."

"You might have waited too long before you came for me, Colby," Zonie declared, rising from the table to hurriedly begin preparations to leave immediately to try to save the young mother-to-be. "Do you have any gas in the truck?" Zonie asked, bustling about the bedroom, trying to think of everything that she might need while delivering the baby. She put some clothes in a bag to take just in case she might have to stay a few days while waiting for the baby to make up its mind.

The child would come when it got ready, she knew. Since it was the first one for Myrt Skinner, it could take all day and night to get the little fellow to come on out and face the world. Zonie would have to go prepared for a long stay.

"Do you have gas in the truck, Dalker?" she asked again, facing her husband, still sitting at the table eating contentedly, as if nothing was urgent about his nephew's plight.

"Yeah, there's plenty gas in it," Dalker replied, sopping his plate clean with a scrap of bread. "I put a dollar's worth in it last week. There should be plenty. I ain't drove it very much—just when we put up the hay crop. It didn't use much—just from the hay field to the barn."

"How many trips did you make from the field to the barn?" Zonie queried further.

"I don't know, woman," Dalker blurted out. "I was putting up hay, not counting how many times we went to the field and back. It could have rained on us while we counted out trips."

"Let's get started," Zonie ordered, trying to put some life into the two men. "It may be too late as it is, with that numskull there waiting till the pain was just right to come for help. You ain't run many granny races, have you?"

"This is my first one," Colby replied meekly.

"And it could be your last if anything has happened to that girl while you were playing know-it-all," Zonie threatened. "I'll take matters into my own hand if she's suffered unnecessarily, and you'll wish that you had been born into another family, 'stead of this one."

"Let Colby drive the truck down there to his house," Dalker suggested. "I'll have to come right back to look after things here. Then when you get ready to come home, he'll have to come to tell me. If he has the truck down there at his house, you two can come on back without wasting any travel time. I have a lot of work to do here. You all go on and get that baby birthed."

"Let's go, Colby," Zonie told the confused young father-to-be.

Dalker Skinner watched the two people ride away in the old truck that bounced over the rocks and ruts in the road. The springs and shock absorbers screamed as the truck bounced up and down. A smile spread over the man's face as a scheme began to ferment in the back of his mind. The time had come to rid the farm of a pesky, bossy red rooster. "How will I carry out my plan to annihilate that pile of feathers? I could chop off his head, or I could shoot his eye out with my rifle. But that would be self-incriminating evidence. It's got to look like an accident. Maybe I could kill him, bury him, and tell Zonie that a fox caught him. Nah, she wouldn't buy that, either."

* * * *

Two days had passed. Zonie was still at Colby Skinner's house. Colby's reckoning had been a false alarm, or Myrt was having a hard time in delivering.

"There's no use to worry about that baby, 'cause nature is going to take its course, regardless of what people might think," Dalker reasoned to himself.

The big red rooster was still the boss of the flock. He was just as mean as ever to the young domernecker that Dalker so highly appraised as a good bloodline to breed into his flock of layers. Very few hens were wooed by the persistent rooster. He couldn't spread his inheritance through the flock like that. Something had to be done, and quick!

Dalker was afraid that Zonie would return from her granny run before he could form a plan and implement the action. He had pondered several alternatives, but they were too ludicrous. They were such blatant, outward acts of treachery that he was ashamed to try them. He had been hoping hope on to of hope that Zonie would be home by the weekend—maybe Sunday—but not before he had time to get rid of her rooster. He would have a pot of chicken and dumplings for his loving wife. He missed her so much that he wanted to welcome her home with a good meal, just to start things off right.

It was Saturday morning. A brilliant idea popped into Dalker's head, worked its way to the top of his skull, and popped through a weak space in his scalp. "I'll do it!" he exclaimed as he headed for the corncrib, calling the chickens to the feed lot. "Here, chicks! Here, chicks!" he called excitedly. "Come and fill your craws with some good, tasty corn."

Chickens seemed to materialize from all directions. At least fifty hens hurriedly gathered in the feed lot to be treated with a handful of corn.

The big red rooster placed himself on the outer perimeter of the milling hens, where he could keep an eye on the young domernecker.

As the younger rooster chanced to crow in with the hens, the old cock of the walk gave him a good cuff and sent him scurrying to safety with his hackles raised, showing his cowardice.

"That's all right, big boy," Dalker grumbled, looking hard at the boss rooster. His rooster hurried toward the safety of the barn. As the chicken passed from sight behind the building, Dalker returned his attention back to the red rooster. He dropped a few grains of corn near his feet.

The hens climbed over one another as they fought for a good position to reach the food.

The red rooster worked his way to the center of the milling, squawking hens by pecking his way in. A few grains of corn fell in front of him, and as he hurriedly tried to beat the hens to the punch and pluck the grains from the dry earth, his head was forced downward. He was unable to see what was going on around him. Before he was able to survey his position, Dalker Skinner's rough hands grasped him, and he was raised up to where the chicken and the man could look straight at each other—eyeball to eyeball.

Dalker walked toward the barn, the flock of hens following, anticipating more treats of corn. As the procession passed through the big yard and on toward the barn in the middle of the luscious meadow, Dalker could hear the domernecker crowing loudly in an effort to entice the hens to follow him.

A plan began to fall into place. Dalker stopped by the little stream that meandered through the field, scooped up a handful of clay from the creek, and smeared it over the glossy red feathers of the innocent rooster. He then submerged the chicken in the stream and gave it a vigorous rubbing, soaking the feathers in the tepid water. As he lifted the fowl from the stream, it looked so comical that he had to chuckle at its drab appearance. "Now, you'll look like some other rooster—not like the bossy one that my domernecker fears. We'll have a good fight, and I hope that you come out the loser," he said, holding the chicken out where he could get a good look at it.

Seeing that they would not receive another treat, the hens began to scatter about the meadow in search of grasshoppers and other insects.

Dalker saw his young rooster as it came from behind the barn and raced toward the flock of hens. It stopped several times to crow, to let the world know that he was one happy chicken.

"Come on, young feller," Dalker coaxed. "I'll have to give this rooster a handicap in order to make this fight fair," he said, trying to think of a scheme to make the odds more even. "I've got it!" he exclaimed happily as the answer came to him. "I'll tie some corncobs to your feet, old boy. That way you won't be able to lift your feet high enough to stab my rooster with your long spurs." He searched the barnyard for water-soaked corncobs. After he had made his selection, he went to the harness room where he found two pieces of binding twine. He tied the cobs to the rooster's muddy feet and set him down.

The old rooster walked about, stepping high, trying to rid himself of the cumbersome cobs. When the domernecker saw him, there was no recognition due to the bedraggled appearance of his nemesis.

Thinking that the odd-looking chicken was a stranger in the neighborhood, the young rooster advanced toward the disguised bird with the intent of ridding the premises of another unwanted competitor.

Soon there was a furious battle going on between the two adversaries. The young rooster was doing rather well against the older, more-experienced fighter, but suddenly he fell beneath a crunching blow and began to kick at the air, his head lying in an awkward position. Soon the feet stopped moving as the chicken lay deathly still.

During the heated battle, one of the heavy cobs had been swung with so much force that it had broken the young rooster's neck, killing him dead as a coal bucket.

"I should have known it!" Dalker bemoaned, stamping the ground to vent his frustrations and anger. "I should have known that something like this would happen to my rooster. Why couldn't it have been Zonie's rooster that got conked out?"

There was nothing else to do but accept the situation, since he had been the lone perpetrator of the act of deception, so he picked up the rooster and took it to the house. He scalded and plucked it in preparation for a Sunday dinner of chicken and dumplings. His new bloodline for a laying flock was history. He would have to accept the fact that the dominant rooster would be the sire of a new generation of layers.

* * * *

"Did you kill my rooster, Dalker?" Zonie asked as she bustled about the kitchen on her return from Colby Skinner's house, "Did you get rid of my chicken while I was away and couldn't stop you from doing it?"

"No, I didn't," Dalker replied, lowering his head to hide his embarrassment.

"I know that you didn't kill a laying hen," she continued. "What happened?"

"I got those roosters into a fight, and your rooster killed mine," Dalker admitted. "He didn't actually whip my rooster. I have to tell you that I tried to even the odds for my rooster by tying some water-soaked cobs to your rooster's legs to hold him down so he couldn't fight well. I thought that my rooster could take advantage of the situation and whip your rooster pretty quick, but the cob put his lights out. It broke his neck as if someone had wrung it. That's my rooster in the pot."

"I figured that it was mine when I smelled it cooking," Zonie laughed—so hard that she lost her breath and began to hiccup. "It serves you right, though. I was going to give in to letting you get rid of Ol' Red."

"Now, you tell me!" Dalker moaned. "I know that I shouldn't have done what I did," he replied as he saw the humor of the outcome of the battle. "I just gave the boss a cob to knock my rooster in the head with," Dalker laughed.

Curiosity and a Cat's Tail

"Mom, I'll be going over to Coaley Creek tonight," Marn Cornfield told his mother as he buttoned his shirt at the neck. "They're going to be playing over at Allamander Skinner's house. They have one about ever' Saturday night. There'll be a bunch making music for us to keep time with while we play."

Marn had referred to the art of square dancing when he told his mother that he would be playing that night.

"You've been over there on Coaley Creek every night for the last four or five nights in a row," Fronie Cornfield claimed, stopping near the open bedroom door. She did not enter the room where her son was dressing to go out.

"That's a fine holler to visit, Mom," Marn vowed, laboriously smoothing down his heavily starched collar. He twisted his neck around to try to settle it into the rough band. As he looked at himself in the mirror, a dark-complected gentleman stared back with strong, amber-colored eyes set beneath black eyebrows. He cut a handsome figure in his navy blue trousers and white shirt. His shoes gave off a beautiful shine. One could almost see himself well enough in the glow to be able to comb his hair—slicking down every hair on his head.

"I bet that you've met a pretty girl over there," Fronie teased, pointing a finger at her son.

"I'm just going over there to visit and mingle at the get-together," Marn answered as he finished primping before the scarred mirror on the big cherry dresser. "I'm not interested in the females right now, Mom."

"I'm still wondering why you've gone over there every night this week is all," Fronie stated, turning back to the kitchen and her task of washing the supper dishes.

"I'll see you in the morning, Mom," Marn replied as he passed through the bedroom door to the kitchen. He kissed his mother on top of her head. "Tell Dad, when he comes home from work, that I'm still planning to go with him Monday and apply for that job at the mines."

"I wish you wouldn't go in those dog-holes to make a living," his mother lamented, looking at her strong, young son.

"I just about have to, 'cause Dad has almost committed me to accepting that job," Marn declared. "It's a timbering job, and I'll get paid by the hour, not like the coal loaders, where they lose a lot of money by having to load just the coal in a whole cut. They have to clean up the entire cut, whether or not they get a lump of clean coal out of it, and they don't even get paid for all that rock they have to load. The union will put a stop to that lost work. They're working hard and will have an organization real soon, I hope. Then there'll be pay for everything that we have to do in the mines, with an eight-hour shift. No more working till we drop from the lack of energy to carry out our assignments. I hope the union organizes the mines real soon. And I hope that I can be a part of that organization. Mom, I think things will be all right. Don't worry about me. I'm a grown man."

"I know, son, but I can't help but worry about you," Fronie replied.

"Things will work out all right. I'll be careful," Marn promised as he smiled at his loving mother. "I'm ready to go do some playing over on Coaley Creek," he said, changing the subject. He kissed his mother on the cheek. He had to bend his lanky frame over the short woman in order to kiss her good-bye.

"I still think that you have gone batty-blind over some girl over there in one of those laurel thickets," Fronie called after her departing son.

"Don't ever worry about that, Mom," Marn called over his shoulder as he jumped the paling fence surrounding the house.

Fronnie's words remained in the back of Marn's mind as he walked up the steep, winding path from Bass Creek to Coaley Creek. His mind was on something other than work, hunting, and fishing, the three most occupying activities which were often his endeavors.

The time of year was late fall—just a few days before winter began. It was December 10, 1920, to be exact.

Marn's fancy had turned to love, and it wasn't even spring. He had often heard that a man's mind went haywire and turned to mushy love in the springtime, but he had gone right through that season just like water through a tub with the bottom out of it. He reflected on what he had told his mother a few days earlier. "Mushy love is for the wimps of the world. I'm was going to be a bachelor—forever," he had said. Marn wanted to enjoy life to the fullest, and he didn't want a nagging, sniveling woman in the picture to punctuate his daily routine. He had often said, "There's no woman in this world that can cause me to go batty-blind over her and lose my common sense."

Marn walked up the slope, pulling himself along by grasping small bushes by the path that wound its way up the mountain in a snake-like trace.

Snowbirds flitted through the crisp, cold air. Nuthatches searched for hibernating insects beneath the scaling bark on a dead white oak tree that stood near the mountain path. The little birds spent most of their time going down the tree, headfirst, instead of going up. Their flat-note calls carried on the still evening air.

Marn heard nothing as he hustled up the mountainside. He had met a beautiful girl over on Coaley Creek—only four days ago—and he had been burning up the path as he commuted on foot to and fro to see her.

Dalker Skinner lived about as far up Coaley Creek as he could, without living somewhere else. Mr. Skinner had the most beautiful little girl in the world. Her name was Vann. She was an eye filler, too. She had filled a young gentleman's eye—Marn Cornfield's—and he was almost batty-blind over her already.

* * * *

A noise emanated from the weather-beaten house of Allamander Skinner, Vann Skinner's uncle. From the looks of the numerous horses tied to the paling fence, there was a throng of people crowding the rustic building. At that early hour, no sounds of square-dance music came from within—only the boisterous voices of the crowd as each person tried to talk louder than the rest.

Marn Cornfield eased his tall, lanky frame through the front door. Heat from the huge fireplace in the spacious living room and the milling, talking habitants and guests greeted him with a pleasant warmth.

"Hey, Marn, how are you doing?" Tarncie Skinner, Vann's younger brother, asked as he greeted his new acquaintance.

"I'm doing just about the best that you have ever looked at," Marn replied, chuckling at his own remark. "Sure is cold tonight."

"Yeah, it's just about as cold as a penguin's nose," Tarncie remarked, showing an air of joviality. "Come on in and scrouge up to the fireplace with the rest."

"Thanks, my friend," Marn said, moving toward the crackling fire. He greeted each person he passed as he walked to the front of the room where most of the people had congregated for a warm chat in front of the fireplace.

The crowd opened an aisle as they made room for the new arrival.

Each person shook Marn's hand or gave him a friendly thump on the shoulder, and he returned each greeting in kind. He held his hands out to the lapping flames. Heat from the warm fire caused his hands to ache as cold and numbness were replaced by a tingling warmth. Actually, the affability of his friends gave him more warmth than the crackling fire.

When he felt completely warm again, he began an eye search of the room, hoping to find a pretty girl with whom he could strike up a conversation. Hopefully that pretty female would be Vann Skinner. He saw several pretty girls in the room, but none could compare with Vann. His heart began to feel just a little heavy as he frantically explored the room. "She must be here somewhere," he mumbled to himself, continuing his search.

Vann emerged from the kitchen, accompanied by four young men trying valiantly to gain her attention by making silly remarks and punching one another on the shoulder, trying to see who could make the biggest frog pop up on an arm. They weren't very romantic in their actions. It seemed that she was less interested in them than they were in her, which suited Marn to a tee.

Vann—short for Savannah—began a scrutiny of the room as she hoped to find her new friend from Bass Creek. She espied the tall, handsome gentleman standing near the crowded fireplace. Her heart fluttered as she had to breathe hard to control the excitement that surged through her dainty body. "That's surely a handsome man," she thought aloud as she approached her male friend.

Marn walked toward Vann with a swagger, indicating that he wanted her attention. "Hello, Beautiful," he said, greeting her. "Cold tonight, ain't it?" He knew that the weather was a good conversation starter. Almost anyone could talk about the weather, since it was such a common subject.

"It sure is," Vann agreed, trying to be as coy as possible. "It could turn off and snow before the night's over, though."

"Yep, it sure could do just that," Marn remarked. "I hope it doesn't snow too much, though. I have to go over to Jankins to apply for a job in the mines this Monday morning, bright and early. I don't like to have to wade the snow, unless I'm going foxhunting or something like that. But do you know what? I could wade the snow all the way up to my belt just to get to look at you for ten or fifteen short seconds."

"Oh, you're just joshing me," Vann giggled, dropping her head in a coquettish move. "You wouldn't go to that much trouble just to look at plain old me."

"There's nothing plain about you," Marn rejoined, praising the shy girl. "There's outer beauty showing, and I know very well that you are chock plum' full to the gills with inner beauty. Why, a person could skin you, and you would look beautiful without any hide on you at all—just standing there raw."

"I know you're just joshing me now," Vann blushed, dropping her head, an indication of her embarrassment, not because the conversation was off-color or anything like that, but there was a bunch of people around. She felt that they would overhear what was said.

"I wish there was someplace where we could go to be alone," Marn said as he gently took Vann's soft hand in his. "We could talk about a lot of things if we were alone by ourselves. Is there a back porch where we can talk. I know that we can't stay outside for a long period of time, but I would like to chance the cold just to be alone with you. What do you say? Do you want to chance the cold? I'll give you my mackinaw to keep you warm. It's fleece-lined and everything. You'll be sweating like a racehorse in about ten minutes if you wear it. I can keep warm by being near you and touching your hand."

"Dad's around here somewhere," Vann warned her friend as she looked about the room in search of Dalker. She knew that her father would not want her to go out into the cold air to be with Marn. He really did not have anything against the young man, but she knew that he would not want to lose a daughter. She had heard her father speak on the subject one day. "Zonie," he had said, "I had rather lose a hundred-dollar bill than to see my little girl get hitched to some man that might not be good to her. It would be awful quiet around the farm without her. She's a lot of help around the farm, too."

"Aw, come on, Honey. He won't see us leave, and by the way he's been tipping the bottle, he won't realize that you're gone," Marn whispered, guiding Vann through the milling crowd.

A fiddle began to scrape as Ferd Skinner, Vann's older brother, started a tune. Someone plunked a few clawhammer-style notes on a banjo as the picker joined the melody that began to sound like good "playing" music. A guitar was strummed into the melee of sound.

Dancers prepared to play as they began to form sets. A caller stepped to the front of the room and helped to organize the sets. He then began to call the dance in a singsong, sonorous twang.

Marn eased through the door and closed it quietly, knowing well that no one in the room would have heard had he slammed it with all his strength. He did not want to take a chance, though. Maybe Dalker Skinner had good ears placed on the sides of his head. He knew that the gentleman would not want his daughter to go outside in the dark to be alone with a man. "Here, take this mackinaw, Honey," Marn offered. He removed his coat and draped it over the girl's shoulders. He felt her shiver as the cold wind whipped through the opening in the front of the warm garment. He hurriedly buttoned the big coat to stop the frigid draft from chilling the small body.

"That's much better," Vann murmured, leaning against Marn. "But you might freeze."

"Don't worry about me, Hon," he told her as he wrapped his arms around her and kissed her on top of her head. "I'll stay warm by just doing that. I hope you don't mind me snuffing you like that," he breathed, referring to his kissing as "snuffing."

"That was all right with me, but just don't let Dad see you snuffing me here where somebody can see us," she giggled.

"We can see anybody approaching us without them knowing that we are here in the shadows of the porch," Marn whispered, kissing her on the head once more. "Why don't we walk up to your house?" he suggested. "We can sit in the living room and talk and court all we want to? Do you think your dad would object to that?"

"Everybody's here at the playing," Vann replied. "My parents wouldn't want us to be alone in the house with no one to be with us."

"Ask them if you can go. We'll take your little brother with us," Marn proposed. "I don't want you to think that I want to take you up there to be alone with you, just by ourselves. I have all the respect in the world for you. Your little brother, Buck, can be our chaperone."

"I'll ask Mom and Dad if we can go up to the house," she told him.

Vann entered the room to search among the dancers for her parents. She saw her mother sitting by the fireplace, talking to Ferd's wife, Meg. "Hello, Meg," Vann spoke, greeting her sister-in-law.

"Where have you been, Vann?" Zonie asked. "I ain't seen you playing with the rest out there on the floor."

"I've been talking to Marn Cornfield out there on the porch, where we can be alone for a minute without having to gab with everybody else," Vann replied.

"You should stay in the house out of the cold," Zonie warned. "You could take pneumonia out there in that whistling wind. Where's Marn? Is that his coat that's got you all wrapped up from head to toe?"

"Yep, it is, Mom," Vann giggled. "He was afraid that I might get too cold out there in the shadows."

"Get him back in here where he can warm up," Zonie ordered, pointing toward the door and waving her arms as a gesture to expedite her order. "You know that he's like an icicle out there in that blustery wind. I know that he ain't so excited that he can stand the cold wind without freezing to death."

"We were wondering if we could go up to the house and sit in the living room and talk a little. Marn said that we could take Buck along to chaperone us," she stated, before her mother had a chance to object. She had seen a look of surprise flood the older woman's pleasant face.

"That's very thoughtful of him to suggest that someone go along with you to keep an eye on you lovers," Zonie said. "You don't see many men that cordial and gentleman-like. You can go if you can drag Buck away from his play with the rest of the young 'uns over there in the corner."

"Buck likes Marn," Vann called over her shoulder as she hurried to the corner to ask Buck to leave his friends and go up to the house with Marn and her. She knew that she would have a hard time persuading him to go. She would probably have to promise him something special to get him to give in. She had a few sticks of candy hidden in a dresser drawer—just for such an emergency.

"That's a lucky girl to get a considerate man like Marn Cornfield," Meg Skinner told her mother-in-law.

"Marn Cornfield is a lucky man to have a girl like Vann—all googly-eyed over him," Zonie laughed, her chubby body shaking with the laughter.

"Yeah, she is a very lucky girl," Meg repeated.

Vann tempted Buck with the hidden pieces of candy, and soon they were picking their way through the cavorting dancers hopping about the room, enjoying themselves without any rhythm at all in their movements.

They just followed the caller, doing whatever the man said. They were having fun, though, and that was the reason for their being there.

Ordinarily, Vann would have been right there among the frolickers, having just as much fun as anyone, but that night dancing was far from her regimen of activities.

"Did you say that you had two big sticks of candy or two little lumps of candy?" Buck asked as they went through the door.

"I said that I have two big sticks of candy," Vann repeated, gently closing the door behind her. The noise from the dancing people was partially muffled by the closed door. "Let's find Marn and head up the holler to the house."

"I don't see why you need me to go along with you and Marn to do your silly courting," Buck whined as the cold air struck him in the face, causing chill bumps to pop out all over his body. "If it wasn't for the candy, I wouldn't have left the fun and warmth of the corner by the fireplace. Us boys were having a grand time playing crack-a-loo. I had won two pennies from the other fellows, and they had only won three pennies from me. My penny landed on a crack in the floor about every other time I flipped it. I guess I was holding my mouth right. Don't you think so, Marn?" he asked as he looked into the darkness and waited for the man's answer.

"I suppose so," Marn laughed, patting the boy's head.

Buck Skinner had referred to the pitching of coins to see who could place one on a crack in the floor. The person whose coin landed on a crack, or nearest to a crack, won the coins. "Crack-a-loo" was the name of the game.

"You sure have to hold your mouth right to get the penny to flop on the crack," Buck reasoned, skipping along to keep up with the fast pace that Marn had set.

The trip over the rough road was made in about twenty minutes, and the warmth of the big living room greeted the wayfarers as they entered the house.

Marn punched the burning logs and turned them over in order to get more heat from them. Flames rose up to lap at the throat of the huge chimney. He placed a few lumps of coal on the logs for a more intense heat. The room was filled with a warm brightness, making it light enough to see without having to use a lamp.

"Give me the sticks of candy, Vann," Buck impatiently urged his sister.

"All right," she replied, leaving the parlor and going into a bedroom. She fumbled around in the darkness for a moment and soon returned with two sticks of peppermint candy and handed them to Buck.

The boy took the candy and hurriedly devoured it. He seemed to have just inhaled, and the candy was immediately sucked up, vanishing down his throat to his stomach.

"That surely didn't take long," Marn laughed.

"That wasn't even enough to fill a tick," Buck said, burping loudly. "Hey, I got to swaller that piece twice!" he laughed.

"Buck! That was nasty!" Vann stormed, puckering up her face, showing her distaste for the crude remark. She showed her embarrassment by covering her face with both hands.

"What was I supposed to do—spit it out?" Buck asked. "It went back down to join the rest. That ain't nasty. I was just saving ever' bite." He ran his tongue over his teeth to get every morsel of the candy stuck to them, and between them. He made a loud smacking sound as he finished sucking his teeth clean.

Marn laughed at the little boy. He held Vann's left hand in one of his, while his other hand rested on her shoulder. Occasionally, he would "snuff" her, as he called his lovemaking.

The two lovers were so engrossed in their petting that they did not miss Buck when he left the room. They heard the door open and close and saw a big tomcat enter the warm parlor.

The tomcat began to rub against Marn's legs, leaving hairs clinging to the serge material of his pants.

Marn paid no attention to the presence of the cat as he continued to talk to Vann in a hush-hush tone—too low for Buck to hear.

Buck lay in the floor and began to play with something that he had brought into the room on his return from his chore of letting the cat in.

The curious cat ran up to Buck to see what was in its master's hand. It received the object right in the nostrils, causing it to sneeze and snort to clear the stinging substance from its irritated nose.

Buck rolled on the floor and laughed hilariously. He held an empty toothpaste tube from which he was able to squeeze a trace of paste. That was what he had smeared on the cat's nose.

Marn and Vann laughed with Buck. They, too, found the mischievous act humorous.

"What did you do that for?" Vann asked, when she was able to stop laughing.

"I just wanted to show Mister Nosy what I had in my hand," Buck said, squeezing another bit of toothpaste from the discarded tube.

As if on cue, the tomcat ran back to see what Buck was offering—his curiosity not yet sated.

Buck rubbed the cat's nose with the bit of paste, and again rolled on the floor, roaring with laughter. He laughed so hard that he began to hiccup.

Marn and Vann laughed with him, but not as uproariously as they had at first. The incident wasn't as funny the second time.

A third squeeze from the tube did not interest the cat. Instead of showing curiosity as it had before, he turned his rear end to Buck with his tail up in the air. The tail jerked excitedly as he strutted before the courting couple.

Suddenly the tail dropped as the cat gave a hiss and ran from the room.

Buck had poked the cat under the raised tail, causing it to panic with the suddenness of the jab from the mischievous lad.

The tomcat began to scratch on the door, wanting to go outside to get away from his antagonist.

"You hateful thing!" Vann exclaimed, covering her face and running from the room.

"That'll teach him to try to snap my picture," Buck laughed as he continued to roll on the floor.

Marn tried to withhold a laugh, but found it very hard to keep a straight face as he looked at the amused boy. He went quietly through the door in search of Vann. He found her in the dark kitchen, trying to get control of her anger.

Instead of counting up to ten before she was able to control her anger, she counted to twenty. "I should kill him!" she stormed as Marn entered the room.

"Don't worry about it, Vann," Marn laughed. "It was just a little curiosity and a cat's tail."

To Preach or to Plow

"I feel like I've been called to preach, Brother Semm," Zeke Warp-board said as he crossed his legs to make himself more comfortable.

"Only you and the Lord know that," Brother Semm Pilton replied, hunching back on the davenport in the spacious living room. "If you have been called, I don't think you'll have a *feeling* that you have been called. You'll *know* that you have been called when you have that urge to go forth and carry a message to the lost and dying world. You'll have a big lump in your throat about the size of a goose's egg, and you'll try to preach that lump out of your throat. If you have the lump and can carry a message through it to the sinners, you'll feel it gradually go away, and your messages will flow much easier. I believe the Lord uses that lump as a test to see if you are worthy as a messenger for Him. You have to prove that you are worthy before you can go out and preach."

"I think He called me as a circuit-rider preacher, like in the olden days when they went about the country, preaching and getting a little change for the pocket," Zeke said as he looked at his friend across the room. "I think that I can carry the message and make a good living on the side with love offerings from the congregations. If the church is big enough, and I can fill it, maybe I can get enough to buy me a car. I won't have to hotfoot it all over the country, wearing my shoes out."

"Brother Zeke, I think you have the wrong idea about the call to preach," Brother Semm said. "You could have been called to plow instead of preach. You'll have to get your priorities straight. Don't go out with the idea that the Lord will let you make a potful of money for work that is supposed to be free. Jesus said to his disciples in Matthew 10:8, 'Freely ye have received, freely give.' That means without charge. You can't charge the people for preaching. He also said to the same disciples in Matthew 10:9, 'Provide neither gold, nor silver, nor brass in your purses.' I believe that he was saying for us to not take pay for our preaching. He said, 'A workman is worthy of his hire,' meaning that he has to work for a living and preach for free."

"I can't work and preach, too," Zeke protested. "I'll have to do one or t'other, and I think it'll be preaching. I have this gut feeling that I am predestined to do a knockout job of ministering the Word. I'll prepare a good sermon and knock them dead with it, so to speak. I'll give the flock something to think about."

"Now, Zeke, that was in the days when Jesus walked on this earth that I am speaking of," Brother Semm continued. "He went about the country preaching, but he wasn't a circuit-rider preacher. And, Zeke, if the Lord calls you to preach, you won't know what you're going to preach from sermon to sermon. You can't prepare your sermon ahead of time, 'cause in Matthew 10:19 and 10:20, it says: 'But when they deliver you up, take no thought how or what ye shall speak for it shall be given you in that same hour what ye shall speak. For it is not ye that speak, but the Spirit of your Father which speaketh in you.' So, Zeke, watch out how you carry out your ministry. Do the will of the Lord—not the will of Zeke Warpboard."

"Oh, I know just how I'm going to do the Lord's work," Zeke replied, ignoring Brother Semm as if he had not even spoken. "I have studied about it a lot since I felt the Spirit that gave me my wake-up call. I know just how I'm going to do it. You see, Tug Cornfield said that he ain't doing much right now, so he can go and drive me around the country, 'cause he has a good car—a '49 Hudson—runs real good, too, so he says. I'll pay for his gas, oil, and tires with money from my preaching funds— that I am sure to amass as I do my ministering. I'll pay him a nice little salary, too—enough to tide him over for a period of time while we're out on the road. I have a two-burner gas stove, and I can cook two items at once. That will save time and money by cooking our meals. I guess the congregations will invite me into their homes to take meals with them. That will be real economical for me and save lots of money. I can send my wife and ten children a few dollars a week, just to tide them over while they take care of the farm. I'll probably start me a little savings account at the bank. I can add a few dollars each week, and if I get a big love offering from a humongous crowd, then I can put away more savings for a rainy day. I have it all worked out, Brother Semm. I'll start a checking account, too. That way I can just write a paper slip for my expenses. I won't have to carry a big pocketful of change that will keep me weighted down on one side all the time."

"You're counting your flock before it materializes, Brother Zeke," Brother Semm Pilton warned. "You're looking at this calling in the wrong perspective. I think that you should get down on your knees right now. Don't wait till tonight, as so many people do, to talk to the Lord. You must get your priorities straightened out."

"Don't worry about it. I'll make it just fine with Tug Cornfield along. Tug can read the Bible real good," Zeke stated. "He has a pretty good education—went to the public schools for eight years. He can help keep all my finances straight and schedule my revivals. All I'll have to do is preach. He can read the Bible and help me interpret the wording so that I can deliver a good, soul-saving sermon with a message for the flock. I bet you hadn't thought about it like that, had you? See, I have done a lot of thinking about this, and I'm ready to go out there and tell the world just what it should hear."

"I hope you can do just that," Brother Semm Pilton said. "The world needs to hear the right things, though."

"Tug can read good, and he'll help me out when the going gets rough," Zeke declared.

"You were called to preach, and *you* called Tug Cornfield to help you. Is that the way it is?" Brother Semm asked, a smile playing around his somber mouth.

"That's just about the way it all happened," Zeke admitted. "Ain't it just amazing how the Lord works with His servants?"

"Yes, it's surely amazing how He works, and you amaze me the most of all," Brother Semm vowed, shaking his head.

"Me and Tug will start our travels Friday next," Zeke Warpboard continued. "Would you like to take a jaunt down the road with us? You could preach one night, then I could preach the next night. We could take turns, and that way one of us could rest while the other worked for the Lord. We can split the offerings in half and both make a good living from it. Don't you think we could?"

"I don't think I'll join you on your first trip," Brother Semm told his friend. "We're going to start a revival at the Coaley Creek Freewill Baptist Church this Sunday night. Why don't you come by and take part in the services with us? You can get your feet wet, so to speak."

"I'll check with Tug Cornfield and see what his plans are for next week," Zeke replied. "I hope that he ain't working anywhere. Maybe he ain't too busy right now. I need to get started out on the road. If he has to stay here and work, I might take in the services, but I'm afraid that I'll have to get on out there and get things started out right."

"You said just a minute ago that he wasn't doing anything constructive right at the moment," Brother Semm said. "He won't be working at anything, unless he has hired on somewhere, and I doubt that, since work is so hard to find around here."

"He could be tied up in his crops. This is a very busy time of year on the farm, you know," Zeke replied, defending Tug Cornfield.

"You should be getting your crops in, too," Brother Semm reminded his little friend. "Your crops might bring in just a little more pay than your preaching."

"My woman and kids can handle the harvesting of our crops. They won't need me around in the way," Zeke rejoined, defending his reason for going away during the harvest season.

"I suppose you'll be free to share in the preaching in our revival," Brother Semm said. He watched Zeke begin to squirm in his seat. "I expect to see you present throughout the entire running of the revival. Tug won't be in any hurry to get on the road. He'll probably wait for you while you take in the services. He might even come a few nights. Now, I want you to see just how you are to conduct yourself while doing the services of the Lord. Since you haven't preached before or held a revival, you can pick up some important pointers. We'll have a very learned preacher from over in Kentucky. He'll deliver the sermons each night— that is if he is blessed every night. The Lord doesn't give you a message every time you step into the pulpit. If Brother Taylor should come up blank on one of those nights and can't get a blessing to give us a message, we might have to call on you to help us through the services. You'll help us out, won't you Zeke?"

"I don't know, Brother Semm," was Zeke's slow response. "I'm afraid that I might have to get out on the road."

"I want you to get out there and preach," Brother Semm replied, encouraging his friend. "You have to have a message to give. You can't stand up there in the pulpit and hem and haw around and sling slobber all over the church-house floor. You have to have feed for the sheep, and I don't mean for you to come with a bucket of corn to feed to them. And forget about Tug Cornfield as your reader and interpreter."

"I have committed myself with Tug," Zeke whined. "I can't go back on my word with him—not one bit more than I can go back on my promise to the Lord. I promised the Lord to be His servant, and I promised Tug Cornfield that he could be my driver, reader, and interpreter. I'm going to stick to that promise if it kills me."

"It may do just that," Brother Semm predicted, scrunching around on the sofa to find a softer place to sit, since the cushions were frayed, letting the metal coils work their way through the worn material that held them in place. "We know that the work of the Lord is really hard to understand, and the mystery behind it all could be that He called you to preach, and, too, it could be that He will snuff you out like a candle, by calling your number for calling yourself to preach. If I were in your shoes, I would think this matter over very carefully."

"I've been doing some very careful thinking. I'll be the messenger that carries the Word to the lost sheep," Zeke said, rising from his seat. "I guess I'd better be running along. My wife might be 'specting me for supper."

"I'll be expecting you in church Sunday night when the revival starts," Brother Semm added.

"Don't count on it, Brother Semm Pilton. Tug Cornfield might want to leave Sunday morning on our pilgrimage through the country," Zeke replied as he prepared to leave.

"I'll talk to Tug and get him to stay here till the revival ends next Sunday night," Brother Semm promised.

"I just don't think that I can make it this time," Zeke whined as he sought an excuse to play hooky from church.

"You'll be there, or you'll be known as the 'Chicken Preacher,'" Brother Semm laughed. "I'll spread it all around that Brother Zeke Warpboard chickened out on his calling to preach."

"I'll be there!" Zeke retorted. "Me and Tug will get together and study up for a sermon, and I'll write it all down so that I can remember it when I deliver it from the pulpit. You'll hear a sermon that the likes has never been heard. I'll preach the dirty sins right off the sinners' backs. It'll take the whole congregation a week to scrub and scour the floors to clean up the defiled mess that peels off their skins. Just you be ready with them, too, 'cause a little smudging might rub off your rusty hide, too,. Brother Semm."

"Don't write anything down. You can't read it when it's on paper, and you can't take Tug Cornfield up to the pulpit to help you deliver your sermon," Brother Semm told him.

"Don't worry about me. I'll get through it all just fine," Zeke predicted.

"I certainly hope so—for your own sake," Brother Semm called as Zeke passed through the door. "Poor, simpleminded man," the old preacher mumbled to himself, making himself as comfortable as possible on the worn sofa. He opened his Bible and began to read. He chose no certain part of the Lord's Word. The book just chanced to open to Corinthians I, 1:26. The old preacher read aloud. "For ye see your calling, brethren, how that not many wise men after the flesh, not many mighty, not many noble, are called."

* * * *

Having thought about Brother Semm's invitation to preach at the up-coming revival, Zeke went in search of Tug Cornfield. He needed to for-mulate a plan to evade the pulpit at the Coaley Creek Freewill Baptist Church on Sunday evening. He found his friend at Big Onion Gap watch-ing a group of men pitching horseshoes.

"Hey, fellers! Here comes the new preacher," Tug Cornfield yelled, pointing a finger toward Zeke. "Maybe he can bless the shoes so we can pitch better—make more ringers that way, maybe."

"Don't be too hard on him," Toby Cornfield said as he removed a shoe from around the stake, where his pitching partner had thrown the first ringer of the game. "That makes us nine, and you boys are just three. We can go out with this pitch," he said, banging the shoes together to dis-lodge the loose dirt clinging to them. He turned his hat around on his head three times, did two complete 360-degree turns, and stamped his right foot once.

"What was that shenanigan all about?" Allamander Skinner asked as he stood back away from the stake. "With a shine like you cut, I could lose a leg with a wild pitch. Throw us a ringer!"

"That was my good-luck routine," Toby replied, chuckling. "Here come our going-out points. Let another team prepare to face defeat."

He threw his first shoe. It struck the stake with a wobbling blow, caromed off, and rolled into the weeds about twenty feet from the leaning stake.

"You should have put a cowbell on that one so you could find it," Allamander Skinner laughed, slapping his legs excitedly. "Throw us another one, but let it be a little closer, preferably around the stob."

"This one will be a lot better than the other one," Toby promised as he pitched a carbon copy of the first. It rolled to within six inches of the other shoe. "I don't know what's got into me. I can't pitch for snot."

"You didn't cut that shine that time," Allamander said, continuing his crazy laugh.

"Maybe you can get us through the game," Toby stated, stepping back and watching his pitching partner toss the shoes.

"Tug, I need to talk to you," Zeke whispered, taking the big man by the arm and walking him out of hearing range of the horseshoe pitchers.

"What's so urgent?" Tug asked, peering into the bewildered and frantic face of his friend.

"Could you get away Saturday to start our preaching tour?" Zeke asked.

"Why are you in such a hurry?" Tug queried, playing the question game. He knew the reason, but wanted to hear what Zeke had to say about it.

"This calling is working on me. I need to get started making use of it before I lose it," Zeke told his friend, scuffing his foot in the dirt beside the road.

Cars and pickups passed as they sped toward Jenkins, Kentucky, a little town about ten miles from Big Onion Gap. Coal trucks sped by, blowing coal dust over the men and the hardtop road, pulling more dust behind them in their draft.

Several people called a friendly greeting as they hurriedly went about their daily activities.

"Zeke, I can't go with you this weekend," Tug informed his friend. "Me and some boys are planning a fishing trip down on Bass Creek River. Why don't you come along with us? There will be plenty of room in Toby's pickup truck. You might have to ride in the back, but that won't hurt. He's got a good seat for you to relax on. Go with us."

"I can't do that. My calling won't let me do it," Zeke lamented.

"Have you talked to Brother Semm Pilton lately?" Tug asked, smiling genially. "He was looking for you. He said something about you helping in his revival. He told me that some big-named preacher is coming from Kentucky, or somewhere. It would be an honor if you could participate in the ministering to the lost with him. It would be a real caution on your part. It would get you ready to hit the road in your endeavor for the Lord."

"Yeah, he asked me to participate with him. Brother Semm ain't going to preach," Zeke said, staring nervously at his friend. "I think he's going to ask me to preach first, to sorta open the services and get the congregation in a happy, spiritual mood. Then the visiting preacher will close services. I hope we can split the offering, since I'm going to be doing part of the work."

"Yeah, you should be able to share in the take." Tug said, shaking with a silent belly laugh. "Maybe you can get enough for us to take off next week. Give it a try, Zeke. Who knows? You might get started off on the right track, and one of those preacher-paying churches could just snatch you right up to pastor for them with a good salary."

"Yeah, they might!" Zeke said, his face lighting up with a thistle-eating grin. "Yeah, they might just do that. Will you help me prepare a sermon for Sunday night? Would you come over and read to me and help me write a good sermon?"

"Sure, I'll do it, but the agreement still stands, don't it?" Tug wanted to know.

"What agreement?" Zeke asked, looking bewildered. "What agreement are you talking about?"

"The one about my sharing in some of your preaching money. You do remember that, don't you?" Tug said, amused with the growing nervousness of the preacher-to-be.

"Well, there was supposed to be a share for you when we go on the road. Here at home you'll be staying with your family. I shouldn't have to share with you right now," Zeke whined.

"What about your sermon Sunday night? Can you write one by yourself?" Tug asked.

"No, but we ain't out there on the road right now," Zeke stammered.

"Well, the deal's off. You're on your own, my little friend," Tug said, threatening to leave.

"Wait! Help me with my sermon Sunday night, and I'll cut you in on my first offering. Maybe it'll be a big one," Zeke hoped as he grasped Tug's huge arm. He held on as the big man drug him over the rough ground. "Please! Help me get my start," Zeke pleaded.

"Well, since you're twisting my arm so hard," Tug said. "I guess I ought to help you. You sure are a persuasive man, Zeke. You talked me right into taking part of the offering. Thanks a lot! You should be able to talk the sinners into quitting their sinning."

* * * *

The two confidants arrived at the Coaley Creek Freewill Baptist Church late that Sunday afternoon—early enough to implement their plan of action. Though the door was securely locked against vandals, a window high up on the north side of the building wasn't secured against an entrance to the structure.

Tug Cornfield scaled the wall using a locust pole that he had found in the wooded area behind the building. He crawled through the window and was lost from sight.

Zeke Warpboard removed the pole, carried it to the woods, hid it, and went to the front of the building to await the arrival of the preachers and the congregation. He didn't have very long to wait, as cars began to arrive bearing many people in them—most were chock-full. Zeke's heart skipped a beat as he thought of the assignment awaiting him within the building. He hoped that Tug would fit in the lectern. Tug was a big man, but Zeke felt that he was safe—that Tug would be able to hide behind the dark curtain on the front of the lectern. He hoped his plan would work.

Tug would have the sermon and could read it and whisper it to Zeke. In that manner, the two gentlemen could convey a message to the congregation.

"Good evening, Brother Semm," Zeke said, greeting the old preacher. He smiled pleasantly as he extended his hand.

"Evening, my good friend," Brother Semm said, returning the salutation. "Are you ready to give us some good counsel tonight?"

"Ready and raring to hit the pulpit," Zeke said with a positive tone. "I think I can move the congregation to the very entrance to the Pearly Gates."

"That sure sounds good to me," Brother Semm said. "I was afraid that you would get nervous and back out on me right at the last minute, leaving me with the chore of opening the services for Brother Storey Taylor."

Brother Semm unlocked the door, pocketed the key, and let Zeke enter first.

Zeke walked to the pulpit, stood behind the lectern, and addressed Brother Semm. "How do I look, peering over this stand? Can the people see me if I stand just like this?"

"Yeah, they can see you," Brother Semm replied. "Now, come down here, and let's talk about the revival."

"I'll just stand here and be ready when everybody gets here," Zeke said, shifting his weight from one foot to the other. He was getting ready for the Spirit to move him. He could light-foot back and forth while delivering his sermon. "There's no use to sit down and have to get right back up." He heard a snicker under the podium. Tug found his statement amusing.

"Are you happy enough to laugh about it?" Brother Semm asked, looking at the short man standing in the pulpit.

"I'm not laughing," Zeke said. "It must have been a church-mouse."

That statement made the preachers laugh, and a third party found it amusing, too, but was able to suppress his laughter.

The church-house began to fill, and soon there was standing room only to hear the visiting preacher, Brother Storey Taylor.

Preacher Taylor shook hands as he walked up the aisle, his Bible clasped tightly in his left hand, leaving his right hand free. "Hello, Brother Semm," he said, shaking hands with his friend and brother in Christ. He sat down and looked toward the pulpit. "Who is the flowerpot in the pulpit?" he asked, giving Zeke a close once-over as the little man stood up there grinning like a skinned skunk.

"That's Brother Zeke Warpboard. He's going to open the services for you," Brother Semm explained, smiling.

"Looks like he is eager to get into the harness and plow through the sinners who have come to hear some preaching. I hope there are some sinners in here. If there aren't any, we may as well go home," Brother Taylor joked.

"I guess we'll have to go home if there aren't any sinners here, but I imagine there will be plenty for us to worry about," Brother Semm replied, chuckling. "This young man said that he was called to preach. I really don't know. He was called to preach or to plow one. I don't know which, and neither does he," Brother Semm replied.

Zeke found Brother Taylor's joke amusing and cackled like a banty hen that had just laid an egg. He ignored Brother Semm's statement.

"Jolly little fellow, isn't he?" Brother Taylor said as he looked toward the pulpit, where Zeke continued to stand and laugh hilariously.

"That was a good one, Brother Taylor," Zeke reflected. "Do you have any more as funny as that one?"

Brother Storey Taylor turned back to face Brother Semm Pilton, without giving Zeke an answer.

The dust in the lectern caused Tug Cornfield to sneeze. Even though he had tried to smother the sound, it was still audible.

"Somebody is taking a cold, looks like," Zeke said, quickly taking his handkerchief from his pocket and wiping his dry nose. He then blew it to be sure his actions were authentic enough to fool the crowd.

Brother Semm looked at his watch, rose, and walked to the pulpit.

Zeke hurriedly stamped his right foot to warn Tug that Brother Semm was approaching. Otherwise, he did not move. He stood his ground, grinning amicably.

"Let's open our hymnals to page 222 and sing that good old hymn," Brother Semm suggested, opening his songbook. "If there is a quartet here tonight, we would like for you to come forth after we sing a few congregational songs."

"Yes, we have a great quartet with us," Brother Taylor offered, motioning for the singers to come to the front of the room.

The building rang with the song of praise as everybody tried to sing louder than the person next to him.

After the end of the last congregational song, the quartet was ushered to the pulpit by Brother Storey Taylor.

Zeke stood his ground as the singers selected a song which would be appropriate for a revival. Everyone in the building looked at the little man standing in the pulpit. He stood guard as if his life depended upon it, hoping that Tug would not be detected. That sneeze was almost a dead give away for the two strategists.

The members of the quartet continued to look in a bewildered state— at Zeke and then at each other—wondering when the little intruder was going to take a seat. As Zeke continued to ignore the singers, the group leader struck a tuning fork on the corner of the lectern.

Zeke jumped, startled by the sudden sound that the tuning fork made as it struck the lectern, but the grin remained on his happy face.

The people whispered their confused wonder amongst themselves as they looked at the grinning man standing with the four singers.

After several songs by the quartet, Brother Semm said a few words and then asked the visiting preacher to lead them in prayer.

The preachers dropped to their knees, resting their heads in their hands. They were joined by several members of the church as they came forward and in their humbleness knelt on the bare floor.

Zeke continied to stand in the pulpit and grin without even bowing his head.

At the end of the moderately short prayer, Brother Semm said a few more words and then introduced Zeke. "Brothers and Sisters, I want you to meet Brother Zeke Warpboard. He says that he has been called to preach, so I'm giving him a chance to get broke in right. He'll deliver the opening sermon."

Zeke stood before the crowd, unable to speak, still grinning. He stamped his foot as a signal for Tug to read the sermon. "Thank you, Brother Semm," he said. "Tonight, I want to preach to you from the Book of Mark, and if my memory serves me just right, Jesus said to his disciples...."

The little man faltered for a moment as he looked down at his feet, and then at the huge crowd staring back at him. "As I said there at first, if my memory serves me right, Jesus said to his disciples...." Again he stopped and looked down. The sermon lay at his feet. He could not see well enough to read it down there on the floor—if he had been able to read. As he stood there in his anxious state, he heard a contented snore emanating from the closed lectern. Tug Cornfield was asleep.

The big grin vanished from the little man's face, replaced by a look of dumbfounded surprise. "Bust take it, Tug! You went and screwed up the whole sermon!" he said, squatting to peer despondently at Tug, who continued to snore peacefully.

"What have you done, Zeke?" Brother Semm asked as he rose with an embarassed look. "I should have known that Tug Cornfield was in on this. Brothers and Sisters, I don't know what got into those two to cause them to do a stunt like that. What are you trying to prove, Brother Zeke?" he asked, turning his attention to the pulpit and the stammering Zeke Warpboard.

Zeke kept up his tirade, directing it to the hidden Tug Cornfield, still seated beneath the lectern, too embarrassed to show himself as he awoke and realized what was going on.

"I should have known that you were too dumb to help me the way you said you could," Zeke stormed. "All you wanted was some of the offering that we could have got if you had done your part."

"I did as much of my part as I could," Tug protested as he crawled from his seclusion and faced the crowd. "Me and the boys went fishing down on Bass Creek River last night. We didn't get in till daylight this morning. With all that closeness and warmth under that stand, I just slid off into dreamland. If you all will be kind enough to excuse me, I guess I had better be on my way," he said as he headed for the door. A big smile split his homely face as he walked past the bewildered congregation of worshipers.

"I could have been a good preacher if you had read my sermon for me!" Zeke called after his departing aide. "All that you wanted was part of the offering. Now, I won't even be able to get any of it, 'cause of your going to sleep. I guess that you were right, Brother Semm. I was called to plow 'stead of preach," he lamented as he sat down between the two ministers.

Pass the Taters, but Hold the Possum

Cephus Gallmathy stood before the seventh-grade history class that brisk October afternoon. He was in excruciating pain as was evidenced by the mask of misery on his morose face. One could tell that his stomach had been giving him a fit through the morning and early-afternoon class periods, and it was all that he could do to stand before the worn-out group, staring impassively at him.

"Why don't you give us a study period, Mr. Gallmathy?" Esker Seedy suggested to the pathetic teacher. "We'll be real good while you relax and take it easy till the bell rings for us to go home."

"Yeah, we can do something to occupy ourselves," Ham Sedder replied, turning to the rest of the students for their approval of his suggestion. "Me and Gillis Cornfield can go dust the erasers on the rock wall down there in front of the gymnasium, if you think they need it bad enough."

"I've got a good book that I checked out of the library today," Masby Wheddle said, offering the book to the teacher. "Teed Cornfield recommended it to me. That's why I checked it out." He turned to Teed, who sat directly behind him, and said, "It's sure a good book, ain't it, Teed?"

"It sure is. I've read it at least six times," Teed replied, grinning all over himself.

"Thanks, Masby, but I have several books and magazines to choose from," Mr. Gallmathy replied. "I need to average the six-weeks grades and record them on your report cards by Monday afternoon. We need to cover the last chapter of 'The French and Indian War' for a test tomorrow. The test will be a third of your grade, so it is important that we get through the chapter. I appreciate your concern for me, but we will just have to grunt and grind."

Teed felt sorry for the 'Fess, as he and most of the other rambunctious boys called Mr. Gallmathy.

Cephus had just moved from Baltimore, Maryland, where he had taught in the city's school system for a number of years. His doctor had told him that he needed to be where there was a more laid-back atmosphere. The city—his job, especially—had been very nerve-wracking. His health had deteriorated to the point where he would need surgery to remove part of his stomach if he did not slow down and try to relax more.

The word that had circulated about the town of Birchfield was that the new teacher was sort of puny. That is what the people in rural Appalachia refer to when a person is sick, but not too sick to keep going.

"Why don't you just average our grades that we've made on our other tests and homework we've turned in?" Teed suggested. "Most of us have pretty good grades. We can all get along very well without another test to bone up for. We can take an extra test during the next six-week period."

"Part of you might, but I don't fit into that *most* category," Esker quipped. "Aw, shucks, go ahead and average them up. A test could make mine go down and hit the bottom, though. I think it's about to suck mud right now. A test can't make it go any lower. Tear us up with a big test, 'Fess."

Everyone got a good laugh at the amicable Esker Seedy. He was always clowning, keeping the class in a jovial mood. He was no smart aleck—just fun-loving.

"Thanks for the laugh, Esker. That helped a lot, but we must get back to our studies," Mr. Gallmathy said. His strained face had lost some of its pallor due to the vigorous laugh. "Turn to chapter eight."

The students took their books from their desks, making as much noise as possible. Several books were dropped—some on purpose, just to hear the resounding slap against the tiled floor.

Esker Seedy dropped his twice. "Boy, that sounds great!" he said. He picked the book up and searched for the assignment.

Mr. Gallmathy called for quietness and asked a question in an attempt to start a discussion.

The first question was easy, so Teed jumped on the answer like a fox would pounce on a baby chickey-diddle.

"Very good," Mr. Gallmathy remarked, commending Teed for the quick response.

The next question was very easy. Mr. Gallmathy wanted to know which side the Indians had fought for.

"The Indians fit on their own side," Esker Seedy commented. "I bet they fit for the English one day, and the French the next day, just to keep the feud going as long as they could, 'cause they could prosper better that way. They could get guns from both sides and compare them and cull out any duds that they might have got. The red men were supposed to be dumb savages. I'll allow that they were some very shrewd characters, if you ask me."

"We didn't ask you, Esker," Gillis Cornfield snapped. "Let's get to the cankered core of this war and study it real hard so we can take home some real good marks on our 'port cards."

"They could have done that, couldn't they, 'Fess?" Esker said, turning to the teacher, and then turning back to Gillis, with a perfected smirk on his homely face. Esker always gave a little whistling sound as he talked through his buckteeth.

"Yes, that could have happened, Mr. Seedy," the teacher agreed.

"See, smarty Gillis Cornfield!" Esker retorted, smiling almost past his ears. "Did you notice that 'Fess called me Mister Seedy?"

"That doesn't mean anything," Ham Sedder laughed. "He could call a dog 'Mister,' if he wanted to. Why do you think that Indians would fight for both sides?"

"Well, they could keep the argument going, and that way they could keep all the soldiers out of the woods so they could kill a lot of deer for their food. I still say that the Indians were very smart. Look at Teed and Gillis; they are part Indian. They ain't too smart, but I've heard that they're part Indian. Ain't that right, Teed?"

"That's what I've always been told," Teed replied, and then began an explanation for the Indian blood in his family tree. "Dad says that our folks came from North Carolina. My great-great-grandmother on my dad's side was a full-blooded Cherokee, so that would make me some part Indian. I don't know and don't care just how much Indian blood is flowing through my veins. I can't see it, so it doesn't really matter if I'm part Indian or not. Gillis and I aren't going to go to war against the white folks around here, are we, Gills?"

"You're right about that, Teed. We sure ain't going on the warpath," Gillis laughed.

"See? I told you that they were part Indian," Esker beamed. "Everybody had better hold on to your hair so they won't scalp you."

"That will be enough about the Indians for now, Esker," Mr. Gallmathy intervened, rapping the desk with a stick he used as a pointer. "Let's summarize the causes that led to the outbreak of the war. We also want to know what each side gained or lost due to the conflict."

Teed Cornfield asked a question, and soon everyone was captivated by the aura of the review.

Mr. Gallmathy smiled at Teed, showing his approval of the step taken to get the entire class to participate in the review.

After about fifteen minutes of discussion, the subject was changed to a completely different topic.

Esker Seedy, who sat directly in front of the teacher's desk, raised his hand above his head, snapped his fingers to be sure to get attention, and asked a question that nearly knocked Mr. Gallmathy off his feet.

"'Fess, I've just been studying you while everybody else has talked about a war that don't mean cat hair to me," Esker said, with that ever-present whistling sound of air flowing freely through his widely spaced buckteeth. "You sure look pale and peaked. Do you have a hangover?"

"Absolutely not!" Cephus snapped. His ulcer must have made him grumpy and caused him to give such a blunt reply.

The room resounded with laughter as everyone turned to the person sitting next to him to see if he had gotten the gist of Esker's joke.

Teed tried to restrain his laughter. He felt sorry for his gentle teacher.

"Mr. Gallmathy," Esker said, when the noisy students ended their mirthful expressions, "I bet you can't stand as much physical exertion as me, Teed Cornfield, Ham Sedder, and Masby Wheddle."

"Teed, Ham, Masby, and I," Mr. Gallmathy replied, correcting Esker's grammar.

"No! I'm included in the quartet—not you!" Esker stated, without realizing that the teacher was only correcting his grammar, not wanting to take his place in the gang of boys.

"You always state everyone else before yourself," Mr. Gallmathy said, repeating the correct order of the names.

"Well, whatever you say," Esker said, looking around at his cohorts for their approval.

"Why do you say that I cannot stand as much physical strain as you boys?" the teacher asked, his curiosity raised. He wondered why Esker had brought up the question of his strength and stamina.

"Have you ever been out in the woods on a huntin' trip?" Esker inquired.

"No, I have not, and I don't intend to go on one," Cephus answered, a hint of irritation showing in his voice.

Teed figured that since the teacher was so tall and thin, he would be a very vulnerable adversary to lead into the Booger Hill area of the

Cumberlands, the mountain range separating Southwest Virginia and eastern Kentucky. The terrain is very rugged, and in most places it is rocky and there is a lot of underbrush and laurel thickets, making it very hard to walk through. Even the strongest men in the area have a tough battle with the bushes, grapevines, and shoulder-high ground flora. Poor Mr. Gallmathy would be worn to a frazzle if he were to try to best the four rambunctious boys at their own game.

"I bet that you couldn't stand a good possum and coon hunt with us," Esker bantered further, keeping the conversation going.

"Let's forget about opossums, raccoons, and hunting trips and get back to our history lesson, where we can study about the French and Indians," Cephus ordered, but his attempt to carry on a discussion of the lesson was rudely interrupted again by Esker.

"Will you go huntin' with us boys tonight and prove that you can stand as much as we can? Do you want to prove your bragging rights?" Esker asked, snickering, causing the air to whistle through his front teeth.

"There isn't anyone in here bragging, except one Esker Seedy," Mr. Gallmathy stated.

"Season opened night before last, and us boys ain't had a chance to go out, 'cause of school and stuff like that," Esker went on. "The wind is still today, and the temperature is just right to get the possums to stir early tonight. What do you say? Do you want to go?"

Mr. Gallmathy needed the evening to prepare an examination for the next day's class, but before he would let those boys think for one minute that he was a weakling, he would work late into the night—after the hunt, of course—to prepare the test. "All right, I'll go hunting with you, but remember, we can't stay out very late. Remember that we have a test tomorrow."

"Okay!" the boys yelled.

"We might not have a test," Esker whispered to Teed.

"Probably won't," was Teed's quick reply.

Seeing Teed and Esker in conference, the teacher asked, "What did you say, Esker?"

"Oh, I just said that we'll probably ace the test, with you out there with us in the wilderness, discussing the war while the dogs are looking for some game," Esker said, causing the rest of students to laugh.

"What kind of dog do you have, Mr. Gallmathy," Teed queried.

"I don't have a dog," Cephus told him. "I thought that you boys would provide the hunting hounds. You talked up the hunt, and if you don't have dogs, you will have to talk up a bunch of hounds, too."

"Ever' hunter must have a good possum dog—that is if he intends to catch a possum," Esker bantered further, looking around the room at the amused boys.

"You boys talked up the hunt, so you will have to supply the dogs," Mr. Gallmathy stated. "Let's drop the subject and get back to our lesson."

"But you must bring a dog. That's one of the rules for a possum hunt," Esker added.

"You will furnish the dogs. That's *my* rule," Mr. Gallmathy stated firmly. "Now, let's get some studying done before the day elapses."

"But you *must* bring a dog," Esker argued.

"Well, I'll bring a dog," Mr. Gallmathy agreed. "When and where are we to meet for this opossum hunt?"

Teed Cornfield drew a crude road map directing Mr. Gallmathy to the Cornfield's farm. "Be at my house about dark. Here's a map. I hope you can find it," he said. "We'll hit the woods as soon as you get there."

During the rest of the period, Cephus wondered where he could find an opossum-treeing dog. None of his acquaintances in town were hunters. There were many dogs, but how could he tell whether or not one would hunt for an opossum. He happened to think of Miss McSkirt's Boston terrior—a pretty little fellow with a head full of sense. Maybe it could be a true hunter—a good tree-dog. That would be the dog to take on the big hunt.

Miss McSkirt ran the rooming house where Cephus made his home. She had told him once that her dog, Midget, had chased a huge opossum from her sister's henhouse while she visited on the farm a few weeks earlier. He hoped that she would lend the dog to him for the hunt.

"There's no use to study for this test," Esker said as he left the room after the class period ended with the dismissal bell ringing clearly down the hall. "We'll hack him for sure," he went on to say, and the other boys agreed.

"Hack me!" Cephus exclaimed to himself. He knew what "hack" meant. The people in the neighborhood held cockfights. The boys referred to a cowardly bird as a "hacked" rooster. That is when the feathers on the back part of the neck of the chicken rise, showing the rooster's fear of his opponent. "They might hack me," he said aloud, "but I'm going to try very hard to show those boys that I'm game." As he left the room, he heard Esker Seedy talking to his pals.

"Wait till he starts eating a haunch of a possum; that's when the fun will start," the boy said, laughing loudly.

Cephus knew that he was in for an eventful evening—his first opossum hunt, and his first leg of opossum meat. He decided that he would go, regardless of the outcome.

* * * *

The night was dark with no moon to help light the way. The hunters walked along a narrow path which wound through a large beech grove on Teed Cornfield's parents' farm.

Midget, the little Boston terrier, walked along at Cephus Gallmathy's heels and whined pathetically as they crossed fallen trees blocking the way. The teacher found it necessary to help the tiny canine over several. He could not understand why the little dog would not go out with the rest of the pack of hunting hounds—a pack of mixed mongrels. The large dogs had not been seen or heard from for almost an hour.

"They're wide hunters," Teed Cornfield explained when he was asked why the dogs had left and had not reported in for such a long time.

"Could they be out in the woods taking a nap about now?" Cephus asked.

"Man, that hurts!" Teed stammered. "You insult me by questioning my dog's hunting abilities. Those dogs don't come back to check in until they find something to put up a tree. They just don't come in, unless the night is bad and the animals ain't stirring out. Don't worry about them. They'll tree directly. Be patient. A hunter has to be patient, 'cause he can't smell after a possum like a dog can. You'll learn about hunting, that is if you stay around here long enough to get out in the woods and see what goes on while on a good hunt."

Cephus had worn too many clothes. He perspired freely, and when the crisp night air touched the dampness of the lower part of his neck, chill bumps covered his entire body, causing him to react with a shaking convulsion.

As the quintet topped a rise in the path, they heard the plaintive bay of the pack of hounds.

Cephus hurried along to keep pace with the energetic lads. He had lived in the area for only a few months, and his lack of stamina showed.

His two-cell flashlight gave only a faint ray of light. The feeble, yellow glow barely reached the leafy carpet beneath the huge trees. It bounced along with each unsteady step the teacher made.

As the hunters arrived at the tree, they saw the clamoring dogs looking up into a crimson-colored sourwood sapling, making the hills ring with their baying.

After a thorough scrutiny of the leaf-covered tree, Cephus saw two small beady eyes peering back at him. They were much brighter than his weak flashlight, and when the opossum blinked, the woods were in total darkness.

"Let's tie our dogs and let 'Fess' prized hound do the honors of catching the game," Teed suggested, taking a length of binding string from his coat pocket. He tied his dog, Old Carbo, to a small tree and watched as the other boys tied their dogs in the same manner.

Esker Seedy, eager to send the small animal to its doom, began to shake the limber tree vigorously—until the opossum lost its hold on the limb where it had perched precariously.

"Get your ferocious hound dog ready to retrieve the game, Mr. Gallmathy," Teed said as the small creature plummeted to the ground.

Cephus held Midget in his arms. That was an easy task, for the frightened little dog cuddled against his chest. She shivered in fear as the huge hounds barked and carried on, making an earth-shaking roar.

As the opossum met the ground, Cephus attempted to release Midget. He wanted the little dog to have a chance to chase the opossum. As he set the canine on the ground, it ran behind him and peered around his legs, and from that position the little fellow took in the frightening spectacle.

Esker laughed so hard that he fell on a pile of leaves under the tree.

The other boys laughed hilariously and tumbled into the leaves on top of one another, playing a game of pile-on. Esker ended up on the bottom of the pile, kicking to rid himself of the weight of his buddies.

"We'd better get up and do something about confiscating that four-legged monster," Teed said, rolling from the top of the pile of scrambling lads.

Cephus saw nothing funny. The little dog was frightened. He pitied it, but the boys found the incident very amusing.

Rising to his feet after a good scuffle in the leaves, Esker released his dog, and in a matter of seconds the huge hound caught the fleeing marsupial. He recovered the skinny-looking animal from the steel-trap jaws of the dog, while Teed tried to still the other charging, barking hounds.

Upon completing his task of freeing the opossum, Esker instructed the other boys to rake the leaves away and start a fire.

"What are you going to do now?" Mr. Gallmathy asked.

"We're going to skin, broil, and eat this sucker," Teed said, looking up from his cleaning chore to find his teacher staring at him with his mouth wide-open in disbelief. "Ham and Masby brought some sweet taters. That's a delicacy around here. Wait until you taste our meal! You won't want to eat anything else after that."

"I won't be eating any of that scrawny opossum, but I will take a baked potato," Cephus answered, trying to be as sociable as possible by accepting the invitation to dine with the boys. If he should eat that meat, he knew that Teed Cornfield could be right—he may never eat anything else. It could just plain kill him.

In a matter of minutes, the boys had the skin removed from the most pitiful excuse for a repast that Cephus Gallmathy had ever seen. "How can I upset my stomach on that diet?" he thought as he watched the boys skin and dress the opossum.

Ham Sedder and Masby Wheddle raked the live embers from the roaring fire. They placed several yams—wrapped in aluminum foil—on the hot coals and covered them with more embers. With the intense heat, they would soon be baked to a golden turn.

Teed did a quick job of cutting up the small animal. He cut long sticks from small sourwood saplings that were plentiful all around the arena of action. He cut holes in the pieces of meat with a knife and slipped the skewers through them to make a makeshift spit to broil their snack. Soon the meat commenced to sputter and sizzle over the roaring fire.

While the boys talked incessantly among themselves, a scuffle broke out between Teed Cornfield and Esker Seedy.

Teed challenged his friend to a round of wrestling—his favorite sport.

The set-to lasted for only a few seconds as Teed succeeded in securing a good neck hold. He squeezed hard enough to stop the obnoxious whistling of air through his opponent's teeth. He had Esker throttled so tight that the boy's eyes had begun to bulge, but that didn't bother Teed. He was in the match for a win. He got that win as Mr. Gallmathy stepped into the fracas.

The teacher pulled with all his strength, attempting to break Teed's pit bull grip on the choking boy. He finally succeeded in breaking the hold.

"Teed! Are you crazy?" he asked, turning the little warrior around to where he could look him in the face. "You could have choked him to death!"

"Aw, he's tough," Teed laughed. He slapped Esker on the back. "Aren't you, old buddy? He didn't say that he was giving up at any time while I was squeezing his long, rusty neck."

"He couldn't tell you that he was giving up," Mr. Gallmathy said. "You had his wind cut off."

"He'll live, 'cause this ain't the first time I've whipped him at rasslin', is it, Esker?" Teed grinned, checking the red marks on Esker's neck. "Is that raw?" he asked, rubbing the red skin.

"It don't seem to be too raw, but I sure am smarting real bad, though," Esker groaned, wincing under the pressure from Teed's probing index finger.

"It'll heal up and hair over in no time," Teed laughed. He turned to the other boys and challenged them to take him on—all three at once—but did not get an acceptance to the banter.

"I think we have had enough wrestling for tonight," Mr. Gallmathy announced. "You might accidentally roll into the fire and receive a bad burn."

Midget moved nervously as she cowered by Cephus' feet. The aroma of the cooking meat floated about the area, causing the little dog to drool.

The three big dogs were interested in the meat, too. Their tongues were hanging out of their mouths, where long, thick streams of saliva dripped off and fell to the ground as they anticipated tearing into a piece of that broiled possum.

"It's done," Esker said, taking the food from the sticks and serving it to the waiting group, while occasionally rubbing his scuffed-up neck.

"Eat up, men," Teed invited. He watched his teacher inspect the charred morsel in his nervous hand.

"Pass the taters, but hold the possum," Mr. Gallmathy said, using the local jargon as he tried to reject the offer of the meat.

"You have to eat a tater and a piece of possum, Mr. Gallmathy," Esker said.

Mr. Gallmathy looked at his portion and swallowed against a large lump that had welled up in his throat. How could he eat a thing like that? He could not eat pork on his sensitive stomach, and he knew definitely that that little opossum's leg would be his doom if he were to eat it. He thought about pitching it into the bushes behind him, but knew very well that the boys would think that he was a wimp if he were to do that. He watched the boys bite into theirs with vigor. He really did not know whether or not they liked it, but they were chewing vigorously and moving it around in their mouths.

He bit into the food with little enthusiasm. The half-done meat clung tightly to the bone, but he tore at it to try to pull it free. He finally got a bite into his mouth and began to chew.

"How is it, 'Fess?" Teed asked. "You look just a little peaked. Can't you hack it?"

Mr. Gallmathy said nothing as he made a valiant effort to eat the one bite that he was able to force past his clinched teeth. He was finally able to swallow. The half-chewed bite tried to grip his esophagus as he continued to swallow. Finally, he got it down to his stomach, but his ulcer gave it a kick and sent it back. It lodged in his throat and slowly slid back to his stomach. It stayed there for a few seconds, and again, up it came in a very healthy upchuck.

"'Fess can't hold his possum!" Teed laughed, and the rest joined him as they made light of their teacher's inability to keep the meat in his stomach.

Esker extinguished the fire with the water from his canteen and dismissed the hunt. "'Fess can't hold his possum," he laughed, wheezing through his buckteeth.

Cephus Gallmathy was tired as he hurried along behind the strong boys. He had to carry the little Boston terrier, for it was too scared to walk. How could he face those energetic lads on Friday when it came time to hand out test papers—that is if he could make it through the night? From the way his stomach was rolling, he was afraid that he was in for an uncomfortable night.

* * * *

The next day, three of the quartet of boys were absent from school. Only Teed Cornfield was there, and he had a sick look on his face.

"What's wrong, Teed? Do you have a hangover?" Mr. Gallmathy asked with a smile of triumph.

Teed bowed his head and said nothing. He was hacked!

Chickey-Diddle and Dumplin's

Tolley Trent sat in front of the warm fireplace, watching the many-colored flames lap at the throat of the sooty black chimney. As he sat there in a semi-trance caused by the warm glow and dancing flames, he could see knights in shining armor riding into battle. The scene suddenly changed as a dragon came along and gobbled up the knights and horses in one big gulp and then vanished up the chimney. The scene changed again, to a herd of cattle running across a cornfield. A bunch of slopping hogs took the place of the cattle as the flames jumped toward the throat of the chimney and fell back to the burning logs—or did they fall back? They could have gone right on up through the chimney and floated toward the clouds. No, they couldn't do that, Tolley reasoned. The boy watched the action in the fire and daydreamed of Christmas.

Tolley's favorite holiday was only a week away, and he had not yet decided what he wanted to receive in his cap on Christmas morning. Each year he laid his cap out for Santa Claus to put his goodies and one toy in; that was a tradition handed down through the ages in the Trent family. One Christmas, Tolley remembered, he put his father's big hat on the treadle-type Singer sewing machine for Santa to fill to the brim with goodies, and he had hoped for a big toy of some sort instead of the usual ball, yo-yo, or little rubber truck. He had made plenty of room, but Santa did not take the hint. Maybe the lingering aftermath of the Great Depression was cramping Santa's buying power, Tolley reasoned. And with the war going on, times were hard for the Trents.

Anyway, last Christmas Tolley had received the usual little wad of goodies and a yo-yo. The yo-yo lasted about as long as it took him to eat the goodies. When the string broke and the yo-yo came apart, he used the round pieces to skip across the pond down near the barn. When a kid isn't used to having much, he can find a way to make a game of almost anything.

Tolley had five brothers and two sisters, and counting his parents, there were ten in the family. With that many folks to kick shins around the long, narrow table, every meal had to stretch as far as possible. The family lived on a hillside farm and grew most of their food, but food wasn't their only need. There was a need for things which could not be grown on a farm, such as clothing, shoes, sugar, and salt. Most of these items were rationed due to World War II raging at that time.

The Trents had enough to get by with: food, clothing, and a good roof over their heads—no luxuries, though. If there had been luxuries, they wouldn't have known what to do with them, so they didn't need luxuries.

The scene continued to change on the wide-range fireplace movie screen. Birds flew into a huge cloud and came out on the opposite side. Somehow they had changed into sheep while inside the fire-cloud. They, too, flew up the chimney and disappeared, while more visions of different animals danced in the hot flames.

Tolley was brought back to reality when his brother Claude slapped him around the side of the head with a wet sock that the lad had just taken off his smelly foot.

Claude had been out hen-grannying and collecting eggs from the straw nests in the henhouse. Snow had gone down the tops of his brogan shoes, creating a toe-jam slosh, causing an unpleasant odor.

"Claude! I should hang you with that stinking sock!" Tolley shouted, bounding up out of his comfortable seat to chase his younger brother through the house. A wrestling scuffle broke out as Tolley managed to corner Claude on the big feather bed in his parents' room. He gave his brother a good knuckle-rubbing on the head.

"Mom, Tolley's trying to take my sock away from me and put it on. I need it just as bad as he does; maybe more, since he already has two socks on," Claude called to his mother, who at that moment was preparing supper.

"I don't want his old stinking sock," Tolley replied, before his mother had time to reprimand him for his aggression toward Claude.

"You boys had better start your chores," Martha Trent ordered, brushing hair back out of her eyes with the back of her dough-covered hand. "Dad will be home from the mines in a little while. You know what he'll do if he finds you lollygagging around without your chores done. He'll take a two-handed brash to your backsides, so shake into your chores."

"Shakin', Mom. I'm shakin'," Tolley said, twisting his body into as many different shapes as possible while working his way toward the door. "Shake it, Claude," he told his brother, slamming the door as he left the room.

Claude followed suit, twisting and gyrating in the same cavorting manner as Tolley. No one saw his monkeyshine, but that didn't matter; it was a lot of fun for him anyway. He continued to shake and twist on his way toward the door.

* * * *

"It's getting awful close to Christmas, Dad," Tolley said, breaking the silence at the supper table that evening. "Would you all like to have a big gobbler or feznit for the Christmas dinner this year, 'stead of an old, tough rooster?"

"That would be mighty good, son," Tavis Trent replied, eating contentedly. "But where are we going to get a big gobbler? I don't get paid till Friday. Christmas is Sunday, and I'd say that there ain't a turkey anywhere in the woods of Russell County. Now, you might find a feznit up on a point where there's lots of grapevines and dogwood bushes. They do a lot of scratching under grapevines and dogwoods."

"I believe I'll mosey up to Barn Holler and see if I can find a fat gobbler or feznit for our holiday repast," Tolley stated as he thought of going hunting for a wild turkey or grouse. Tolley called a ruffed grouse a "feznit."

"Where did you ever hear the word repast before?" Tavis asked.

"Learned it in school—just today. Thought I'd spring it on you all as soon as possible, so I wouldn't forget about it," Tolley laughed, noticing his father's surprise. "It means 'meal.'"

"Oh. Didn't know what that word meant," was Tavis' answer. "All that education that you're getting in school is making you awful smart, boy. Keep it up and someday you're bound to be President."

"That would be good!" Claude quipped. "Then we could have a turkey ever' Christmas, 'stead of chickey-diddle and dumplin's all the time."

"Dad, have you seen any turkey sign down around the mines?" Tolley asked.

"Yeah. Two came by t'other day looking for a job," Tavis joked, a twinkle playing around his eyes, and a smile tugging at the corners of his mouth.

"Aw, Dad," Tolley groaned, looking at his father. "I know better than that."

"No, son, I ain't seen nary a turkey at the mines, but I have seen lots of people looking for jobs, though," Tavis stated. "I guess we're really lucky that I'm working a day or two now and then. We're hanging in there, but it sure ain't easy. Roosevelt's gonna change things, though, and I hope how soon he does."

"I've heard that for the last ten years, but things ain't so rosy, the way I see it," Martha quipped, breaking a piece of bread for Maxie, the baby girl.

"I know, Hon, but it's better than it was ten years ago," Tavis told his wife. "I'm working now, but I sure wasn't then. If Ol' Santy ain't got too thin to hold his britches up, maybe we'll have a pretty good Christmas this year, after all."

"It would sure be a real caution if Tolley could bring home a big gobbler or fat feznit," Martha said, looking at her son. "You're gonna try, ain't you, Tolley?"

"Yep, I'm gonna give it the ol' Trent try the first thing in the morning, Mom," Tolley promised. "I might be able to track a feznit up in the snow. That way I'll know he's around and I'll be ready for him. I might get a ground shot at him. I'll shoot him while he's scratching for grapes. They say that it ain't showing good sportsmanship when you shoot one that ain't on the wing, but I can still be a sport about it all; I'll carry him out of the woods. He won't have to walk, and that will be showing sportsmanship enough."

That statement got a big laugh from the entire family, as everyone enjoyed Tolley's humor.

* * * *

Stinging snowflakes struck Tolley's face as he walked into the gusting wind. The snow was almost sleet, he noticed. A thin layer had frozen on the six-inch accumulation already on the ground. His heavy brogan shoes crunched through the frozen snow as his weight forced his feet toward the dark ground underneath.

Old Feisty, the little bench-legged feist dog, bounded along over the snow. His ten-pound body wasn't heavy enough to break through the frozen crust.

Tolley followed far behind the fiery little canine, unable to keep within a hundred yards of the charging animal.

Old Feisty stopped suddenly and sniffed the wind, an indication that he had scented game close by. His tail began to whip back and forth as the spoor became hotter. Jumping upon a fallen tree to search for the pursued scent, Feisty gave an excited yelp, giving Tolley the message that he could get his gun ready for the bagging of the quarry. He stopped at the base of a tall hickory tree, sat down on the frozen snow, and began to bark incessantly as he looked into the branches above.

There was a sudden pounding in Tolley's ears as he hurried up the steep grade. His feet crunching through the crusty snow slowed his pace, but he still hurried along as fast as he could, excited that he had a chance to shoot some game. The pounding grew in magnitude as he neared the barking dog.

As he came near the tree, Tolley began to search for a small gray animal. He was sure that a gray squirrel was somewhere in that tangle of limbs jutting out from the thick bowl of the tree. It just had to be up there somewhere. Feisty had never lied to him before. There had always been a squirrel at the end of the dog's bark.

A gust of wind lifted the long hairs on the fluffy tail of the little animal as it clung to the tree. When the wind died down, the squirrel's tail hairs settled against the shaggy bark of the tree.

Tolley could no longer see the squirrel, but he knew it was up there. He would flush it out of its hiding place when "Ol' Gitter," his twelve-gauge shotgun, belched her pellets of lead into those branches.

As the boy raised the gun to get a good bead on the critter, he heard that thumping sound again. It sounded like a grouse drumming. It was unusual for one to drum when snow was on the ground. They drummed during the spring and strutted their stuff as they tried to impress the hens. Why would one be drumming in the snow?

He lowered his gun in order to get a bearing on the sound. Maybe he could bag the bird, and then bag the squirrel. He knew that the squirrel would stay where it was, but the grouse would fly away when it heard the report from the gun. He was in a quandary as to what he should do.

The wind had picked up considerably, and the snow had begun to fall in larger flakes, whipping against Tolley's cold cheeks, causing his face to tingle and sting with the onslaught of the flying ice. With the roaring wind whipping the snow by his ears, he was no longer able to hear the drumming of the grouse. After several minutes of listening and trying to quiet the excited dog, Tolley decided to shoot the squirrel, if he could get a bead on it again. As he looked into the branches once more, he was unable to pinpoint its position. Finally, he saw the tail hairs, moved by the gushing wind, and aimed Ol' Gitter toward that spot. As he raised his gun, he heard that grouse start drumming again. The drumming was so loud that he could almost feel the pulsation right in his ears. That bird was close, but where could it be? It was snowing so hard right then that he probably couldn't see it if it were to fly up right in front of him.

Tolley lowered his gun once more. The drumming stopped immediately. "What is that thing trying to do to me?" he asked aloud.

Feisty looked at his master but did not give an immediate answer.

Tolley decided to flush the bird out of its hiding place and take his chances of hitting it on the wing. He knew that it would be a hard target to hit, but he surely could not locate its position in that whipping, swirling snow. He made a circuit of the tree, in about a fifty-yard radius, without flushing a chickadee, even. When he returned to the tree, where the little dog sat and continued to bark, he once more searched for the elusive squirrel. As he aimed toward the spot where he knew it should be, that confounded drumming began again, closer than ever that time.

"Feznit or no feznit, I'm gonna get me a squirrel," Tolley mumbled, aiming at the little lump high up in the tree. As Ol' Gitter belched lead, smoke, packing, and that loud boom, the animal plummeted toward the blanket of snow beneath the tree.

Tolley broke the gun down and inserted another shell in the barrel as quickly as possible, preparing to shoot the grouse on the wing. Nothing moved except for the little feist dog as it retrieved the dead squirrel. The wind had abated somewhat, and the snow had lessened in its efforts to cover the earth. Where could that feznit be?

"Drum again now, feznit," Tolley called to the stillness. "Are you chicken to drum again?"

There was no answer from the grouse; if there had been a grouse drumming up on that point. Tolley raised the gun to see if the grouse would drum again. It didn't. In the meantime, Old Feisty had treed another squirrel.

As Tolley picked up the dead squirrel and pocketed it, the excitement of the hunt seized him once more and that drumming began again. "So that was it," he cried. "My heart was thumping in my ears from all the excitement of getting to kill a squirrel, and I thought it was a feznit drumming." He hurried toward the barking dog.

* * * *

"Chickey-diddle and dumplin's ain't so bad, are they?" Tolley declared, dipping a large helping onto his plate, right after his father had asked the blessing on the family, their health, and the food that Christmas day. "The pieces of squirrel meat blend in good with the rooster meat, don't they?"

"It sure does, son," Tavis agreed as he looked at his big family sitting around the table. "We seem to have plenty. Just think, there are people out there," he began, moving his hand in an arc, "that have hardly anything and are still happy. We should be thankful for what we have, even though we don't have that big gobbler gracing our table today. Chickey-diddle and dumplin's will be plenty."

"Yeah, Chickey-diddle and dumplin's will be enough," Martha echoed, sighing contentedly as she watched her family enjoying the sumptuous meal.

Time and a Turnip

Tanner Leatherwood lay in the secluded comfort of the tall hickory's shade. He had lain in that same posture for nearly an hour. Nothing stirred about his position of alluring ecstasy. Occasionally, a whining gnat tried to dab its way into the lad's half-closed eye, or was it his a half-opened eye? Whichever, it was applying its life's profession of pestering. Tanner lazily brushed the tiny insect aside, stirring for that purpose only.

The quiet was suddenly interrupted as Hosh Kaney came barreling out of the underbrush.

"What's chasing you?" Tanner asked, bounding to his feet, ready to flee from a phantom pursuer.

"Ain't nothing tailing me, Tanner," Hosh panted, almost out of breath as he flopped to the ground.

"What's the matter then?" Tanner asked, sitting down beside the expended boy. "What's wrong? You came in here like one of those pro ball players sliding into second base."

"Give me just a minute to catch my breath, and I'll tell you the news," Hosh puffed, gulping big mouthfuls of air.

"How far have you run in that gear?" Tanner asked, and waited for the puffing lad to answer.

"All the way," was the only reply Hosh gave.

"All the way from where?" Tanner queried, growing anxious with the incoherent boy lying prone upon the ground. "Boy, tell me what I need to know. If I'm supposed to respond to some crisis, then I want to get a good start before it's too late."

"Your brother got arrested and socked in jail just awhile ago," Hosh gasped, after he had rested enough to talk in sentences instead of phrases.

"What did he do that was bad enough to put him in jail?" Tanner asked. He shook his friend's shoulders, trying to hurry the answer.

"I can't talk with you shaking me like a snake-killing dog on a copperhead. Turn me loose and I'll tell you all about it, if you don't shake my goozle out," Hosh begged, pushing against the hands gripping his shoulders.

"What happened?" Tanner asked impatiently.

"You know the Much-and-a-Plenty-Food Grocery at Big Onion Gap," Hosh began. "Well, Dee-Mo was in there—just looking—when Gimpy Sledd 'cused him of shoplifting some 'matoes. Gimpy tried to corner Dee-Mo in the produce section. Dee-Mo didn't think too highly of that idea, even though he was innocent of any 'cusing that Gimpy did to him. When Gimpy got pretty close to him, he chucked one of the biggest turnips that he could find in the turnip bin at him. It caught Gimpy just above his left ear and knocked him colder than a crock of kraut."

"How do you know that it happened just that way?" Tanner asked, continuing his interrogation.

"Well, you see, I was shopping with Dee-Mo when it happened," Hosh admitted.

"How come you didn't get caught and put in the jail with Dee-Mo?" Tanner queried further.

"Well, when Gimpy 'proached Dee-Mo, 'cusing him of stealing, I hid behind the back door," Hosh stated.

"Are you guilty of stealing, too?" Tanner asked as he continued to ply his friend with questions.

"No, I'm not guilty, and Dee-Mo ain't guilty, either," Hosh declared.

"Well, if you boys weren't guilty of anything, then why did you act like you were?" Tanner wanted to know, amazed with the action the two boys had taken when confronted by the store owner.

"Well, we weren't buying anything, and usually young boys don't go into a grocery store just to look around. We were only looking, though," Hosh said, defending his innocence. "Now, it would be understandable if we had gone into a hardware store and gawked around at the bolts, nails, paint, saws, hammers, 'lectric stoves, televisions, 'frigerators, bicycles...."

"You don't have to name everything in the store. I get the picture." Tanner interrupted the boy's listing of the store's inventory. "You should have stayed there and helped Dee-Mo explain to the grocer that you all hadn't done anything wrong. When you ran, that gave him all the evidence that he needed to accuse you of lifting goods."

"I got scared and left in a hurry," Hosh said. "Dee-Mo had already thumped Gimpy with that turnip. Gimpy plopped to the floor, limp as a rope."

"You should have stayed and helped Dee-Mo," Tanner growled, rebuking his friend for running away. "Why didn't Dee-Mo run out the back door with you? When Gimpy plopped down on the floor, out cold, the way should have been clear to run."

"The cashiers and stockboys all ganged up on Dee-Mo and rassled him to the floor, just like a pile-on at school," Hosh replied. "He didn't have a chance to run. They swarmed over him like a passel of flies on a car-killed possum."

"I knew that something like that must have happened, 'cause he would have shagged it on out of there like a gander after a grasshopper if they hadn't jumped him," Tanner mused.

"Dee-Mo busted two of the cashiers' noses pretty bad," Hosh recalled, laughing about the fracas. "Their noses looked flat as a beaver's tail, smeared all over their faces, with blood just a squirting all over the place. It was a sight to see, Tanner!"

"Do you mean to tell me that he busted the women's noses with his fists?" Tanner asked.

"No, he didn't hit them with his fists," Hosh said.

"Good! I wouldn't want him to be fighting with women," Tanner sighed, relieved.

"He kicked them in the face 'stead of busting them with his fists," Hosh went on. "Everybody was holding him so he couldn't hit anyone, so he just up and kicked them. He was a wild man."

"Have you told Dad and Mom about the incident?" Tanner wanted to know.

"No, I've not told nary a soul but you," Hosh said. "I just came up to here, hoping you would be around. I just took a guess on your where-abouts and came out lucky on my figuring."

"We'd better mosey on down off the hill and go tell my parents about Dee-Mo," Tanner suggested. "They might want to do something about him."

The two friends discussed the happening as they walked the two miles to Tanner's house.

"What in tarnation has that boy gone and done this time?" Lilburn Leatherwood asked when he heard the news of Dee-Mo's demise. "I've tried to teach that boy that he can't go into stores and browse around and not get questioned about his conduct while in the store. If he's innocent like you say, Hosh, then I'll go down there and kick Gimpy Sledd's butt so hard that he'll have to take his hat off when he goes to the toilet, and I mean that, too."

The two boys had to laugh when they heard Lilburn's threat. As they kept up their uproarious guffawing, Lilburn had to break his serious moment and chuckle with the lads.

"I'll run over to Big Onion Gap and see what it'll take to get that scalawag out of jail," Lilburn stated. "Somebody from the sheriff's office should have come and let me know about it. I'll vote again' him next year at election time, and I'm sure I can turn several more votes again' him."

"Maybe Dee-Mo didn't tell him that he's your son," Hosh wondered.

"That's about what Dee-Mo would do. He's a sly little scutter," Lilburn said.

"I don't see why he chucked Gimpy with that turnip when he could have walked out with Hosh," Tanner wondered.

"Fill up the radiator in the truck while I change my duds. We'll go up to Big Onion Gap and see what we can do to get that boy out of jail and back here to the house," Lilburn said. "Dicy, where's my clean britches?" he called to his wife, who was in the kitchen puttering around at a never-ending job of some sort.

"They're hanging on a nail behind the door in our room," Dicy replied. "Don't get in too big of a hurry. I'm going with you. I'd like to give that sheriff a word or two to mull over before 'lection day this fall. He had no right to go and 'rest my baby without any grounds, other than chuckin' a turnip against Gimpy's head. I'd loved to seen Gimpy flop on the floor when Dee-Mo scuzzed him a good 'un with that turnip. You know, just for a little I wouldn't pay our charge-bill at the store. He hadn't ort to press charges again' Dee-Mo."

"We'll get it all straightened out in a few shakes when we get up to Big Onion Gap," Lilburn promised as he changed his trousers.

Tanner had just finished pouring the last bucket of water into the leaky radiator of the old rattletrap pickup truck when his spruced-up parents emerged from the house. He opened the door for his mother as he had seen valets do in the movies when they opened limousine doors for royalty in England.

"Thank you, young man," Dicy laughed, marveling at the actions of her chivalrous son.

"You're welcome, Madame," Tanner said, bowing to his giggling mother.

"Get in here, you two. Quit your corny acting. We have to get to town sometime today," Lilburn ordered.

The trip was made without a boil-over due to the leaky radiator. They didn't even have a flat tire, which was unusual.

* * * *

"Lilburn, I had to arrest your son," Sheriff Onsby Bush began, trying to prevent an anticipated outburst from the agitated parents.

The trio took seats facing the nervous law officer and stared at him without speaking, hoping to make him nervous. They hoped to cause the sheriff to give in and release Dee-Mo into their custody without first having to pay a fine or post bail—if the offence was serious enough to warrant bail money.

"You both know that I was elected to uphold the law, regardless of who might break it," Sheriff Onsby said, continuing his explanation for making the arrest. "I like you folks, but that's not the question here. If my brother should happen to break the law, I'd have to arrest him. So you can see I had to take the action I did concerning your son."

"You don't have a brother, Onsby," Dicy retorted.

"Well, Mrs. Leatherwood, that was just a figure of speech," Sheriff Onsby replied. "Now, if you folks will just pay the money to have Dee-Mo released into your custody, we will get this over with. Your son will have to be arraigned and stand trial for a misdemeanor. You'll be informed of the trial date."

"What's a 'meanor, Sheriff Onsby?" Lilburn asked, giving the lawman a confused look.

"Well, your son broke the law—an act of misconduct, so to speak," the sheriff said, trying to explain to the parents that what their son did warranted an arrest. "I couldn't just turn him loose, because Gimpy Sledd swore out a warrant and pressed charges against your son. There was nothing to do but arrest him and incarcerate him."

"You could have brought him out to the house where we could have kicked his butt a few times. That would have straightened him out," Lilburn said, his face turning red with anger.

"That wouldn't do any good," Sheriff Onsby averred. "That would only cause him to rebel against you, and just might cause him to go do something worse the next time he is in such a predicament."

"When I see that little Gimpy Sledd, I'm gonna kick some butt," Lilburn threatened.

"You mustn't make threats toward Mr. Sledd, Lilburn," the sheriff warned.

"He's in for it—just as soon as I lay eyes on him," Lilburn continued his threat.

"If you feel that way about it, I'll have to lock you up with your son," Sheriff Onsby declared.

"You wouldn't do that, would you Sheriff?" Lilburn asked, surprised.

"I would have to do just that," the sheriff stated.

"What in thunderation can I do to revenge my son, if I can't do some butt kicking?" Lilburn wanted to know.

"You'll have to hire you a lawyer and make a defense of your son's innocence—if he's innocent," Sheriff Onsby advised.

"Do you know any good lawyers in town? You see, no one in my family, as far back as I can remember, has ever been took to court for anything," Lilburn explained. "This is the most embarrassing thing to me and my folks. There had to be a bad tater in the hole at some time, but I hoped that it would be in somebody else's brood 'stead of mine. Now, I don't want a shyster of a lawyer, Sheriff Onsby. I want a good one. I'm sure we can clear Dee-Mo, but I want a good lawyer to make it real clear that my boy ain't a thief."

"I'll send a good attorney out to your place this week," Sheriff Onsby promised. "I believe your son, so I'll do everything that is in my power to help clear him. The lawyer should be out to your place by the first of the week."

"You'd better help him, 'cause we'll vote again' you when you run for re-election next time," Dicy Leatherwood threatened.

"Don't worry about it," Sheriff Onsby said. "Now, if you'll just pay this fifty-dollar fee to make it legal for me to release Dee-Mo, then everything will be just fine."

"Ain't that awful high for just his first time to be locked up?" Lilburn asked. "What about around ten dollars? That would be enough to get a little boy out of jail. He ain't but fifteen, going on sixteen."

"I don't set the bail rates," Sheriff Onsby stated, smiling broadly.

"Somebody ort to set 'em, and they ort to set them reasonable enough so poor people could get out of jail without having to spend their life's savings all at once," Lilburn lamented.

"I know that it's high," Sheriff Onsby apologized, "but I don't set bail. I just collect the money. Let's go over to the jail and get that boy released," the sheriff suggested as he rose and donned his hat.

The trio of Leatherwoods followed the sheriff to the jail and received Dee-Mo into their custody.

"A lawyer will be out to see you by the first of the week," Sheriff Onsby told the departing family.

* * * *

"This is Dee-Mo's lawyer, Wash Bleecher, from over at Big Onion Gap," Lilburn said, introducing the attorney to Tanner one evening a week after Dee-Mo's release from jail.

"Howdy," Tanner spoke, greeting the lawyer.

"How are you, young man? I'm very pleased to make the acquaintance of another of this fine family," Wash Bleecher spoke, looking over the group of ragamuffins lounging about the room.

"Listen, Bleecher, you had better get Dee-Mo out of his predicament," Tanner threatened. "If you don't," he continued, "you're in for some trouble with me and my friends. My folks will take whatever the court does about this case. That's 'cause they're law-abiding folks. But I'm not as easy going as they are."

"Don't get excited," Wash Bleecher said, smiling at the young man's mettle. "Give me a chance. I have to know just what the boy did. We have to prove to the court that Dee-Mo is innocent. It's not easy to convince a judge that someone who has been caught red-handed, so to speak, is innocent. I've spoken to Dee-Mo. Now, I'll have to prepare my case. Don't jump up and down and yell about it. We have to keep a calm head. Things will work out fine, but everyone will have to be cooperative. Don't come to me and ask for help, then go jumping heel over hoe handle in a rage. We have to work together on this. Don't threaten me. Do everything you can to help me; that way we can prepare a good defense for Dee-Mo."

"I just don't want Dee-Mo to go through life with this smeared on his record," Tanner said. "I get pretty ruffled where my brother is concerned. This is the first time he's been involved in something so drastic. I know good and well that Dee-Mo is as innocent as a day-old chickey-diddle."

"I told Bleecher everything about the case that I know, and Dee-Mo told him all that he knows about it," Lilburn allowed. "I'm about convinced," he continued, "that we should have him plead guilty as charged. That would save time. It would also save us some money. And he'll tell the truth, whether or not it'll help him. He's just like your mother, concerning the truth."

"But Dee-Mo says that he's innocent of any wrongdoings, other than hitting Gimpy with a turnip, and that was an accident, he says." Tanner replied. "If he's too honest in this case, he could cut his throat. We'll have to let Mr. Bleecher handle things for us, I guess. He didn't take anything unlawfully. He was just looking around and wishing. He's honest, and there's nothing wrong with honesty—in its rightful place, of course."

"Now, you listen here, son!" Dicy exclaimed. "I grew up in a family that told the truth, and I have tried to teach my young 'uns to be honest and truthful. I'll see that Dee-Mo is honest, jail or no jail." She was on the riled side, and it was unusual for her to act in that manner. She was so easygoing.

"Well, Dicy, Hon, the truth is okay in the right place, but look at Dee-Mo's problem. He's in the position where the truth ain't going to help much. You must remember that your brother, Amon, told the truth, and he had to go to jail for a spell," Lilburn explained.

"Yeah, but Amon was framed from the start to the end," Dicy retorted. "If t'others had told the truth like he did, then they would have gone to jail, too—the way they were supposed to. But, no, they were wimps and turned state's evidence again' him. He'll never forgive them for doing that."

"He must have already forgive 'em, 'cause they're all shagging around together again after he got out," Lilburn reminded his wife, telling her that people will forgive.

"Mr. Leatherwood," Wash Bleecher began, "if your son should admit his guilt, his punishment would be less severe. By that I mean he would pull a shorter sentence, but it will most likely be probation. He could be acquitted altogether. You people seem to think that I am incompetent as an attorney. Give me a chance to defend him. You have him convicted already."

"I just don't want him to plead guilty to something that he's not guilty of," Tanner said. "If you don't get him out of this, we won't pay you anything for your efforts."

"I intend to defend him, but with all this distrust floating around the room, I just don't think I will stand a chance with you. The case is a simple matter, but trying to get through your thick heads is a bigger case than Dee-Mo's," Wash Bleecher stated. "If it wasn't for my good friend, Onsby Bush, I would never have taken the case. I'm doing it for him."

"Sheriff Onsby said that he would send us a good defense lawyer out to talk over the case," Lilburn said.

"Did you fellers draw up a contract?" Tanner wanted to know.

"Sure did, son," Lilburn said, smiling broadly. "Now, Bleecher will *have* to defend Dee-Mo."

"Let me see that contract, Dad," Tanner said, reaching for the paper.

"I guess we'll have to stand up to our part of the bargain, son," Lilburn informed him.

"Yeah, looks like we will," Tanner agreed, folding the paper and laying it on the coffee table.

"You people just don't trust anyone, do you?" the lawyer said. Before he got an answer to his statement, he continued. "Well, if you don't have any more evidence to give me, I guess I had better head back to town and start preparing my case. If I need any more information, I'll be back out to see you; if not, I'll see you in my office about an hour before the trial begins on August twelve." With that last statement, he left the room, got into his car, and drove up the highway to Big Onion Gap. Lilburn, Dicy, and Tanner walked out on the front porch and watched the car until it went around a curve in the road and out of sight.

"Well, you see, it's this way, son," Lilburn said as he watched the lawyer drive away, the car stirring up a cloud of dust that floated on the still air. "He could win this case and still not get paid. I may not be able to find the money to pay the old legal-maker. Do you know that he didn't even ask for a retainer? That's 'cause Sheriff Onsby told him that I'm good for the fee. I may even fool the sheriff."

"Listen here, Lilburn, you'll pay the fee, even if it takes everything that we have and that you can borry," Dicy stated. "We have to be honest, even though we don't have much money. "I'll sell Ol' Pigger, and you know that I would rather have her than my right hand. Ol' Pigger is the best brood sow that we've ever had. She drops twelve pigs ever' time. That's the same as money in the bank—something that we can count on. She's due to drop anytime now. In six weeks I can start selling the pigs at fifteen dollars a piece. That'll buy shoes and clothes for the young 'uns to start school."

"I ain't gonna sell Ol' Nubbin, no matter what happens to Dee-Mo. I need that horse to make a scratch-living on this farm," Lilburn declared.

"Dad, you know better than that," Tanner laughed. "That horse isn't worth what your son is to you."

"I know it, but I sure want to keep my horse. He's the best brute that I've ever owned," the man bragged.

"Let's not argue about this," Dicy advised. "But I do have the best sow in these parts. I don't want to sell her, but I will if I have to."

"Maybe we won't have to sell anything," Tanner said. "It's chore time, so I'll go slop the squeal-boxes." He went to the corncrib to get a basket of corn to feed to the hogs.

Eager squeals could be heard as the sow ran back and forth along the hog-lot fence.

Old Coaley followed along behind Tanner, playfully biting his master on the ankles. With the slightest sound somewhere out in the woods, which was inaudible to Tanner's less sensitive ears, the dog was off at a swift run toward the stream that meandered through the farm.

Maybe it was a fox nosing around the henhouse. Or maybe a coon in search of crawdads and frogs in the creek.

"What's the dog after?" Lilburn asked as he stood on the front porch and listened to the baying hound.

I guess it's a fox. Ol' Coaley just crossed over the ridge," Tanner answered. "I don't think it was a coon, for he'd have treed it before now."

"It's pretty dark out there. You'd better come on in," Lilburn said, turning to go back into the house.

"I'll be there in a bit," Tanner replied. "Tell Dee-Mo to come out here for a minute."

Dee-Mo joined Tanner in the pig lot. The brothers sat for awhile, talking about many things, but the subject of the upcoming trial returned often.

"What do you think the outcome of the trial will be, Tanner," Dee-Mo wanted to know. He scuffed his foot in the dust of a dry pig wallow while waiting for an answer.

"I don't know. I can't imagine just what will take place," Tanner said, pondering his brother's plight. "We'll just have to let the lawyer take care of our problems. That's what he's getting paid for."

"From the way he talked the other day, he doesn't know good soup from apple butter where the lawin' is concerned," Dee-Mo laughed.

"Yeah, I guess you're right, but we'll just have to trust him," Tanner said.

* * * *

The courtroom began to fill, and by nine o'clock it had overflowed its capacity. People continued to crowd into the room, filling the aisles. Several children sat on the floor, while others leaned on the little banister that separated the spectators from the lawyers, jury, and judge's bench. The kids were fascinated with the goings on. They watched in awe as the lawyers shuffled through their case papers.

Dee-Mo sat at a desk with Wash Bleecher. The two were in a quiet conversation, getting the facts straightened out, going over the final details while everyone else waited for the judge to emerge from his chambers.

The kids peeped through the banisters and whispered to Dee-Mo, trying to get his attention so they could wave at him.

Tanner looked about the courtroom. People from all walks of life were present. Lawyers were there, of course, and miners, since there was a slowdown in orders at the mines. The miners had come to town to relax and talk to fellow workers and friends.

Farmers sat and talked about livestock and crops and discussed the weather. They did not know what to do about it, though, and it was a good thing they couldn't, because there would have been a big mess up had they been able to control the weather.

"Do you suppose Dee-Mo will get out of this all right?" Ratio Cornfield, a friend of the Leatherwoods, asked as he joined Tanner on the long bench.

"Well, I suppose so," Tanner replied. "I gave the lawyer his orders of the day."

"What kind of orders?" Ratio asked, showing a set of strong, even teeth as he smiled genially.

"Just orders," Tanner said, shrugging his shoulders.

"Just what did you tell him?" Ratio continued to ask, trying to get Tanner to reveal the type of orders that he had given to the lawyer. "I'm curious as to what you told him."

"They were just orders. They don't concern you nary a whit," was

Tanner's curt reply.

"Boy, you're a stubborn cuss—just like your daddy," Ratio chuckled. "Well, its all right to be independent like that and say what you feel. That's like Lilburn to a tee. Me and him used to have some good times when we were young. I still remember the time that me and him. . . ."

Ratio Cornfield's story ended for the moment as everyone began to rise.

The judge emerged from his chambers with a cough and throat clearing, loud enough for everyone to hear and take as a gesture for silence.

Ratio Cornfield rose and motioned for Tanner to do likewise, but Tanner remained seated. He wasn't going to stand in honor of someone who might sentence his brother to jail or the reform school. His mind was changed when a deputy goaded him in the ribs and told him to stand along with the rest.

"Stand up, young man," the heavyset deputy ordered. "That black-robed man is Judge Breading, and you're supposed to stand in his honor when he enters the room."

After the judge had made himself comfortable, the bailiff said, "Court is now in session—Judge Breading presiding."

The judge rapped his desk with his gavel. "Let's have the first case," he ordered. He turned to the court clerk.

The clerk stood, licked his thumb and index finger, and shuffled through his book of cases. "The first case on the docket is Beecher versus Beecher," he whined.

"Your Honor," a tall, well-dressed gentleman, an attorney, said as he rose, "may I approach the bench?"

"You may," Judge Breading replied.

"That case was settled out of court. Dock Beecher won't be suing his wife for support. She agreed to give him an allowance," the lawyer reported.

"Next case!" Judge Breading snapped.

People versus Duttle," the clerk replied.

"Your Honor," another well-dressed attorney replied, "Tut Duttle paid his fine for an illegal muffler."

"Next case," Judge Breading stated.

"Goshie versus Seedy," the clerk read.

"Your Honor," another attorney said as he rose to face the judge, "that case has been postponed."

"Why are we holding court this session if all the cases are settled outside the courtroom or postponed? Next case. No, wait a minute! Is there a case to be tried today? If not, we will adjourn court, and I'll go fishing."

"Your Honor, there is one case to be tried today," Wash Bleecher announced, rising to approach the judge. "People versus Dee-Mo Leatherwood is scheduled for today."

"There are so many cases settled outside the courtroom these days that I believe the court is going broke," Judge Breading complained.

"Your Honor, Judgie-Pudgie," Dee-Mo said, facing the judge, "that case was settled outside the courtroom, too. My lawyer thinks differently, but me and Crooked are good pals now. Ask him and see."

"I just be dabbered if I'm a pal to that stinker!" Gimpy Sledd retorted, rising from his seat beside his wife on the front row. "I'll never consent to a settlement with him. My head still hurts from that turnip thumping he gave me."

"I could have hit you harder," Dee-Mo said, rising. He grinned all over the room.

"Sit down, young man!" the judge ordered. "Court will come to order."

"Well, Judge," Dee-Mo said, "I thought that I might pull one on him." He laughed and pointed toward Gimpy Sledd.

Gimpy Sledd was the first witness to be called to testify. After he was thoroughly interrogated by both the prosecuting attorney and the defense attorney, he was allowed to leave the witness stand.

Dee-Mo Leatherwood was called to testify. He swaggered to the witness stand, plopped down, and grinned a friendly hello to everyone.

"Dee-Mo Leatherwood, do you swear to tell the truth, so help you God?" the bailiff asked.

"Amen, good brother, I sure do," Dee-Mo quipped.

The prosecuting attorney, Dunn Asken, approached the stand with a smile. "State your name, please."

"Dee-Mo Leatherwood," the lad replied.

"Is that your real name or a nickname?" Mr. Asken inquired.

"It's my real name, I suppose, 'cause it's the only one that I have," Dee-Mo said with a thistle-eating grin.

"How old are you?" Mr. Asken inquired, continuing the interrogation.

"I'm fifteen, going on sixteen. I'll be old enough to quit school soon. It can't be too soon, either," Dee-Mo said, smiling comfortably.

"Young man, do you have anything to say in your own defense?" Mr. Asken queried.

"Yes, sir, I sure have," Dee-Mo stated. "I have all good things to say for myself, and nothing good to say for Ol' Crooked Sledd."

"Young man, don't call anyone a nickname," the judge commanded.

"I didn't call him a nickname. I called him a real 'propriate name," Dee-Mo answered. "He's as crooked as a quiled-up blacksnake. He's just as sneaking, too. I'm sure that you know how a blacksnake sneaks up on a poor spar-bird and swallers it down without giving it a fighting chance. Well, Ol' Crooked Sledd over there is just as sneaking. He tells his customers that he has the best stuff for the best price, but he don't. Now, that's sneaking!"

"Wait just a minute," Gimpy Sledd stammered, facing the judge and lawyers. "Are you going to permit that cranky brat to ruin my business? Some of my best customers are present."

"Some of your best dummies are," Dee-Mo laughed. "They can't see straight to let you cheat them right out of their money. You say that they're your friends, but I know better. When they pay their grocery bills, you smile right big, showing your fine bridgework, but when they go outside, you cuss right big because they don't buy more groceries. I know 'cause I was hid in your store one time and heard you." He smiled around the room as the people roared with laughter.

The judge rapped with his gavel and called for order. "Let's cut out the nonsense. This is a time for seriousness, young man," Judge Breading stated sternly. "I don't like for people to make false accusations."

"Judge, I told you the truth all the way. Bless a terrapin, Judge, I certainly have told you the truth," Dee-Mo said seriously.

"You sound like you are making up a big story," the judge said.

"But, sir, I have told the truth," Dee-Mo cried.

"He's your witness, Mr. Asken," the judge said, addressing the prosecuting attorney.

"Now, Dee-Mo," Mr. Asken began, "where were you on the eighth of September, about three o'clock in the afternoon?"

"I don't know," Dee-Mo answered quickly. "You see, I don't keep up with the calendar. We had a calendar once, but Dad got in a hurry one night and took it to the toilet with him."

The room burst into laughter again, and once more the judge called for order as he rapped his desk with the gavel.

"If I don't have complete quietness, I'll have to order a deputy to clear the room," the judge threatened.

The room quieted to only a big grin.

"Young man, let's quit trying to be funny and get serious," Mr. Asken said. "Do you know how to be serious?"

"All right," Dee-Mo said. "After thinking about it a little, I do 'member where I was. I was over at Much-and-a-Plenty-Food Grocery shopping around."

"Did you take anything from the store?" the attorney asked.

"Objection!" Wash Bleecher shouted, rising to his feet.

"Overruled," the judge replied. "Answer the question, Dee-Mo."

"Now, son, did you take anything from the store?" Mr. Asken inquired once more.

"Nope, sure didn't," Dee-Mo quickly replied.

"Why were you in the store?" Mr. Asken queried.

"Shopping," Dee-Mo answered.

"Shopping for what?" Mr. Asken queried further.

"Oh, just shopping to be shopping," Dee-Mo responded.

"You had to be shopping for something," Mr. Asken said.

"Nothing in particular," Dee-Mo answered calmly, shrugging his shoulders.

"You have told us that you did not take anything from that store," Mr. Asken stated.

"Yes, sir, that's right," Dee-Mo quickly replied. "I've told you that three or four times already."

"Did you hit Mr. Sledd with a turnip?" the attorney asked.

"Well, as for hitting him directly with it, I would have to say no," Dee-Mo admitted.

"What do you mean by 'directly?'" Mr. Asken inquired.

"Well, you see," Dee-Mo began, "I can throw real straight. I threw at a washtub that was hanging on a nail in a supporting post. I aimed to knock the washtub off the nail. You see, Gimpy had me hemmed in a corner of the produce section. He didn't ask me any questions about what I wanted. He just started accusing me of taking stuff, but I hadn't touched nary a thing. I wanted to cap that washtub down over Gimpy's head and get out of there. The turnip wasn't balanced right, so I hit the post. The turnip bounced off and hit Gimpy on the head. Actually, I didn't mean to hit him."

"Why were the police called?" Mr. Asken inquired.

"'Cause Gimpy Sledd couldn't act like a man and ask me nicely if I wanted to buy something. He had to smart off and accuse me of something that I didn't do." Dee-Mo said. "If he had had a reason to think that I was in there to steal something, then he could have been man enough to ask me point-blank if I was trying to take anything. I may be rambunctious and all like that, but I will not steal anything. I have been taught better. My parents have never had reason to be disappointed in me. You can ask me questions all day, but I have nothing else to tell you. Those are the true facts, and if Gimpy will tell the truth, then his answers won't be any different from mine."

"That will be all. You can step down," Mr. Asken said.

Dee-Mo rose, looked at Tanner, and winked. He seemed to be sure that he would be found innocent of any wrongdoings. He left the witness stand and went back to his seat by Mr. Bleecher.

After all the witnesses had been questioned, Judge Breading retired to his chambers to study the testimonies and to deliberate a decision.

Dee-Mo sat by Wash Bleecher and talked incessantly. Occasionally, he would look back at Tanner and grin, and Tanner would grin back. The people in attendance would look at the two boys and grin. The room was full of grinning people.

"Let the attorneys and defendant approach the bench," the bailiff ordered as the judge entered the courtroom.

Dee-Mo jumped to his feet and danced his way to the front of the room.

"Young man," the judge said as he peered over his glasses, "I know that you think you did nothing wrong when you hit Gimpy Sledd with that big turnip, but you did. I hate to do this, but I'm going to fine you one hundred dollars. I could give you some time in the reformatory, too. Maybe that would cool that brash tongue. If you had not been such a smart aleck with your answers, maybe I could have overlooked your quandary this time. Son, I just don't think much of a smart aleck."

"But, Your Honor, I don't have a hundred dollars," Dee-Mo replied, staring at the judge in disbelief.

"Well, that will be three months in the reformatory if your father can't pay up," Judge Breading stated.

"Dad doesn't have as much money as I have, and I'm plumb broke," he said, smarting off once more. He could not let good enough alone. He had to stick his foot in his mouth every time it flew open, and if he kept his foot in his mouth much longer, he would catch a case of athlete's foot of the tongue.

"I want to see the attorneys, the plaintiff, and Dee-Mo's parents in my chambers," the judge ordered.

As the entourage left the courtroom, everyone in attendance looked at his neighbor, wondering why there was a conference.

Dee-Mo looked about the room, waved to friends, and smiled at Tanner. He wasn't worried about his future. He wasn't the worrying kind.

After a period of fifteen minutes, the judge returned to the courtroom, followed by the lawyers, Gimpy Sledd, and the Leatherwoods.

"Approach the bench for your sentencing, young man," the bailiff ordered.

Slowly, and with a completely different attitude, Dee-Mo rose and faced the judge. He dropped his head as he realized that he would have to pay for his little caper at the grocery store. And, too, he realized at that moment that maybe he had smarted off just a wee bit too much during the trial.

Tanner looked at his brother as the boy stood before the judge with his shoulders slumped in a show of depression. There was a grinding pressure at the pit of Tanner's stomach. He felt more depressed as he looked at his watched brother. When he looked at his parents, standing with the attorneys, he saw smiles on their faces. How could they smile when Dee-Mo might have to go to the reformatory?

"Dee-Mo Leatherwood, I have decided to put you on probation for one year for that little caper with the turnip. You know that I could have given you some detention time in an institution. Mr. Sledd agrees that maybe you didn't really do anything wrong before you popped him with the turnip. Mr. Leatherwood says that his size-twelve boot will keep you in line while on probation, but you will have to report to my office each month. I am certain that you will agree to further your education. With the fact that you will be in school, I think that probation is stiff enough punishment. Your record won't be lily-white, but you can live with it. I probably did some things about that shady when I was your age, but we won't get into that. Remember that I am giving you another chance. Be thankful that you have parents who care about you. Court's adjourned." Judge Breading rapped the gavel smartly and left the room.

Dee-Mo shook hands with Wash Bleecher and ran to hug his parents, giving Lilburn's big boot a quick once-over. He turned toward the crowd as he received a round of applause.

Tanner gripped his brother's hand. "You're a nut, Dee-Mo," he said. "You sat up there on that witness stand and smarted off. You should have known that the judge wouldn't put up with your shenanigans."

"I know that I'm a little too smart for my own good. I guess that I have just a little too much vinegar for the salit," Dee-Mo laughed.

"You almost got some time in the reform school because of a turnip," Tanner said as he playfully shoved his little brother toward the door.

Betch'ye

Three men sat on a bench situated in the corner of the park in the little town of Mullinsville. Three bone-handled, sharp-bladed Case knives worked meticulously, shaving long, thin slivers from smooth, even cedar sticks. The shavings fell, spiraling in a cork-screw decent, to the growing pile at the feet of the whittlers.

The conversation had been at an ordinary pace, like the whittling action—slow—and there had been a lull for awhile.

Finally, the silence was broken as Manning Seedy spoke. "The 'lection is starting off real low-key, ain't it?"

"Hadn't noticed much," was the slow reply from Cody Skinner, continuing his quest to shave the longest and thinnest sliver from his cedar stick. "Who's running this year?"

"Ain't you keeping up with the campaign for the vacant seat on town council?" Manning asked, surprised. "Here you are, one of the most avid of all the election watchers, and you don't even know who the can-dee-dates are?"

"My health has been poorly here lately. Ain't been out much. I've just got to be tol'able in just the last week or two," Cody replied, not breaking stride in his whittling, watching the slivers fall as he continued to carve his stick.

"Sorry, didn't know you was sick," Manning apologized. "Had I known you was ailing, I'd have brought you about a gill of 'shine to perk you up a might."

"It would have took more than a gill to quench my problems, pal," Cody told his buddy. "I've had the blind staggers and been plain dauncy at the table. Can't eat hardly at all."

"You need about a gallon of bitters that's been working and blending for nigh on to about a two-month draw to get the kinks out of your system," Manning drawled.

"Yeah, bitters is good for what might ail you—spring time 'specially—but I'm on the mend right now, might be ready for the 'lection after all. Show me a stump and I'll make you a good campaign speech, just to give you the gist of how a good 'lection should be run. I can garner a good crowd to stand and gawk openmouthed at a great orator. Bring on the crowd, boys," Cody Skinner said, smiling.

Manning Seedy and Mayo Coalfield looked at each other in surprise as they saw their friend come to life, after he had just told them that he was on the verge of a permanent disability.

"Just the thought of my bitters brought the ol' boy back from the very edge of eternity, looks like," Manning said, a dry chuckle thumping around in his throat.

"Wasn't your bitters so much as the memory of the good 'lections in the past," was Cody's quick reply.

"Whatever it was, we should call it a miracle cure and can it up for the future generations to use to overcome their sickness," Mayo quipped as he whittled and thought about his complaining friend's recovery.

"Who'd you say was running for the vacant seat on the town council?" Cody asked once more.

"John Jay Sprungtrap, the Republican, and Cubbie Willpower, the Democrat, are vying for the coveted position." Manning told his friend, continuing to whittle contentedly.

"Not much of a choice there, is it?" Mayo Coalfield replied, pondering thoughtfully the political matchup. He continued to whittle, watching the shavings fall slowly to the ground, as though he had no interest in the upcoming election.

"You boys know that John Jay Sprungtrap is having a hard time trying to recover from a slander case in which he is solely involved, except for his wife, Lotta Sprungtrap," Manning said, stopping for a breath of fresh air before continuing with his gossip. "She's the one that John Jay slandered out in public. You can see that he is in deep slop—up to his chin, to be exact. When a man has a gossipy wife, and she is again' him, what chance has he in winning a bid for election to a high office like town councilman?"

"No worse than his opponent, I would say," Mayo Coalfield drawled, whittling on his stick, as if he had very little interest in the election as a whole.

"You're right there, pal," Manning continued, "but that don't make either of them lily-white, you know. Cubbie Willpower is no top-notch can-dee-date for the Democrats, you know. I guess you already heard that Cubbie is in court right now, trying to defend himself on charges of polygamy. He's such a speech maker that he made two speeches the other day on the witness stand, which, try as hard as they might, the court deputies couldn't stop the flood of listeners from leaving the court room. Two jurymen jumped out the winder because they were Republicans and again' Cubbie's stand on the issues. The judge had to call on the town constable and the county sheriff to round up the jurymen and force them back in order to get the case back on track."

"You mentioned the issues. What are the issues?" Mayo asked with interest.

"Your guess is as good as mine, Mayo," Manning replied. "The only issue that Cubbie has for a run is to run from his wives. He has three, you know. That's been brought out in the campaign. All the skeletons get woke up in the closets during a heated campaign. After the election, everything will get back to normal, though. Cubbie is having a hard time campaigning and defending himself in court, all at the same time. It'll be a miracle if he comes out of this one on both feet and running. But you can never tell about twelve folks on a jury. You just don't know how they're thinking about the case. Only time will tell. We'll just have to wait and see," he said, watching the shavings fall to the ground.

"Nary a one of them is fit to carry the banner for their party," Mayo stated, rubbing his smooth whittling stick with his rough fingers.

"What do you mean by that?" Manning asked, staring thoughtfully at his friend and confidant. "Somebody's got to win. Even with a tie, somebody's got to win. The mayor would pick somebody, and you know that the mayor is a Democrat. So you can see who would be the winner in that case."

"I betch'ye nary one of them wins," Mayo argued.

"We'll have to wait and see," Cody Skinner spoke up, breaking his silence. "Somebody's gotta come out with the long end of the noose. From what you've been telling us about each one of them, neither would be much of a swing on a high limb. How's Cubbie's trial coming along?"

"Well, not too good from what I hear," Manning declared. "Two of his wives are suing for divorce and half of his estate and earnings, and a part of his future earnings. On the other hand, the other wife is willing to settle for a legal separation and one-third of his estate and life's earnings. Now, that's what they're telling about it. You can never get the truth of a matter where a divorce is involved. There's allus two sides to a board, and you don't know which side is the roughest. But you can see that

Cubbie is a pathetic choice to carry his party's banner. Did you hear them on the battery set t'other night? They had a dee-bate."

"Naw. I don't have a battery for my radio," Cody replied. "Anyway, I wouldn't have listened to it anyway."

"Well, they had a dee-bate, and a good one to boot. You'd have laughed at most it it," Manning chuckled.

"Was it that funny?" Mayo asked, showing a growing interest in the tale that Manning began to relate.

"They were dee-bating on the problems of juvenile delinquency and the town's growing birthrate and unemployment problems. Cubbie thinks that there could be something done about so many pregnancies out of wedlock. He believes that these girls should get married. He said in the dee-bate, 'If I was a single man, I would marry an unwed mother.' The moderator laughed so hard at that statement that he drowned out the voices of the dee-baters. The moderator laughed 'cause he knew that it would be pretty hard for Ol' Cubbie to become a single person, since he's already married to three women. He went on to say that he believed that the marriageable boys in town and roundabout should get out and look for these good-looking girls and talk marrying-talk to them. They could get married and have a wife and a family already started. That should give them good reason to quit loafing and start to work at some kind of a job that he, himself, would create if elected to Mullinsville Town Council."

"What did John Jay say in rebuttal to that statement?" Mayo asked, continuing to whittle on his stick and watch the shaving pile grow.

"That statement was a throat-cutter, and John Jay took as much of an advantage of it as he could. John Jay was afraid to laugh at Cubbie's statement about being a single man. He figured that his wife was listening to the dee-bate, and he was afraid that she would crack his head if he said anything about the unwed girls. His wife knows that girls can make a few innocent mistakes during their difficult teenage years, but they can't make the mistakes without some teenage boys along to make the same kind of mistakes that the girls make. She made one of those innocent mistakes when she was much younger, and John Jay reminds her of it ever so often. The slander case came from some of his reminders. He forgot that he was in public when he reminded her of it the last time. That put him in court, with his wife as plaintiff. When John Jay got on the subject of clearing the town of loafers, he held the floor until the airtime ran out and the moderator had to turn the program off. Cubbie didn't have a chance to respond to the mud that John Jay slung at him."

"Those two fellers should have been born mud daubers, since they're such good slingers in their campaigns," Cody declared.

"Yeah. I guess you're right there, Cody," Manning said, rising and brushing the shavings from his worn pant legs. "I guess," he continued, "that I'd better mosey on home and tell Girty that she needs me."

"She don't need much if she needs something like you," Cody Skinner chuckled, following suit, brushing his pant legs.

"Betch'ye nary one of 'em wins," Mayo Coalfield wagered, leaving the company of his good friends.

"Betch'ye *one* does," Manning called over his shoulder as he walked along the sidewalk.

"Betch'ye," was Mayo's one-word reply. He shook his head slowly as he turned toward home in deep thought. He wondered about the character of the candiates. Their backgrounds were about the same, he realized.

John Jay Sprungtrap had the men of the town backing him, because they were envious of Cubbie Willpower, since he had three wives—good-looking ones, too—while they had only one jabber-box.

The women's church groups and civic orgainizations had not given either candidate their support, because they could not support a polygamist, nor could they support a man who would slander his own wife. They had no preference in the upcoming election.

The loafers and unwed mothers had not voiced an opinion. They really didn't care which one of the candidates won.

* * * *

Mayo Coalfield shuffled his feet in the pile of shavings beneath the bench on which he sat, nervously awaiting the outcome of the election. He gazed at the clock high on the courthouse tower. The time was five minutes till seven o'clock. "It won't be long now," he solemnly spoke.

"Sure won't, ol' pal," Cody Skinner quietly agreed.

"I have a five-hundred dollar bet on this election, "Mayo informed his friends.

"What!" Manning gasped. "You mean to tell me that you bet on one of them mangy curs?"

"Had to bet on somebody. An election ain't an election if you don't make a little side bet on somebody," was Mayo's hearty reply.

"Yeah, but them two!" Manning exclaimed. "I just can't figure you out."

"Don't try, Manning. That's too much for your little brain to stand," Mayo laughed.

"I noticed that you've been plenty nervous all day," Cody stated, looking at fidgety Mayo.

"There goes Cubbie with a carload of voters. Reckon they'll get there in time?" Mayo wondered.

"Sure! Ol' Cubbie'll stop the clock if he has to, and argue that the time is wrong," Manning responded as he watched the long hand on the courthouse clock approach the seventh hour.

"There goes John Jay on his last trip. He's got a minute and a half to vote his people. He has at least five to follow Cubbie's load," Cody stated.

As John Jay and his five voters got out of the car, the clock began announcing the arrival of seven o'clock. The courthouse doors closed immediately, leaving John Jay and his supporters outside. A loud banging could be heard by the three spectators on the park bench. The door opened and the late voters were admitted to the voting room.

"I hate to see that," Mayo groaned.

"Are you for Cubbie Willpower?" Manning asked, surprised.

"No, but I have a bet," Mayo said, rising.

"I wouldn't have bet on Cubbie," Manning told his friend.

"I didn't," Mayo intoned.

"Good! I'd hate to see you lose money like that. It's kinda stupid to bet your hard-earned money on an election, anyway," Manning argued.

"They should have the votes counted by eleven o'clock tonight," Mayo predicted. "I think that I'll go home and listen to the finals on the radio. I'll see you later."

"Did you take time to vote today, Mayo?" Manning asked.

"Yeah—once," Mayo slowly replied. "Did you?"

"Yeah—once," was Manning's deliberate answer.

* * * *

"In today's municipal election in Mullinsville," the news commentator began as Mayo Coalfield flipped on the radio to listen to the results of the election, "there was an upset."

Mayo's heart skipped several beats as he awaited the results of the vote tally.

"Here is the unofficial results, given to me by the election head-quarters in town," the newsman continued. "I have covered much of the campaign, and, my friends, the campaign got pretty hot at times, with mudslinging all over the place. A newcomer has crashed the election for town councilman, and I hope that he will represent his contituents well. Cubbie Willpower received 273 votes, while his opponent, John Jay Sprungtrap, received 270 votes. That is only 543 votes. I have been informed that a total of 1503 votes were cast. That leaves 960 votes for the unknown candidate. Who were those votes cast for? None other than the phantom—the write-in candidate. Our new councilman is Mayo Coalfield. Mr. Coalfield received 960 votes. No one knows what tactics he used in his campaigning, nor his party affiliation, but there is one thing for sure: he won the election. I hope he serves us well."

Mayo sighed in relief, smiled broadly, flipped the radio control off, and relaxed in silence.

* * * *

"I won't take your money, boys," Mayo Coalfield said. He stood in the door and looked at the dejected faces of John Jay Sprungtrap and Cubbie Willpower standing on his front porch, the day after the election. "I don't want your money. I'm against gambling. I made a bet with each of you boys, without the other knowing it. Cubbie, you thought I was betting on John Jay. And John Jay, you thought I was betting on Cubbie. I fooled both of you. I just wanted to let you know that you can't win an election the way you waged your campaign, and look at your back-grounds! The people want honesty in office. I'm gonna give them just that. I just wanted to betch'ye and prove that I could win. And I did just that. Betch'ye won't bet with me again."

Shake a Leg

Teed Cornfield was six years that day, many, many, many years ago. He was clean and shining as a big, red apple with dew on it. He had a pinkish-red tint due to the scrubbing he had given his tender skin. He had scrubbed four or five layers of skin from his little body.

His mother, wanting him to be clean on that first day of school, had done some scouring, too—probably more than the little fellow had done in his efforts to get the rust off. He had missed a few places—maybe.

The two-mile walk to school that morning was no obstacle for Teed. He was six years old and big, he thought.

As he walked along with his big brother, Judge L., and sister, Skatney, other red-faced boys and girls, who had been scrubbed clean for that exciting day, joined the growing procession. Cousins, friends, and neighbors joined them as they passed the numerous houses along the road. Soon there was a small army marching to battle against a bunch of books.

Judge L. and Skatney attended the big one-room school that sat in a field about two hundred yards from the little schoolhouse which Teed was to attend. Actually, his school was a small church-house. There were so many students on Coaley Creek that the real schoolhouse was overcrowded. The members of the Freewill Baptist Church were kind enough to grant the Wise County School System use of the desperately needed building.

On that first day, the students from both schools met in the big building to organize the different classes.

Before the students were summoned into the classroom, they had time to run and play long enough to get a little dirty.

Teed stepped in "doggie doo" with his new brogan shoes. He then became an unhappy little fellow. Things had certainly started off on a bad note for him.

When the bell rang to take up books, as the beginning of classes was called, the students formed two lines—boys in one line, girls in another. In that order they marched inside.

Teed sat with Judge L. He felt protected by his big brother. While he sat there, feeling protected and important, a big boy named Buck, about the same age and size as Judge L., looked at the little fellow with a humiliating grin.

"You stepped in doggie doo, didn't you, little boy?" Buck said.

When Buck said that, Teed burst into a snubbing cry. He snubbed and jerked so hard that he almost lost his breath.

"You didn't have to say that to little Teed, Buck," Judge L. said. He was amused with the little fellow's plight, but wanted Teed to know that he would protect him.

"I was just having a little fun with Teed," Buck laughed.

"I know you were, but he's just a little shaver. He's scared 'cause this is his first day of school," Judge L. replied.

Each time Teed looked at that big boy, he saw a churlish grin. That caused the kid to burst out crying again. He knew what that boy was thinking.

"You stepped in doo, little boy," Buck would say.

That first day of school was a nightmare for poor Teed, but the following day was much improved. He had grown up a lot overnight, he thought, and he was ready to face everything by himself.

Skatney walked Teed to his school that morning and left him standing there on the playground. He had a lost-and-all-alone feeling as she went to her classes on the other side of the big field. He had that desperate feeling for only a very short time. Teed saw kids playing games and joined in their recreation—uninvited. There was no protest to his crashing their frolicking about. He was accepted as one of the group.

There was no indoor plumbing in that little building. Therefore, there were no bathrooms—only outhouses for rest rooms.

Teed's first task as a full-fledged student was to draw a bucket of drinking water from a well at a farm about a quarter of a mile from the schoolhouse.

Satch Hood, a second grader, and Teed went to the farmer's well with a two-gallon bucket in which to carry the water. When they left the well, the bucket was full. Since the boys were so small, they had to help each other in their efforts to carry the pail. They were never in step as they carried the bucket between them. The unsteady walking caused the water to slosh out on their clothes.

Two wet, bedraggled kids arrived at the schoolhouse with a small amount of water in the bucket—about half a gallon. That which they had not spilled, they had poured out to make the bucket light enough to carry. There was just enough of the precious liquid for each student to have a sip to help quench his thirst.

The primer, first, and second grades were all in that one crowded classroom.

Each Sunday, the church pews were placed where the congregation could sit on them, and the desks were stacked in the back of the room. After the Sunday church services, the men of the church stacked the pews and put the desks in place for the students on Monday morning. There was a weekly changing of the seats.

There was a stage at the front of the church-house, or schoolhouse— whichever. It was a schoolhouse that day. The teacher, Miss Wills, had put a desk at each end of the stage. Teed happened to be one of the lucky students who got to sit in one of the special seats, while Satch Hood sat in the other seat at the opposite side of the room.

Miss Wills gave a recess period about ten-thirty that morning, and the kids had some good games going as soon as they could get outside and get unorganized. Children have a difficult time organizing games.

After fifteen minutes of exciting play, the bell rang to take up books. The children marched back into the building with less enthusiasm than they had shown when they left it earlier.

The students had been back in the room for only a short time—ten minutes at the most—when Satch Hood asked Miss Wills for permission to be excused to go to the rest room.

"You were supposed to use the rest room at recess period. That was the purpose for the break," Miss Wills informed the boy.

"I know," Satch whined, "but we were having so much fun that I forgot to go to the toilet. Please, Miss Wills, let me go," he begged. "I really have to go, and you'll be sorry if you don't let me get up and go."

"Are you threatening me, young man?" Miss Wills asked with a stern voice, but there was a twinkle of amusement playing around those soft, pleasant eyes.

"No, ma'am, I'm not threatening you; nature is," Satch said. "If you don't let me go this minute, nature is going to take its course, and I don't have anything to do with what it does. I never question the acts of nature, and in this little situation, I don't think that you would want to question my needs right at the moment."

"Well, all right, but hurry. Shake a leg," Miss Wills told him.

The rest of the students laughed as Satch made a mad dash for the door and the seat of comfort that was a little distance below the schoolhouse.

"Quiet!" Miss Wills snapped, and everyone stopped talking. She wanted to start classes, to proceed with her instructions with the primer class. She used flash cards with pictures and words on them.

When Miss Wills said, "Shake a leg," Teed stood up on the stage, raised his right leg, shook it and said, "Shake a leg! Shake a leg! Shake a leg!"

All at once a big paddle appeared in Miss Wills' hand—just like magic—and Teed got his first paddling on his second day of school.

There was a moment of silence as Teed sat down at his desk with his head bowed so the other students couldn't see that he was crying. The suddenness of the turn of events was more painful than the actual paddling. He thought that he had done something funny, and the other students did, too, but Miss Wills did not find it very amusing or entertaining.

Teed did not want to look at the flash cards when it came his time to show his intelligence. He tried to ignore the cards, and the teacher, because he had already shown his intelligence—just before he received that pants-dusting. He finally raised his head, after a coaxing threat, and said, "Cat." He was correct. That was what he thought the word was, for there was a picture of a cat on that card—a little yellow kitten with a blue ribbon around its neck.

He figured that he must have been correct since Miss Wills said, "Very good!" and turned to face the rest of the students.

Satch Hood sent an encouraging grin across the room to Teed, to attempt to bolster the little fellow's injured ego.

The morning classes passed very rapidly, even though the teacher did not shake a leg.

At lunchtime the kids ate their food as rapidly as they could without choking on the half-chewed sandwiches.

Teed did not have to chew his food very much. His mother had packed his lunch of buttermilk and corn bread in a four-pound lard pail that he used as his lunch bucket. He swallowed the last spoonful and threw the bucket into a bunch of weeds on the playground and ran to join the games already in progress.

As Teed hurried along, he noticed that the smaller kids were running around with their faces turned toward the sky. He could not tell what they were doing, but whatever it was, they were having a great time. He did not even attempt to figure out the name of the game they were playing. He could not spare the time to check out the small-kid games. He was in a hurry to join the big kids in their play, to show them that Teed Cornfield was as tough as anyone else.

There was a pretty little boy in Teed's class—the primer—named Timmy Blue.

All the girls were chasing Timmy, like little girls will do when they like a boy. Teed watched as the other boys chased the girls.

"Nyah, nyah, nyah," a boy would say. "You can't catch me and you can't hit me." He would do that to get attention and then run, hoping to be chased and hit by one of the girls. A little girl, in a half-hearted manner, would chase a boy away, then return to chase Timmy Blue in earnest.

Teed saw that they were having a great time and decided to join the action. He ran up to a big girl, bigger than anyone in the second grade, and said, "Nyah, nyah, nyah," like the other boys were doing to get attention. To his surprise, the girl chased him. He ran among the scampering kids, hoping that she would catch him. He soon got his wish when she caught him with little effort.

The girl's name was Josie Milt, and Teed found that she had a good pair of feet on her. She overhauled him in a very short time and hit him on the arm.

Teed thought that he was going to die right there on the playground. Nothing had ever hurt him like that thump on the arm. Josie hit his arm so hard that a frog popped up on it—big enough to croak—and he thought that he was about to croak, too. That lick on the arm made him hump and gimp around in pain. His fears of another thump were relieved when Josie Milt left him to join the other girls still mauling poor Timmy Blue.

Teed continued his humping and gimping around in pain. He was just like a whipped rooster, all hackled up, hurting with no one paying any attention to his misery. He had received a paddling earlier that morning, and then a thumped arm that felt as if it would fall off at any moment. Right then the big old world looked very unfriendly. He needed Judge L. to console him.

To beat it all, Josie Milt hit him, not because she liked him, but because she *didn't* like him. He thought she liked him when she first thumped him, even though the lick was just a tad intense for a love pat.

"You know," Teed, mumbled to himself as he watched the action centered around the popularity of Timmy Blue, "if he's getting popped as hard as Josie Milt hit me, he'll be beat to death before lunchtime is over."

Teed stayed at a safe distance from the arena of action. He certainly did not want to be hit by Josie Milt, or any of those other little girls.

The bell ending lunchtime was a blessed reprieve for poor Timmy Blue. He looked like something that had been run through a threshing machine. His shirt was out of his blue jeans, his shoes untied, and his pants cuffs were down to the ground. The cuffs had been neatly rolled up a couple of turns. They were much too long for him.

Teed could not understand why parents bought their kids' pants too long. They always did. Maybe they figured that the pants were just the right size, since the children were growing so fast. The clothes were usually worn out long before the little fellows could grow enough for them to fit properly.

As the students marched into the schoolhouse, in their respective lines, Timmy Blue sported a happy, winner's smile. His face was red and sweaty from all the running that he had done in order to evade total annihilation. Sweat dripped from his chin.

Teed was envious of Timmy. That little boy had had so much fun, while he had received so much pain. He was at the rear of the line of boys—an unhappy child. A mask of pain and a trace of a tear were on his face as he humped and gimped along, steering clear of Josie Milt. That frog was still trying to jump off his aching arm.

Teed sat down at his desk on the stage, where everyone could look at him and see his pain and dejection. If every day was going to be that rough, he had already received all the education that he wanted, even though he had not learned his three Rs.

Lumber-Jims

The rays of the summer sun slanted through the canopy of foliage high up near the top of Beartown, one of the highest points in the Clinch Mountains. The light shone about the floor of the forest in a halo-like glow, making the scene a spectacle of pure beauty. A stillness hung over the picturesque setting. Nothing stirred, except for maybe a dog-pesting gnat, which at that moment was flying from the closed eye of a boy lying prone upon the ground to another boy, the first one's cousin, about the same age, lying in a hunched position against a new-made stump. They had made that stump just a few minutes earlier by felling a huge red oak tree. After having used a cross-cut saw to cut their timber, they decided to take a breather. They ensconced themselves in a relaxed posture to while away some time—resting.

Jim Potter and his cousin, Jim Tanner, had been ordered by Zeb Tanner, one Jim's father, and the other Jim's uncle, to cut timber to rive wood shakes to re-cover the barn roof. The boys had started the job, but would they finish it? Starting a job took a lot of effort for those two fellows. Getting out of the bed in the morning was a huge endeavor for them.

Zeb had his hands full just trying to find work to keep the boys busy. Finding a job for them was one thing; getting them to do that job was another. The old fellow would try anything. He knew that they would finish his order, but when?

The still heat became more oppressive even though the area was shaded by the tall oak trees growing on the semi-steep slope up above the barn. The boys were perspiring under the humidity on the forest's floor. Their shirts were open to their belt lines, exposing bare chests—no under shirts in the summertime for them. Those outer garments would certainly come off, if they should decide to go back to work anyway soon. For the moment, though, they would remain where they were, hot or not. They would only get hotter by moving around in an effort to remove their shirts. That would be a wasted effort, they reasoned.

"Jim and Jim!" the roaring voice of Zeb Tanner carried through the still air, causing the first stir from the idle boys in the last hour. "I ain't heard a zing out of your saw or a thwack out of your axes for a long time. What's going on? Have you gone on strike?"

Zeb Tanner lumbered up the steep hill, grasping the sprouts and saplings by the path in his efforts to pull himself along.

Jim and Jim each opened one eye only enough to barely make out the movement of the man as he approached their resting spot. That was the only movement that was made, no effort to rise and commence to work as they had been so instructed to do. There was no reason to jump and shake at the mere thought of Zeb ordering them to do so. They had faced him before with the same impudence. Why jump now? The old fellow might bark, but the boys knew for a certainty that he wouldn't bite. Maybe bite a little, but not very hard. They just lay there enjoying their relaxation as long as they could, knowing that their rest would end as soon as Zeb climbed the hill.

"On your brogans, boys," Uncle Zeb ordered, almost out of breath from the long, hard climb up the hill. "You'll never get your job behind you—along with your butts—without some work. You've got the log on the ground, now saw it up in shake lengths and rive out the lumber so we can cover that barn. Let's shag it along now."

"Yeah, we got the tree on the ground, Pop," Jim Tanner replied, stirring feebly. "We can cut it up and rive out the boards some time next week, I hope."

"Yeah, it ain't raining, so what's the big hurry?" Jim Potter asked, moving only to knock a dog-pesting gnat out of his face. He then fell back into his relaxed state.

"Shake your heels and dust your britches, boys," Zeb yelled, "and let's get into the swing of things. Now!"

"Okay, Pop," Jim Tanner moaned, beginning to pull himself together to rise.

"Okay, Unc," Jim Potter said, following his cousin's movements, grasping a sapling to aid him in his attempt to stand on his wobbly legs— they had gone to sleep while he had lain for so long without moving.

After the boys got going in first gear, they made short order of sawing a shake-length cut from the felled tree.

"Set that block of wood on its end, then set down here and rest for a spell," Uncle Zeb invited, taking a bottle of clear liquid from his hip pocket. He uncorked it and took a swig from it, smacking his lips to show just how much he enjoyed his refreshment. "Set down. I'm tired and I guess you all are, too. We don't want to wear out the froe and maul all at once."

"What you got in that uncorked bottle, Unc," Jim Potter queried, looking at the liquid-filled bottle in his uncle's unsteady hand, knowing full-well what it was.

"Rhumatiz medicine, Nephew," Zeb said, smacking his lips loudly, trying to savor all the flavor in the pungent drink. I try to take a little of it ever' day. I'm just about down in all of my joints."

"If you're down in all of your joints, Unc, the medicine must not be working very well," Jim Potter laughed.

"It will if I give it enough time," Zeb moaned, trying to settle himself in a comfortable posture against the side of a stump. "Just give it time, boy. It takes time, that's all."

"Give me a snort of it, Unc," Jim Potter suggested.

"Naw, boy, you don't need this stuff. It might stunt your growth," Zeb told his nephew.

"Stunt my growth? I'm already as big as a skinned horse!" the young man retorted. "If I get any bigger I'll be too big to work and get around good. Give me a drink of that stuff so I can stem the growth right now and not get any bigger."

"The bigger you are the more work you can do," Uncle Zeb said, taking another drink from the bottle. He made a wry face, indicating that the liquid was a high-proof quality drink.

"Come on, Unc, give me a swig of that toad juice," Jim Potter begged. "I've tasted it before. You can't keep it hid from me and Jim. We know where you hide it. We found a whole nest of bottles in the barn loft. We drank all we wanted t'other day, so give us a swig so we can enjoy your rhumatiz cure."

"You boys don't have rhumatiz," Zeb uttered, taking another drink. The level of the liquid fell another half inch in the bottle.

"If we can drink it along with you, while you're being cured, we can be preventing the disease from infecting us, Dad," Jim Tanner said, entering the confab.

"You might have a point there, son," Zeb agreed, showing that the statement had sunk in, although his brain had a fuzzy spot covering the gray matter of thought.

The bottle was passed from one to the other in a circular movement around the stump, where each drinking participant rested. The bottle continued to make its slow laps around the stump until it was empty.

"We won't need that anymore," Zeb said, licking the bottle opening, trying to get every drop. "Just getting my money's worth," he replied as he saw the boys watching his actions. He then threw the decanter into a clump of rhododendron down the hill below their resting place.

The shattering of glass told the trio that the bottle had made contact with a rock somewhere in the bushes.

Zeb took another bottle from his hip pocket, uncorked it, and took the first drink—a big gurgling one—and handed it to one of the Jims to start another circuit of the stump.

At that moment, Zeb did not know which Jim was which. It really didn't matter which was which, he thought. They were both named Jim, after him, of course, and they were his kin. Zeb was named Jim, too. He was Zeb Jim Tanner.

"What's that?" Jim Potter asked, cocking an ear to his right. It was to Zeb's left and Jim Tanner's back, since they were sitting with their backs to one another.

"What's what?" Jim Tanner and his father asked at the same time.

"That rattling sound out there," Jim Potter said, pointing toward a laurel bush. "Sounded like a big rattler to me."

"Probably a jarfly," Zeb mumbled, closing his eyes. "You know how a jarfly'll rattle like a rattlesnake when it's been disturbed all of a sudden. They'll rattle that way, probably just to scare the living daylights out of you, and it does just that."

"Sounded like a rattler to me, and I sure believe that it was a rattler," Jim Potter intoned. "I'll chuck one of these chips out in his direction, and that way he'll tell me if he's really there." He threw the chip of wood in the direction of the rattlesnake sound. The buzzing sound came back toward the three immobile men. "Told you it was a rattler."

"Ah, just leave him alone and he'll leave us alone," Zeb grunted, nodding sleepily.

The buzzing of the snake's rattles quieted down, allowing the men to rest in peace.

Zeb groaned and moved his right leg to take the pressure off his heel. The old fellow had his heels dug into the soft dirt on the hillside to keep from sliding down the slope. That movement set the rattlesnake to singing again.

"Just like attending a concert, ain't it?" Jim Potter remarked, trying to settle himself more comfortably against the rough bark on the stump.

"What about a concert? What's like a concert?" Zeb asked without moving more than his lips.

"That singing rattler over there in the bushes on his stage. He's entertaining us with his one-line, one-note song," Jim Potter told Zeb.

"Yeah, he sure is cutting a rusty all right," the old man replied. "Do you suppose," he continued, "that he's been disturbed by somebody or another snake of some kind?"

"I've not heard anybody or seen anyone around out there in the bushes," Jim Tanner said. "Could be the rattler's nemesis, the blacksnake, or something nosing around in the rattler's territory, looking for something to swaller down."

"We might see a good shake-down, chew-up fight. I bet one of them is scared and the other's glad of it," Zeb muttered incoherently.

The bottle continued to circle the stump, stopping long enough at each sitting to further quench the thirst of the inebriated men. The bottom of the bottle was slowly moving toward the top. That was what it seemed to be doing—to the drinkers. There wasn't much liquid in the container at that moment. It would soon be empty and have to join its broken brother in the rhododendron patch.

The men's coordination, though they weren't moving much, was slowly deserting them, leaving three prone, idle masses of muscles propped up against the stump. Blurred visions, drooling lips, and slurred words had taken over.

"I see a big snake coming out of the bushes over there next to the rattler, Unc," Jim Potter said, breaking the silence. "He sure ain't a black snake, though, as I had expected he would be when he got here. He's as green as grass on a hillside and as long as a short piece of railroad. Look at him slinking around there."

"I see him, but he ain't green," Jim Tanner said, peering into the bushes. "He's pink and got a blowing-viper's mouth on him. He'll make short order out of that rattler. He'll gobble him down like a dog eating a wienie."

"You boys must be color-blind," Uncle Zeb groaned. "That snake is blue. He's a blue racer-snake. All three of them might gang up on the old rattler and demolish him all at once."

"If each one will just share the entree and not be too greedy and try to take it all, they can sup well today," Jim Potter grunted.

"Could," was the one-word reply from Jim Tanner as he slipped into an unconscious state.

The other two men followed suit, snoring peacefully, leaving the rest of the world to itself. There was a snoring trio propped up against the stump. The bodies were almost comatose, with dog-pesting gnats gathering at the corners of the drooling lips and closed, watery eyes.

The distant rumble of thunder caused the three sleeping men to begin to stir. Flashes of lightning lit up the dark clouds hovering over the mountains to the west.

"I guess that we'd better rattle our hocks on down off the mountain and search for some shelter," Uncle Zeb suggested, rubbing the sleep, and the big wad of gnats, out of his eyes and corners of his mouth. He smacked his lips to try to get rid of the nasty aftertaste of alcohol in his mouth.

"Do we have to move?" Jim Potter asked, protesting the very thought of having to get up. "The snakes might gang up on us and rid the mountain of people 'stead of ridding it of the rattlers. I don't hear Mr. Rattler out there on his stage anywhere, do you all?" He threw a chip of wood into the bushes. Nothing but silence came back to him. The snake was gone. Maybe he had been eaten up by the herd of multi-colored snakes that the drinkers had seen. The odd-colored snakes were gone, too. "Good riddance!" the boy muttered. "They ate each other."

"I don't remember any snakes. Could have been a dream that you had," Uncle Zeb reminded the young man. "I don't remember seeing any snakes or hearing a rattler, did you, son," he asked, facing Jim Tanner.

"Nary a one, Pop," the boy replied.

"See, Jim," Uncle Zeb began, "it was all a dream or in your mind. You probably had just a tad too much of my rhumatiz medicine."

"I saw a snake, and heard a rattler, and you two fellers told me that you saw snakes, too. It was not a dream, I tell you!" Jim Potter retorted.

"Well, they ain't here now, if they ever were here," Uncle Zeb said, rising stiffly to his feet. "Let's shag it on down the mountain."

"I know that I saw a green snake," Jim Potter argued. "I saw it with my own eyes, and you saw snakes, too, with your own eyes. Don't stand there and tell me anything different. You two saw them. You just don't want to admit it."

"Maybe so, son. Maybe so," Uncle Zeb laughed.

"Maybe so," Jim Tanner echoed.

The clouds had become darker, and a rising wind began to lift the leaves on the oak trees on the mountain, exposing their light-colored undersides. The sun had already set, before the men had awakened, leaving the space beneath the heavy canopy of leaves dark and eerie in the early twilight.

"Let's shag it on down the mountain, boys," Uncle Zeb suggested once more. "We'll get back to this job early in the morning. It's too late to do anything now, and one more rain won't hurt the barn roof any more than it is now. Let's go."

The old man and the boys slowly shagged it on down the mountain.

Uncle Sturble Preaches

Teed and Gillis Cornfield and their cousin, Jubal, sat in the back of the big Coaley Creek church-house, on the last pew. They sat over against the wall where they would be the least conspicuous. They were washed and scrubbed to a shiny pink.

The moderator of the church, Trankle Cornfield, had invited Brother Sturble Cornfield to preach the sacrament sermon.

Brother Sturble rose and in a deep, sonorous voice, slowly got into his text for the day. Soon he was into his delivery as the Spirit touched him. He began to tell the large congregation what it should do to get to Heaven. After the Spirit touched him, he began a singsong chant. He surely was ready to preach that day!

"If you don't turn from sin—hack, you sure will fall by the way—hack, and not make it—hack," he shouted to the solemn congregation.

He was getting carried away in his sermon, and the brethren of the church were "amening" each time he made the hacking sound at the end of each sentence. He was preaching so hard that he did not take time to swallow. The saliva thickened and turned frothy-white. White spray flew from his mouth and floated to the cracked, varnish covered wood floor. He tried to swallow several times but couldn't. He just blinked his bulging eyes in his efforts and swallowed some of his words. His last "hack" was just a feeble grunt.

Teed, Gillis, and Cousin Jubal sat in the rear of the room and listened to Uncle Sturble preach, and watched him spit little flecks of frothy slobber over the floor.

Gillis began to snicker. He covered his mouth with one hand and pointed to Uncle Sturble with his other hand.

"What are you sniggering about, Gillis?" Cousin Jubal asked.

"Uncle Sturble can't preach anymore, 'cause he just swallered his hack," Gillis laughed, and that made Cousin Jubal laugh out loud.

People turned to see where the noise came from. Many put fingers to their lips in silent gestures to quieten the trio of boys.

Jubal bowed to them and whispered, "Will do." That made Teed and

Gillis laugh out loud, causing heads to turn again, as if on swivels. Fingers went to lips, and Jubal bowed again. His actions weren't as funny that time. He didn't say, "Will do."

Uncle Sturble was still croaking, hacking, and spraying frothy spit all over the floor as he continued to preach.

Teed figured that the preacher should wipe his mouth pretty soon. He was waiting for that to happen.

Uncle Sturble wore a blazer-type jacket over his freshly washed overalls. He always carried a red bandanna-type handkerchief in his left coat pocket to use when he preached each Sunday.

Teed could not understand why his uncle waited so long to wipe his mouth. Surely he knew that it needed to be wiped.

The old minister was so carried away in the fervor of his sermon that he did not take time to wipe the unappealing dry spittle off his fast moving lips.

Teed knew that Uncle Sturble should wipe his mouth soon. With all the foamy spittle flying, the power of his message was fading fast, and the congregation had ceased "amening" as the preacher searched for words to continue his sermon.

Finally, Uncle Sturble's hand stole toward his pocket, and as the excited boys sat on the back-row pew, waiting excitedly for something to happen, they inched toward the edge of their seat.

In his excitement, Cousin Jubal slid from the pew and landed on his backside on the floor. He thrashed about for awhile, trying to regain his composure so he could rise and return to his seat. While he was still on the floor, thrashing around, a funny thing happened that brought him to his feet in a hurry.

As Uncle Sturble pulled his hand from his coat pocket, a pair of gaming dice flew from the handkerchief gripped tightly in his big hand. Unbeknownst to him, the two cubes had been neatly wrapped in his handkerchief, and when he gave the handkerchief a healthy snap in order to unfold it and get the wrinkles out, the dice rolled and bounced over the floor. They stopped—in the snake-eyes position—in front of the good brethren who had been "amening" the loudest.

Uncle Sturble had been doing a good job with his sermon delivery, but that ended with a final "hack" that had lodged in his throat.

There was a moment of pin-dropping silence. Then very slowly a murmur went through the congregation as people looked at one another in surprise.

Teed, Gillis, and Cousin Jubal screamed with laughter and headed for the door to escape the wrath of Uncle Sturble.

"You devilish boys will hear from me!" he warned as they ran out the door and hit the yard at breakneck speed.

The lads dashed into the wooded area surrounding the church-house. They could hear Uncle Sturble as they hunkered down in the bushes to await the aftermath of the dice-slinging incident.

"Those devilish boys snuck those dice in my pocket, knowing well that I would have to use my bandanner to wipe my mouth with," Uncle Sturble said, giving a lame apology. "Sing a song while I get control of myself. Then we can take the sacrament and have a good foot washing."

Teed could hear what Uncle Sturble said, since the door was open on the side of the building next to his hiding place in the bushes.

"We can't miss the foot washing, boys," Cousin Jubal told Teed and Gillis, laughing uncontrollably.

"What's so great about people dabbling dirty feet?" Gillis asked, laughing with Cousin Jubal, even though he did not know why his cousin was so tickled.

"Let's sneak up to the winder and watch," Cousin Jubal suggested, continuing to laugh without control.

"They'll hear us, and Dad's in there," Teed said.

"We'll be real quiet, and the noise from the excitement inside will keep them from hearing us," Cousin Jubal assured him.

"You're going to have to grab a hold of your laughing box if they ain't going to hear us," Gillis said as he continued to laugh with Cousin Jubal.

"They can see us through that winder, boys," Teed warned. "It's just a little ways behind the preacher's pulpit."

"Shucks, boys, that bunch'll be too busy scrubbing rusty feet to notice us. They won't even look up. We're safe as can be," Cousin Jubal stated. "Don't fret yourself so much, Teed."

The boys stole toward the rear of the church-house, where there was a low-level window. They squatted down and peeped in, hoping that they would not be discovered by the preacher, or anyone else in the building.

Teed was worried. He was afraid that his father would spot them as they looked through the window.

Marn Cornfield had always said that Teed and Gillis were to sit in church and listen to the preaching, whether or not they agreed with what the preacher said.

Teed knew for a certainty that Gillis and he would get a good seat-dusting when they got home. Maybe they did not listen to the sermon that Uncle Sturble had delivered that morning, but they knew that they had done wrong and needed to repent. Teed would have to repent to his father, too, but he knew that his father wouldn't accept his apology. He dreaded the whipping that he was sure to receive, but those dice rolling across the floor had made him laugh. There was no way that he could have suppressed that laugh, even if it had meant his life. He knew that things would take on a more serious demeanor after his father had finished with him when the church services were over.

As Teed looked through the window, he could see that Uncle Sturble had finished washing Talmage Seedy's dry, rusty feet. They looked moist and clean for a change.

It was time for Talmage Seedy to wash Uncle Sturble's big feet.

"Get some clean water there, Brother Talmage," Uncle Sturble directed.

"This water looks pretty clean, Brother Sturble," Talmage replied.

"It may look clean enough for you, but it sure ain't for me," Uncle Sturble said, sternly arguing his point for clean water. He did not want to wash after a dirty-foot like Talmage Seedy.

"No, it sure ain't clean enough," Cousin Jubal whispered, falling to the ground, laughing so hard that he lost his breath. He had to sniff a few extra times to get his breathing air back.

"I don't see why wanting clean water after Talmage Seedy washed his feet in it is so funny," Teed wondered. He had to laugh, too. Cousin Jubal was so comical, kicking around on the ground and sniffing incessantly.

"You'll see pretty soon," Cousin Jubal choked out, continuing to guffaw.

Brother Talmage emptied the dirty water by pouring it outside the church-house door. He refilled the washbasin and placed it in front of Uncle Sturble. "Is that clean enough for you?" he asked.

"I guess it'll do," Uncle Sturble grumbled, removing his right shoe and sock. He placed his big foot in the pan. His heel fit in the basin, but his toes stuck over the opposite side. "Man, that water's cold!" he complained, lifting his foot above the water level.

"Put your foot back in the pan," Talmage ordered, none too friendly. "If you were living the way you should be, the water would feel warm to you," he said, looking at the preacher's foot.

"I'm living right!" Uncle Sturble retorted. "Whether or not the water feels cold to my feet don't mean that I'm not living right. You should know that I'm living right. You heard that sermon awhile ago."

"I heard you hacking and saw you slinging white slobber all over the floor. I also saw you sling your craps dice across the floor, but that don't mean that you were doing a good job with your preaching and hacking. Do you have your dice loaded?" Talmage asked, smiling.

"They were not my dice! I told you that before. I can get somebody else to wash my feet," Uncle Sturble blurted out, starting to rise.

"Sit down and hold still," Talmage said. "I'll do it, but with a foot that big, I'll probably have to get some help from another brother."

"Wash it and hush your big mouth, Brother Talmage," Uncle Sturble stammered. "Else folks have to wash feet, too, you know."

Talmage Seedy proceeded to wash the preacher's big foot. When he finished, he wiped it with a not-so-dry towel. "Now give me that other railroad car. I'll buff it up and put a good shine on it, too," he said, referring to Brother Sturble's humongous foot.

Uncle Sturble removed his left shoe, and when he slipped his sock off, he exclaimed, "Them devilish boys! They've done it again!"

There was his big foot, completely covered with a dark brown substance. He looked at it for a few seconds—unable to speak. When he did finally regain his composure, he tried to explain to Brother Talmage, and the rest of the congregation, the reason for his black foot. "I washed both of them last night," he said, beginning a feeble explanation for his dirty foot. "Those devilish boys put something in my sock. It looks like walnut stain and some kind of grease, probably lard to make it stick good. They put that stuff in there just to plague me, and this sure is embarrassing."

"Put it in the pan. I'll scrub and scour it till it shines like t'other 'un," Brother Talmage said, trying his best to stifle a laugh.

"No, just let it go. One will be enough for this sacrament," the solemn preacher intoned. He put the discolored sock back on his dirty foot.

Cousin Jubal screamed with laughter and raced toward home, followed by Teed and Gillis.

"Boys, I'll get one good stropping for this little escapade, but I have to tell you, my friends, it was worth every lick that I'm sure to receive," Cousin Jubal laughed. "Did you ever see such a black foot in all of your born life? It looked like a big coal hopper sitting there on that floor."

"I'll agree with you, Cousin Jubal. That black foot and that pair of dice were really funny," Teed reminisced. "But what will be waiting for Gillis and me when Dad gets home won't be worth the laugh we enjoyed." He could not understand how his cousin Jubal could face his predicament with a laugh. He thought about the situation momentarily. He then began to laugh without control as he ran along the narrow path toward home. There was only a whipping waiting for him. He could face that, for he had been thwacked numerous times and knew what to expect.

Gillis just ran and laughed.

Water's Too Hot

That Sunday morning was the beginning of a beautiful summer day. Breakfast was over and the morning chores were finished. The older folks were preparing to attend Sunday worship services at Coaley Creek Old Regular Baptist Church.

"Where's my red tie, Ma?" Marn Cornfield asked his wife, Vann, who was taking her bath at the kitchen sink.

There was no bathroom, so a bath was a sponge off.

"A sponge off is just a lick and a promise—one lick today, and a promise of another one later," Marn often said, with a big toothy grin.

"It's in the top dresser drawer where you allus keep it," came Vann's reply.

"Yeah, here it is—right in front of me," Marn stated.

"It should be the only red thing in the drawer," Vann said, scrubbing her face with the wet washcloth, muffling her words.

"It is, but the drawer was closed, and I couldn't see it," Marn called back.

Koodank Cornfield sat on the couch, listening to the conversation. He wasn't going to church with his parents that Sunday. Brother Dump was home for a week of vacation, and Koodank had a lot of playing to do with Dump's sons, Barkoot and Stumper, and Clem's sons, Kardon and Wheddle.

Dump lived in Yorktown, Virginia, while Clem lived beside his parents on Coaley Creek.

There were many different kinds of games that Koodank wanted to play, and since Barkoot and Stumper were interested in sports, the games would most likely involve some type of ball. Since it was about the middle of summer, the first game would probably be baseball.

Marn and Vann, Dump and his wife, Clayora, and Clem and his wife, Sofiejo, walked the short distance to the church-house at the mouth of the hollow.

Dump's trips home brought a lot of excitement to Koodank, Kardon, and Wheddle, who were always ready for the many different events which were planned for the boys during the two-week vacation.

Barkoot reported to the young lads about the differences between Yorktown and Coaley Creek. He often brought new games to teach to his cousins and young uncle.

Most of the older children were in Baltimore, Maryland, making their fortunes. Everyone who left Coaley Creek to work in the cities usually made a crock full of money—much more money than they could possibly make in the coal mines on Coaley Creek. Their work was much easier, too.

Clem was more of a homeboy. He had returned to Coaley Creek after having worked in Baltimore for a number of years. He was working in the "truck mines," as the small mining operations were called.

The coal had to be transported by trucks to the railroad to be loaded into coal hoppers. That was the reason they were called "truck mines."

Teed, Gillis, and Friday were still in high school, and Koodank attended a little one-room school about two miles down the road from the Cornfields' residence.

Having played an exciting, high-scoring game of baseball, the quintet of rowdy boys searched for something else to do. When they found nothing else that was exhilarating, they resigned themselves to the necessity of aggravating Clem's daughters, Doe and Dew. Dump's daughters, Zip and Tweet, could expect to take a little pestering from the rambunctious boys.

Tweet found it necessary to occupy the two-seat outhouse. She had the trots from eating too many green apples. In an uncontrolled haste, she began hotfooting and gimping toward the seat of comfort. Unbeknownst to her, there posed an unfriendly obstacle.

Between the little girl and relieving comfort was a mother hen and her chickey-diddles, contentedly scratching in the path in search of a breakfast of bugs and worms for the ravenously hungry chicks.

Little Tweet was terrified by the presence of the hen blocking her approach to the lonely little building. As Tweet advanced toward her planned destination, the hen ruffled her feathers and began chasing Tweet back toward the house.

The old hen was daring the little girl to enter her turf, and it seemed that the hen was going to be challenged seriously by the little girl.

There was one thing for sure, and Tweet would vouch for that surety, she needed to be on her way to the building which stood just beyond the chickens. It was very evident that she needed to fight her way through to her goal, and soon, or there would no longer be a need for confrontation with that hen. The hen would surely be the winner of the standoff. If something did not happen soon to make the hen move, Tweet knew that something else surely would.

Koodank, Barkoot, Kardon, Wheddle, and Stumper arrived on the scene, and with dirt clods from the garden, they drove the hen and chickey-diddles away from the access route to the toilet.

The boys had watched Tweet as she tried to get past the hen. They laughed because she was in so much discomfort.

"You should have done something sooner!" Tweet shouted in anger, racing to the outhouse.

"That wouldn't have been much fun," Kardon said, slapping his legs and laughing at the little girl.

"I didn't think you were going to hold out there, little sister." Barkoot laughed, continuing his harassment of Tweet.

To make things even worse, the boys began pelting the sides and roof of the building, using dirt clods as ammunition.

"Hurry, Tweet, someone else might want to occupy the comfort seat," Barkoot shouted as he heaved a huge lump of dirt that showered the building like a load of buckshot.

"We didn't eat so many green apples like you did," Koodank said, heaving another clod against the flimsy, crack-filled door.

Tweet screamed as she was showered by the small particles of dirt that sifted through the cracks as the clod burst into many pieces.

"Help!" Tweet began to scream hysterically, "Help me, Zip!" she called to her big sister. "Bring Doe and Dew and help me out of this place."

As the three girls raced to Tweet's rescue, the antagonists fled the scene, and the barrage of clods ceased to rain havoc on the sides, door, and roof of the building.

The boys laughed for a while and commented on how much fun it had been to see someone as uncomfortable as Tweet in her standoff with the hen. The lads knew that the hen had won the battle of attrition. The fowl had the upper foot instead of the upper hand, since chickens have no hands.

The five boys meandered about the farm, going first to the barn where they played by rolling in the hay loft, then to the woods where they rode out trees. Tiring of the latter, they sat down on a log to talk for awhile, returning often to the fun they had had while pestering poor little Tweet.

"Let's walk down to the church-house and sit around until Dad and Mom and the rest come out of the meeting," Koodank suggested.

"Yeah, let's do that," Barkoot agreed.

Anything was all right with Wheddle and Stumper, and since Kardon was quiet and more reserved than the two tykes, he followed, neither in agreement to the suggestion, nor in opposition. He was glad that Barkoot and Stumper were home for a visit and would be in favor of anything that was pleasing to the rest.

They arrived at the church-house and took seats on some huge rocks, plentiful all about the building. While sitting on the rocks talking and telling jokes—a favorite pastime—Wheddle and Stumper had to be reminded to not laugh out loud.

They enjoyed the jokes that Koodank and Barkoot told and laughed to show it.

"You'll disturb the church services," Barkoot warned them.

"Sorry about that, Barkoot," Wheddle apologized. He grinned, showing a wide gap between his teeth caused by the removal of a couple of his baby teeth.

Stumper only smiled and said nothing.

The side door to the building opened, and a stream of water gushed forth, splashing on the grassless yard.

"What was that all about?" Wheddle asked, astonished by the jet of water.

"I don't know," Barkoot said, looking at Koodank and Kardon for help in solving the water mystery.

"Don't ask me. I don't have the slightest idea what's going on," Koodank declared, watching the church-house door.

Kardon shrugged his shoulders. That was his way of saying that he had no idea of what was happening.

Without their knowledge of the event, that was a day of sacrament at the church. The congregation was having a foot washing—the sanctified members were.

"Maybe somebody forgot to take a bath this morning, and the others are making him wash before they'll let him stay in church," Wheddle wondered. "A body can smell real raunchy when he ain't had a bath in about a week."

"I don't see how he forgot to take his Sunday bath, do you?" Stumper said, turning to his companions for their thoughts on the matter.

The door opened once more. Another stream of water came from a washbasin.

"They've got another dirty person in there," Wheddle reported. "I saw the washpan that time. They're sure cleaning up the flock today."

"I know what they're doing," Koodank smiled, realizing what was taking place. "They're having a foot washing."

"What's that for?" Stumper queried, showing his curiosity.

"They must get it from the Bible," Koodank said. "They do that ever so often. I've heard Dad speak about it. He said that Talmage Seedy has dirty feet ever' time they wash one another's feet. They're always dry and rusty. He said that old man must wait for the foot washing so somebody can wash his dirty feet. That way he can get out of washing them. That's supposed to be the honest truth, too, and I believe ever' word that Dad says about Talmage."

"I'd believe anything that Paw says," Barkoot replied.

"Anyone would believe Paw." Wheddle said, agreeing with Cousin Barkoot.

More water was thrown from the church-house door. The foot-washing services continued.

A loud shout came from a woman in the building as she felt the Spirit and vented her happiness in a shout of praise.

Not knowing the reason for the shouting, Wheddle looked at the other boys and said, "That one's water must have been too hot."

That broke up the waiting. The larger boys began to laugh hilariously as they ran toward the house.

Little Wheddle missed the humor of what he had said. He followed the running boys, trying to catch up—to find out what he had said that was so funny.

Fat Teed

"You sure are fat, Teed," Gillis called up to his brother as Teed climbed farther up the maple tree that he intended to ride out.

"What do you mean when you say that I'm fat, Gillis?" Teed asked. Actually, Teed was skinny as a stunted grapevine.

"You can ride out big trees," Gillis stated, trying to explain his reason for saying that his brother was fat.

"It's not that I'm fat," Teed returned, getting a little irritated with Gillis. "It's because I'm a big boy."

"It's 'cause you're a fat boy," Gillis laughed.

"If you were big enough to weigh as much as I do, would you be fat? No, 'cause you're not fat, and I'm not fat, either," Teed said, answering his own question.

"If you're bigger than I am, you're fat, Teed," Gillis quipped, continuing to quibble in his childish way.

"If I were smaller than you, and you could ride this tree out, would you be fat?" Teed asked, growing madder as they continued to bicker. He was a high-tempered kid, and Gillis could always get his dander up. Teed knew that his little brother just liked to argue, and Gillis had no grounds for his pugnacious attitude.

"I wouldn't be fat 'cause I'm not fat now, Teed," Gillis said. "My ribs are showing. Look!" He raised his shirt, revealing his skinny, little body.

"Yeah, your ribs are showing, and a knot's going to be showing when I get down and chuck your head with my knuckles. I've had enough of your arguing," Teed threatened, growing more irate. Gillis really had him going right then.

Even though Teed often threatened the little fellow, he would not have hurt him. There was too much love in his heart to do anything like that.

Their arguing ceased as abruptly as it had begun as Teed called down to Gillis. "Watch out, Brud." He them attempted to bend the tree toward the ground. Slowly it bent over, going down, down, down, until his feet touched the ground. When he released his hold on the sapling, it rose slowly, giving off a swishing sound, trying to get back to its upright position.

"That must have been a lot of fun, Teed!" Gillis said, jumping up and down with his eyes wide-open with excitement.

"Sure was, Brud," Teed said. The Cornfields shortened "brother" to "brud." "Go ahead and try it once." Teed invited.

"I'm on my way up right now," Gillis replied as he started climbing. With his little hands and feet gripping the tree, he resembled a short-tailed monkey as he inched his way up the swaying sapling.

A maple tree, maybe twelve inches in diameter, had fallen during a severe storm at some time in the past. The place in which it had tried to grow was in a very rocky area. The soil was so deficient of the needed nutrients for survival, and the rocks were so numerous, that the small tree had little or no chance of becoming a large one. A small number of roots still clung to the sparse soil, searching for sustenance, keeping the tree alive.

Over the years, since its demise, the limbs had tried to reach for the light above, so they had turned upward, searching in their natural way for the sun's much-needed rays.

The limb which the boys were using for their entertainment had grown rather straight, with just a little bend in it. That was the direction in which Teed had made his first effort to ride it to the ground.

"Here I come, Teed," Gillis yelled as he threw his weight out to start the limb downward. It bent slightly, but would not give Gillis the exciting ride that he had anticipatied. He was just a little too light to force it down. "I need some assistance in the form of help from my ol' buddy, Fat Teed," he yelled, holding to the limb with a bulldog grip.

Teed shinned up the tree. With his weight, along with that of his brother, the limb bowed to the ground, bearing the two boys with it. When they released it, it whoosed its way back to a normal position.

"Ain't that fun?" Gillis shouted with excitement as he looked at the maple limb, swaying back and forth.

"Sure is," Teed agreed as he began to climb the tree once more.

That entire Sunday afternoon was spent riding that limb to the ground. Suppertime and chores ended the good fun for the day.

"We'll hit this place bright and early in the morning. We'll either wear that limb out, or it'll wear us out. Let's give it a try," Teed suggested.

"You can bet your rotten apples against a crippled toad frog that we'll be here bright and early," Gillis promised, running toward the house.

"Me and Teed's got a nice ride-out tree down there below the corn crib," Gillis said to no one in particular as the family sat at the breakfast table that Monday morning. "We're gonna climb it and ride it out all day."

"Or till we get too tired to climb," Teed said as he attempted to help Gillis with his announcement of their plans for the day.

"Teed will get tired before he climbs a tree," his father said, spreading gravy over two fluffy biscuits. The gravy began to soak into the soft texture of the steaming biscuits that Vann had just taken from the oven. Marn dipped more gravy and spread it over the soggy bread. He began to eat, thinking that the bread would devour his gravy before he could.

"I'm gonna climb that tree right after morning chores," Teed announced. He surprised himself by telling his father that he was going to do something instead of asking for permission to do it.

Marn Cornfield was a very strict parent. "Teed," he began, "you'll be in that tater field hoeing taters and chopping weeds. That'll take care of your plans for the day."

"Hoeing taters!" Teed whined, showing his disappointment.

"Yeah, hoeing taters," his father assured Teed, letting him know that he had heard correctly.

Teed hated potatoes worse than any chore that had to be done on the farm.

"Why today?" Gillis asked. "We've found a good ride-out tree. Can't the taters wait till another day?"

"No, they can't wait," Marn said, smiling.

The brothers had found that good ride-out tree, but they would have to forget about riding it out that day. There was such a large field of potatoes that most of the day would be spent in their efforts to plow, chop weeds, and hoe them. Hoeing potatoes was a very slow task.

Teed often wondered why so many potatoes were planted each year. If he had looked at the number of people sitting around the big table, he would have known why.

Dump, the oldest brother, would plow between the rows to stir up the dirt so the rest of the workers could put it around the tender potato plants. Plowing also took away much of the necessity for chopping weeds.

"Me and Friday can go tree riding," Gillis said, beaming with excitement as he wiped a glob of gravy off his chin with the back of his hand. He then rubbed his hand on his pants, using them as a napkin.

Gillis and Friday were too small to do any serious hoeing. They would have done much damage if they had been permitted to try to help. That was why Marn would not turn them loose in that field with a hoe where they could devastate the potato crop.

Teed's bubble of excitement had burst. There he was, facing a day of gloom. He hoped how soon he could grow up and become a man. He certainly would not live on a farm and work hard to make his living. He knew for a certainty that he wouldn't plant a big field of potatoes if he should have to follow in his father's footsteps and become a hillside farmer. He liked potatoes about as well as any food there was, but not good enough to go through the pains that went with tending to them while they grew. Maybe he would eat something different—something that didn't take much effort to raise. He figured that he would just eat candy and wash it down with pop. He wouldn't have to plant pop and candy and then hoe them to make them grow. He could play all day long. Then when he got hungry, he could go to the store and buy some candy and pop. That would be a simple way to make a living. He wouldn't have to worry about planting, weeding, and hoeing his food.

"Get your chores done," Marn ordered, pushing his chair back from the table.

The children rose together. None dawdled behind. They knew better than to do that. They knew that their father had a remedy for such impudence, and it was firm, so they jumped to it as soon as he spoke.

Teed began hoeing potatoes and fighting those old biting flies, while Gillis and Friday were somewhere else. They were playing in the good ride-out tree. He was sure of that, and the very thought made his job in the potato patch almost unbearable. He wanted to be in that tree—not hoeing taters.

"Wake up, Teed. Help us hoe these taters," Judge L. said, "If you don't help a little, we'll never finish."

"I don't care," Teed mumbled, cutting a weed from between two potato hills.

"You may not care, but Dad will," Judge L. told him. "He'll chuck your head with his knuckles. That is if he don't take a two-handed brash to you."

If Teed's father was threatening, and a threat from him was very seldom made, he often told the kids that he would use a two-handed brash when he did his correcting of them. A "two-handed brash" is a big switch.

"It would be better to be chucked on the head than to have to hoe these old taters," Teed whined. He was in no mood to care.

"There might be better things than hoeing taters, but it sure ain't head chuckings," Judge L. said. "You'll have to hoe these taters, even after you get a head chucking."

Judge L. changed Teed's mind with his words of warning. There was a little more effort put into his work as he struck the weeds with harder blows and dug dirt with more endeavor.

During one of his numerous idle moments, Teed saw Friday at the end of a potato row. She was almost hidden by a large potato plant. It was only once in a while that he could see her as she moved about. She used an empty meat can to dig the dirt from a potato hill and put it in a pile at her bare feet.

Teed had no idea how long the little girl had been playing there, because he had been too busy feeling sorry for himself and trying to shirk his responsibility of hoeing potatoes. He watched Friday play for a little while longer. Finally, his curiosity got the best of him. He had to speak to her. "Where's Gillis, Friday?" he asked.

There was no answer. She continued to dig in the potato hill with the empty meat can. She dipped more dirt and put it on a growing pile at her feet.

Teed had to ask her a second time. "Where's Gillis, Friday?"

She was so engrossed in her play that she did not hear him. At least she acted as if she had not heard. After the second attempt to get her attention, she looked up. Her head was just above the potato plant. Her blond ringlets blocked her vision, causing her to have to lean backward to focus on Teed, letting the ringlets fall to one side.

"He's down there below the corn crib. He's hung in a tree that he was trying to ride out," she said, continuing to dip dirt with the meat can.

"Why aren't you there with him?" Vann, who was hoeing a row next to Teed, asked.

"Because Gillis wanted me to come and tell Teed to hurry down there and get him out of that tree," she said as she continued to play contentedly.

"Why didn't you tell us?" Vann asked, laying her hoe between the potato rows.

"You were busy, and I got to playing with this can and having so much fun that I plum' forgot to," she replied, unmoved by the need to inform her mother of Gillis' plight.

"You should have told us about Gillis needing our help," Vann said, reprimanding the little girl for not telling her imediately that Gillis needed help to get down from the tree.

"I forgot to, but I would have remembered if you had asked me about Gillis," she replied, still unconcerned about her brother.

Teed threw his hoe to the ground and raced for the tree which held Gillis captive, while Vann followed at a slower pace.

Everyone else continued to hoe potatoes like nothing had happened. Predicaments, such as the one Gillis faced, occurred so often that no one became overexcited about them.

When Teed arrived at the good ride-out tree, he saw Gillis suspended about twenty feet in the air. He was too light to force the limb to the ground.

Teed shinned up the tree, trying to climb up as near to Gillis as he could. As he reached his brother's position, Vann arrived.

"I think I can reach him from here, Mom," Teed called down to her. He needed to move a few inches closer. He could see that his little brother was tired and would not be able to hang on much longer.

Gillis had gripped the limb so long that the blood had stopped circulating in his fingers, causing them to turn blue.

Just as Teed reached Gillis, the limb began to bend under the added weight.

As Gillis felt the limb begin to bend, he relaxed his hold and fell.

Teed's weight had forced the limb closer to the ground and Vann's outstretched, waiting arms.

Vann saved the little fellow from breaking some of his bones. "Are you all right, Gillis?" she asked, but got no answer.

"Where's Friday?" Gillis asked, instead of answering his mother.

"She's in the tater patch, playing with an empty meat can," Teed told him.

"Did she tell you that I needed help and to come quick?" Gillis asked.

"Yeah, she told me after I asked where you were," Teed replied.

"I told her to hurry, that I couldn't hold on very long, and those rocks looked big and hard below me," Gillis cried. Tears of joy streamed down his cheeks.

"Well, Gillis, I'm thankful that you're safe," Vann said, hugging the little boy to her breast. "Son, please don't play in dangerous places like this anymore," she warned as she kissed him on top of the head.

"I won't," he assured her. "And another thing," he continued, "I'm glad I'm safe—thanks to Fat Teed."

Well-Off

Bennie Barkoot Cornfield went to college. That was a much-talked-about event on Coaley Creek. Most of the people in that area did not attend high school, much less go to college. Barkoot went away to a university in another state—University of North Carolina. He got a store-bought education. That is what his Uncle Meck Lorenzie said it was. In a sense, it was a store-bought education as his uncle called it. Bennie Barkoot had to pay for it.

Uncle Meck Lorenzie was talking to Marn about Bennie Barkoot's way of getting an education, compared to the regular way of getting an education on Coaley Creek.

"You know, Marn, your grandboy should've stayed here on Coaley Creek like your boy Teed did," Meck Lorenzie said.

"Yeah, we allus think that our boys should stay around here, but we just don't have the work for young people graduating from college, except for the mines," Marn explained. "No young boy in his right mind wants to work in the mines if he can find something better, with a good education to go with it. I work in the mines—I know."

"That boy should've got the *real* education like everybody else does here on Coaley Creek," Uncle Meck Lorenzie declared.

"I know," Marn began, "but the seventh grade and experience just ain't enough for men today. They have to go to college."

"Where does that boy live at?" Meck Lorenza queried.

"He's over in Meek County," Marn told him. "He got an engineering degree in agriculture. He's cleaning out the creek where they had a big flood in the spring. That's the type of work he does for the state. Anything that goes wrong, that's caused by nature, he has to try to fix up for the people living in that area."

"He's living fifty miles from home, over there in Meek County," the old fellow stated.

"No, Unc, he's not living away from home," Marn laughed. "His home is over in Meek County. He moved over there."

"Here on Coaley Creek will allus be his home. He just ain't here,"

Meck Lorenzie asseverated. "What did you say he was doing over there, Marn?" he asked again.

"He's cleaning out that stream that flooded and caused a lot of damage last spring," Marn replied.

"You mean to tell me that he had to go away to college and spend big money just to learn how to clean out a creek?" the old man uttered. "I've been cleaning out our creek nigh onto seventy years, and I don't have a college education. I can't understand why he spent so much money to go to college to learn how to clean out creeks. I think I would have spent my money on something else, 'stead of going to college to learn that. How long did it take him to learn about cleaning out creeks, and how much did it cost him?"

"He went to college for four years," Marn informed him. "I don't rightly know what it cost him, but I'd say it cost a pretty penny."

"Well, he could have learnt under me in about a week, and the only cost for him would have been for the gas to get over here on, 'cause he could have stayed with me and eat from my table at no cost at all," Teed's uncle declared.

"He learned more than just cleaning out creeks. That was just one thing that he was taught to do," Marn said.

"Well, I still say that he could have learnt it a lot faster under me, and it wouldn't have cost a whole lot," Meck Lorenzie intoned.

"Well," Marn began, "it costs for tuition, room and board, food, clothes, books, and some type of car to go back and forth to his classes."

"Why didn't he stay with your boy Dump and go from there?" he wondered.

"It's too far to drive back and forth from here. It's at least three hundred miles from here," Marn smiled.

Uncle Meck Lorenzie was ninety-one years old, alert and very spry for that advanced age. He did not understand the need for an education beyond the seventh grade, as far as classes went at Coaley Creek Elementary School.

Teed enjoyed listening to Uncle Meck Lorenzie talk. The old man's philosophy on life and education were all right. The simple life that he had lived was all that anyone needed, he thought. He explained his theory about getting an education without having to spend so much money.

"You can't include food, clothes, and living quarters as necessities for getting an education," he began. "A man has to eat, even if he don't go to college. And he has to wear clothes, too. And a body has to live some place—education or no education. That boy should protest having to pay out extra money for all the things that he had to have for ever'day living."

You couldn't do anything with Uncle Meck Lorenzie. He had an answer for all problems. Teed did not agree with his reasoning, but dared not to disagree openly with him.

Teed and his father left their elderly uncle sitting on the porch talking to himself.

"A store-bought education. What is this world coming to? Going to college to learn how to clean out a plain ol' creek" he mumbled to himself.

* * * *

Bennie Barkoot moved to Meek County to work. One day while visiting the folks on Coaley Creek, he invited Teed to go over and spend a few days with him, and since Teed wasn't working steadily at the time, he agreed to go. Barkoot told his uncle that the visit wouldn't cost him anything.

Learning that there would be no expenses on the trip, Teed quickly made up his mind to go to his nephew's house to visit. Anything free makes Teed a good buddy to anyone, but he liked Bennie Barkoot, his educated nephew.

Teed had no car at that time, so he had to thumb his way over to Barkoot's house. Since it was Sunday, there was very little traffic, causing Teed to have to walk more than he had anticipated. He hitched three rides of approximately twelve, fourteen, and eighteen miles, respectively, and walked another ten long, hot miles to get to the house.

Teed found a beautiful house which sat on a sloping lot. It was nice and big—much larger and nicer than Teed's simple house on Coaley Creek.

Barkoot made big money and could well afford such a house. Teed wasn't envious of his assets—just astounded by them. He enjoyed visiting with his nephew and family that Sunday afternoon.

When the evening grew dark, Barkoot's older son, Basil, turned on the porch light for a basketball game.

Basil and Teed formed one two-man team, while Gaston, the younger son, and Barkoot formed the other team.

Actually, Basil and Teed won the game, but to keep Gaston and Barkoot from crying, they let up and did not play so hard. They felt that anyone could be a good winner. They just did not want to find out the type of losers Barkoot and Gaston were, so they played it safe—they lost.

Barkoot's wife, Tess, and daughter, Tootsieleigh, refereed the game and chased the ball when it went out-of-bounds. They did not like chasing the ball to the bottom of the hill, though, but someone needed to, and since they weren't included in the game, the chore fell to them.

Barkoot had scheduled the beginning of a job for the following day. He invited Teed to go along with him.

Teed promised not to get in the way, for he didn't know the scientific procedure of cleaning out a creek, and, too, he just wanted to enjoy watching someone else work instead of doing the work himself. He needed a long, quiet vacation.

* * * *

"Teed, let's go over to talk to Col Modut about those people on Dodger Creek," Barkoot suggested as he finished his breakfast the next morning.

"All right, Barkoot, I'm ready," Teed said, drinking the last sip of coffee in his cup. "Who is this Col Modut?"

"He's the best-informed citizen around here," Barkoot declared. "When I have a job anywhere in this county, or the adjoining counties, he informs me of the temperament of each family. He knows the best ways to approach them. You can't rush these people into accepting you. They don't accept a stranger, especially if that person should work in a governmental capacity as I do."

As they rode along in the pickup truck, Teed looked at the strange surroundings. He had never been to Dodger Creek.

"I have some bulldozers and end-loading equipment coming on low-boys this morning," Barkoot spoke, breaking a lengthy silence. "I'll have to see that the equipment is off-loaded. We'll start at the mouth of the stream and work our way toward the head of the hollow. I would like for you and my inspector to go with me to talk to some people who live by the river where we are to commence our operations."

"Sure, I'll go with you," Teed said, accepting the invitation.

Barkoot pulled into Col Modut's driveway, got out, and approached the elderly gentleman. After cordial greetings were exchanged between the two men, Barkoot asked a question. "Uncle Col, could you tell me about those people up the road about a mile, in that big bend where all the trees and debris are piled up on the south side of the stream? What are those folks like?"

"Well, son," Col Modut began, twisting around in his straight-backed chair, "those folks are well-off. Whoop Hodat passed on awhile back. You'll find that Mrs. Hodat is a tough old lady. Stand up to her, boy. Don't let her or her sons, Dew and Zech, cow you into leaving without gettin' your job done."

"It doesn't matter if they are well-off, Uncle Col," Barkoot replied. "We do this work for the rich as well as the poor. We don't charge for it. Therefore, we can't slight anyone."

"Well, I just thought that I should let you know that they're well-off," Mr. Modut repeated.

"Thank you, Uncle Col," Barkoot said. He turned to Teed. "Come on, Teed. Let's get my inspector, Hack N. Sputum, and go to see those people."

"Don't let that old lady cow you into leaving before you get started on your job," Mr. Modut warned.

Teed looked back toward the house as they left. He could not see Mr. Modut sitting on the porch due to the dust boiling up behind the moving truck.

"Why do you call Mr. Modut 'Uncle Col' instead of 'Mr. Modut?'" Teed asked.

"Well, Uncle Teed, it's just out of respect. When I call him that, he thinks that I'm in need of his help in some way," Barkoot stated. "Uncle Col's all right."

Barkoot stopped for Hack N. Sputum and headed upstream in search of the Hodat's residence.

"Hack, you come with me. Let Uncle Teed stay in the truck while we talk to Mrs. Hodat," Barkoot suggested as he turned the vehicle into the driveway leading up to the porch.

"I'm not going in that place," the inspector avowed. "I'm not showing any disrespect for your authority over me, Mr. Cornfield, but look at those two big men sitting there. They're as big as two grown giants. They could sweep this creek clean with me if they so desired. Why don't you take Teed with you? He can talk the horns off a billy goat."

"Thanks, Mr. Sputum," Teed said, as nicely as he could, "but I'm here at Barkoot's invitation, and I won't interfere in your work, so I'll tarry awhile with this pickup truck."

"Come on, Teed," Barkoot invited, stepping from the vehicle. "Just back me up. I don't know these people."

"I don't know them, either," Teed retorted. "There isn't any use for both of us to get thrown out, beaten, or shot," he continued, trying to let Barkoot know that he had rather be somewhere else right at the moment.

"Oh, come on, Uncle Teed. You can back me up," Barkoot said, closing the door and facing the strangers on the porch.

"Don't worry, Barkoot. You're big enough to whip an elephant," Teed vowed, trying to give him encouragement.

"I know, but there are two on that porch," Barkoot declared.

"All right, let's go," Teed told his nephew, trying to show a little boldness.

They left Hack N. Sputum sitting in the pickup truck, grinning all over the place.

Zech Hodat sat on the porch with his feet hanging over the edge, rocking back and forth. He seemed to be just a tad off—maybe a tick or two short of a full minute. His appearance and actions made Teed think so, but the man could have been acting, just to throw everyone off guard before he made his move to attack.

Dew Hodat looked a lot like his brother. Dew was taller than Zech, but weighed less. Though he had a lighter build than his brother, he was a huge person.

The two visitors approached the low porch with caution, and as they neared the silent people, Zech put his hands and arms over his head to protect himself. He seemed to be afraid that Barkoot might try to inflict some type of harm to his head. By the way he had covered up, he was as safe as a turtle in its shell. No one could have penetrated that pile of big arms.

Dew Hodat showed no emotion at all. He stood there as stoic as an Indian. The only movement he made was that of his hands going up and down the insides of his galluses.

Barkoot sidled past Dew, not wanting to get too close to him.

Teed moved in the same manner—right behind his nephew's huge body. He was completely protected. If anyone should get thumped, Barkoot would receive the blow, missing Teed completely. Teed was no runty coward, but why should both men get attacked by that giant? He saw no future in that.

The drone of engines could be heard as trucks brought the equipment which Barkoot was to use in his cleaning project. The big trucks stopped at the bend in the stream where the cleanup operations were to commence. The machine operators began the task of off-loading the big end-loading equipment and bulldozers.

Teed was watching the operators in their efforts to park the big trucks beside the narrow road. That time lapse had let Barkoot get ahead as he approached Mrs. Hodat, sitting comfortably in her padded rocking chair at the end of the long porch that spanned the entire length of the house.

Teed caught up with Barkoot without a clout from Dew's big fist. Maybe he wasn't as mean as he looked, but Teed wasn't taking any stupid chances. He felt like a hackled rooster trying to find its way out of the arena of possible action. He cowered behind his big nephew.

"Hello, Mrs. Hodat. How are you today?" Barkoot spoke, politely greeting the lady.

"Hello to you, young man." Mrs. Hodat returned the greeting with an elderly, rasping voice.

"Ma'am, I'm Bennie Barkoot Cornfield. I'm here to clean up the devastation caused by the spring flooding," he said to the quiet lady. "I see there is a huge logjam making a mess of things there in the bend of the stream. We're trying to help everyone in our efforts to clean up the area. It doesn't matter that some people are in better financial shape than others. There is no charge for our services. We want to clean up the entire area before another flood should happen to come. If we don't clean this stream right now, you could be flooded again the next time a big storm moves in."

Barkoot had made a good, fast speech. Teed figured that his nephew wanted to give his reason for being there before Mrs. Hodat could have her big sons throw him out.

"Did you say that you're going to do it for everybody, young man?" Mrs. Hodat asked.

"Yes, ma'am," Barkoot replied, feeling that he was on the right track now that one of the silent bunch was willing to talk to him.

"You can do the cleaning, but don't mess up my medder," she stated, pointing to the meadow.

Paper, plastic jugs, and plastic pop bottles cluttered the grassy strip of land that Mrs. Hodat had referred to.

"I'll do my best, Mrs. Hodat," Barkoot said, smiling with delight. "I'll try to leave it in better shape than it is right now. I'll have the trees cut into the correct lengths for your winter fires."

"Just be sure that you don't do any damage with your big 'nozers, young man," she warned.

"I'll do my best, Mrs. Hodat," Barkoot promised. Teed smiled as the woman referred to the bulldozers as "'nozers," but he made sure that she did not see that he was laughing.

Barkoot could do no more damage than the flood had already done to the little grass-covered lot by the side of the stream.

Teed stayed as close to Barkoot as he could while walking toward the pickup truck and the waiting inspector, Hack N. Sputum.

Operations were soon under way. Work went very well for awhile, without any interruptions. The chain saws roared as the operators cut the fallen trees.

Barkoot was kept busy checking on each phase of the cleanup. "Stack that brush neatly," he instructed the man in charge of that detail. "Don't ram your chain into those rocks under that log," he cautioned a saw operator.

There was so much going on that no one noticed the presence of Dew Hodat. "Are you gonna clean for that bunch up the holler?" he asked as soon as he could get Barkoot's attention.

"We're cleaning for everyone on Dodger Creek," Barkoot told him, tossing a limb on top of a growing pile of brush. "Why do you ask?"

"We don't like them. And, we don't get along with them," Dew Hodat declared, scuffing his big shoe in the loose sand and gravel by the creek.

"We're doing this cleaning for everyone, not for just you people," Barkoot stated as he continued pile brush. "Who are those people, and why do you dislike them?"

"They're the Bunkins, and they don't get along with anyone," Dew said, kicking a plastic pop bottle that lay near his big foot. He watched intently until it splashed into the stream, then turned back to face Barkoot.

"Have you tried to get along with them?" Barkoot asked, stopping his work to look directly at the big man who continued to kick pop bottles into the stream.

"No. And I'm not going to try to get along with them," Dew drawled.

"It's their problem—not mine."

"Usually there are two sides to every disagreement," Barkoot said.

"Yeah, there are two sides—ours and theirs—and we're right. They're the ones that are wrong," Dew said, explaining to Barkoot that he was on the right side of the dispute.

Teed could see that his nephew was about to get riled, by the extra grunt that he put into slinging the tree limbs out of the way, and the way he responded to Dew's peremptory statement.

"I have to clean for that family, too. It's my job," Barkoot stated emphatically, but in as mellow a tone as possible. He did not want Dew Hodat to misunderstand the need to be stern in his stand on the principles of helping each family without showing any favoritism toward either party involved in the ongoing dispute, whatever the controversy was.

"Well," Dew said as he turned to leave. Just that one word was all that he said as he departed. He didn't say, "Well, I'll be back," or, "Well, go ahead and clean," or, "Well, break my elbow and tell me howdy." He just turned and walked away.

Barkoot directed an order to the chain saw operators. Work resumed in full swing.

Things were going fine, or it seemed that they were from Teed's vantage point on a big rock under a huge ash tree that provided protection from the hot sun. He looked toward the house from time to time. He could not relax, since Dew Hodat had given up too easily.

After a very short time—just long enough for Dew to report to his mother on Barkoot's plans for cleaning for everyone on Dodger Creek— Teed saw the big man on his way back. He was sure that the man had another message from his mother.

"Dew is on his way back down the hill, Barkoot," Teed called out, notifying his nephew of the man's return.

"Thanks, Uncle Teed," he said over his shoulder as he continued to work, undisturbed by the approaching messenger. He wasn't as perturbed by those folks as Teed was. Barkoot had to contend with the Hodat-type often. Maybe by ignoring them, they would not be so persistent.

Teed nodded to Dew as the big man passed his perch on the rock. He wanted to be civil toward the big fellow. He could have turned that big rock seat over on top of Teed with little effort.

Dew never even noticed Teed. He slouched on toward Barkoot with a look of perplexity on his solemn face. Maybe he was tiring from so many fruitless trips to the creek and back to the house. "Mom said for you to leave immediately, if not sooner," he said on his arrival.

"Doesn't she want this place cleaned up?" Barkoot asked. "This," he continued as he pointed to the debris strewn about the area, "is an eyesore for the entire community."

"Move out is all that she told me to tell you," Dew said, speaking in his bulldog-growl voice.

"Did she say why?" Barkoot wanted to know. "I have to have a reason to move. I have to answer to my supervisors."

Teed could see that Barkoot was getting a little agitated with that bunch of Hodats. He was afraid that the boy might pop a shirt button pretty soon. His face was beet-red, and his juggler veins were puffed out like two blowing-vipers. He expected an explosion of some kind, but it did not happen.

Barkoot wanted to get his work done but could not due to the interruptions by the Hodats interfering with his progress.

"Mom just said to move. She said that you're going to help the Bunkins up the holler," Dew stated.

The situation seemed to be getting very serious. That was the way it looked to Teed. He did not say anything. It wasn't his squabble. He just hoped it wouldn't get out of hand and maybe turn into a nasty situation.

"I'll move out after I finish this tree," Barkoot said, with the irritation of the disturbance showing in his voice.

"Now!" Dew Hodat snapped.

"Let's move out, men," Barkoot ordered. "Come on, Uncle Teed. Let's get to a phone. I need to call my supervisor while the men are loading the equipment. Be sure to tie everything down securely before you move out," he instructed his men, who immediately began to carry out the order.

"I'm ready," Teed said, heading for the protection of the truck.

Hack N. Sputum was already in the truck, prepared to leave. He had sneaked away during the argumentive fracas between Barkoot and Dew Hodat. He wanted to be prepared for a quick getaway in the event of an altercation.

As the three men rode along in the pickup truck, Teed could see that Barkoot was disturbed. Thought wrinkles were piled up on his forehead.

"Boys, we might have to back up and punt on this play," Barkoot finally spoke, breaking a long period of silence. "I have to finish this job and clean Cubbie Creek next. These two projects need to be finished before winter begins and snow starts to fly. I don't have much time left. Let's go over to Uncle Col's house and speak to the old fellow. He may be able to help persuade Mrs. Hodat to forgive and forget her differences with the Bunkins long enough for my crew to finish this job."

Col Modut was sitting on the porch in his straight-back chair as Barkoot drove up to the house and parked.

Barkoot got out of the truck and approached the elderly gentleman, while Hack N. Sputum and Teed remained seated in the vehicle. "Uncle Col," he said as he approached the porch where Mr. Modut sat, contentedly shaving slivers from a cedar stick with his white-handled Case pocketknife, "I had to cease operations up at the Hodat place. Those people are crazy! They ran me off. You told me that they were well-off, but you didn't say anything about their being crazy."

"Well, you found out that they're well-off—just like I said," Mr. Modut calmly replied, continuing to whittle shavings from the cedar stick.

"So, 'well-off' means 'crazy!'" Barkoot mused, rubbing his chin thoughtfully.

"That's what I said. They're well-off," Mr. Modut repeated, a hint of a smile playing around his wrinkled mouth.

"I learn the meaning of new words and phrases all the time," Barkoot stated. "If I stay around here much longer, I'll be talking just like the rest of these folks. I need to get to a phone to talk to someone about these people. I have to get back to that site as soon as possible."

Bennie Barkoot slid behind the steering wheel, started the engine, and raced down the road in search of a telephone.

The Crowin'est Rooster

Ham and Domer Sedder walked along the narrow path from the spring to the back porch. Water splashed from their pails as they hurried along in the anticipation of ridding themselves of their burdens. The chore had come at a very crucial moment. Ten long minutes of valuable training time were lost. The spring was nearly one hundred yards from the house, and the path was uphill most of the way on the return trip. That inconvenience in their chore was humongous.

"What did you find out?" Ham queried.

"Too much," Domer said, showing concern.

"Too much?" Ham echoed, hurrying to keep up. "How's that?"

"I hung around in the bushes back of the barn near their training grounds," Domer began. "Their shortest time was four seconds. That's as close as they could check it, with no stopwatch. I heard them say that one could hold out for six seconds."

"Six seconds!" Ham exclaimed.

"Six seconds," Domer assured him.

"That can't be," Ham went on, doubting the news. He climbed the last rise in the path, puffing as he tried to keep up. "Ol' Red Ballard can hold out for five and a half seconds, and I believe with some more work, he can go six, but he can't do any better, no matter how much we train him."

The boys set their buckets on a bench on the porch and sat down to rest. Their conversation kept at a fast pace.

"We surely have some competition," Domer spoke, after a brief rest. He rose from his seat on the edge of the porch and descended the steps to the yard.

"I agree with you," Ham said, following his older brother.

They walked down another path that led to the barn. A long "Er-er-er-errrrrr" bugled from the throat of a huge red rooster.

"That's the crowin'est rooster I ever heard in all my born days," Ham avowed as the boys watched the big rooster in a chicken pen by the barn.

"That's what got us into this predicament, my friend," Domer stated flatly.

"I didn't think anything about it when I said that Ol' Red Ballard could beat any rooster in this part of the country at crowing," Ham apologized. "We could tell Tass and Masby that we were only joshing about Ol' Red Ballard being the crowin'est rooster around."

"Never back down on a bet," Domer said. "You'll learn why by the time you get as old as I am."

"Yes, Grandpa," Ham quipped as he thought of his brother's statement. Fifteen wasn't old. It wasn't much older than thirteen. Maybe Domer felt old after having made the bet with Tass and Masby Wheddle.

As Red Ballard arched his neck to crow again, Domer fished his father's stopwatch from its seclusion in a front pocket, snapped the switch to the timer, and watched the second hand move slowly around the dial.

When the rooster ended its challenging call, Domer snapped the switch to stop the movement of the hand. After a close scrutiny he said, "Five and a quarter seconds. He's failing real bad, Ham. He did better than that yesterday."

"He'll do better if we just give him time," Ham blurted out, trying to encourage his despondent brother.

"We don't have time—that's our problem," Domer groaned, staring at the ground in deep thought.

"We have two more days of training until the contest," Ham said.

"What can we do in two days?" Domer asked seriously, timing the rooster during another challenge.

"We can give the ol' bird two more days of workout is what we can do," Ham laughed, enjoying his own witticism.

"Oh, you," Domer replied, slapping his younger brother playfully. "You've just become a teenager and you're a problem to me already."

Ham jumped about and asked, "How would you like to be young again, Grandpa? Can you remember what life was like way back then?"

"Oh, I can still remember my younger days," Domer mumbled as he began to time the rooster again.

"Did anyone see you get it—the watch?" Ham asked, becoming serious.

"Bust it, Ham, you caused me to lose time on him! No, nobody saw me," Domer growled. Very carefully, he dropped the watch back into his pocket. "Get him out of the pen. We'll have to massage his goozle some more."

Ham opened the door to the cage, crawled awkwardly inside—grunting all the while—and lifted the gentle fowl into his arms.

The rooster pecked at the white buttons on Ham's shirt, thinking they were grains of white corn.

Ham handed the big chicken to Domer, who in turn began to massage the long neck.

Domer placed his thumb on the back of the rooster's neck and two fingers against the esophagus and trachea. He then moved his fingers back and forth along the long, skinny neck.

The boys figured that the massage would stretch the vocal cords without injury to the rooster, and thereby enable him to crow for a longer period of time. How well it would work they didn't know, but that was what they were trying to discern.

"Where are we going to get the money to cover the bet that we made with Tass and Masby?" Ham asked as he made a thorough contemplation of their predicament.

"I don't know," Domer came back, without interrupting his workout. He pulled up on the lower part of the neck, causing the rooster's eyes to glaze and close under the pressure.

"Looks to me like you have him throttled a little too tight, Domer. Let up just a tad on his goozle, 'cause he's going batty-blind when you press too hard!" Ham exclaimed. "Do you think that this will help any?"

"I wouldn't swear to it, but we have to do something, and this is the only thing that I know to do," Domer said, continuing to massage the long neck. "This won't hurt him any at all, so let's keep it up for a little while longer. Time will tell."

After several tedious minutes of workout, Domer released the rooster into its quarters.

Red Ballard arched his neck—as if he knew what the boys wanted—strutted about, and crowed a challenge to every rooster in the neighborhood. There was an immediate answer from the opposite side of the building.

"How long?" Ham asked, stretching his neck in order to see the face of his father's watch.

"Six seconds!" Domer chimed excitedly, smiling all over the place.

"Six seconds!" Ham echoed. "That's better than he did on his last try yesterday. Do you think he can better that before the weekend? Do you think it would do any good if I rubbed his neck some more?"

"If you quit blabbering so much, you might have time to, but that will be enough for today," Domer told him. "We don't want to go too fast, 'cause we might make him sore and hoarse."

"How long did you say their rooster crowed?" Ham asked, referring to their opposition.

"It was a guess. They were using a regular watch with a second hand," Domer began. "They could have been off a fraction of a second, and that means a great deal in a contest like this. Their rooster crowed for close to six seconds. Like I said, they could be off a fraction of a second."

"That's a long-crowing rooster all right, but I believe that Ol' Red Ballard will do better than their rooster by the weekend," Ham avowed.

"He's got to," Domer said seriously. "We have a lot on this bet. If you had kept your big mouth shut, we wouldn't be in this predicament."

"I said what I said 'cause I meant what I said. I believe that Red Ballard is the crowin'est rooster in the world, or in this part of it, and I'm gonna prove it—around here, that is. Don't you have any faith in our over-grown chickey-diddle?"

"We'll know Sunday afternoon about three o'clock whether or not he is the crowin'est rooster in the whole world," Domer said. "I have a little faith, but I'm afraid that my faith won't help that rooster crow any better than he can right now."

The training period ended for the day, and the conversation ended as the two boys walked toward the house.

Ham had the task of returning the watch to its place in a bedroom closet. He was lucky. There was no one in the room as he sneaked through the house unnoticed. "I did it without getting caught," he told his brother as he emerged from the house with a thistle-eating grin.

"Now, if winning the contest is that easy, we'll be in pretty good shape," Domer stated.

* * * *

Sunday dawned warm and clear. There was no air stirring—just as the boys had hoped.

Domer and Ham were at the rooster-pen behind the barn. A long "Er-er-er-errrrrrrr" sounded on the still morning air.

"Six and a quarter seconds!" the excited voice of Domer Sedder echoed through the trees about the farm.

"Give him plenty water," Ham suggested. "We want to keep his goozle wet," he continued, referring to the rooster's neck.

"It would be just like Ol' Red Ballard to choke up and croak out a little sound of about a half second," Domer muttered, fearing that there was a possibility of losing the bet. He had not figured out a way to cover the wager. Where could he and Ham get ten dollars? Two weeks had passed since the wager was made. Two weeks, and still no money to cover the gamble. They couldn't call off the contest. Their father had taught them to be honest and keep their word. Domer wondered if his father had meant for his sons to keep their word and cover a ten-dollar bet. He really didn't think so, but still he couldn't back out.

Even though the boys had tried to raise the cash, they were unable to. Surely something would happen, and in their favor, they hoped. Tass and Masby Wheddle should know that there was no danger of their backing out of the contest so late in the game.

It finally came to the point where Ham could no longer keep his feelings to himself. "Domer," he began, "we'll have to put up Dad's watch as bet coverage."

"Gosh, no! Ham! We can't do a thing like that," Domer exclaimed.

"That's our only alternative, Domer. I've thought about it, and there's no other way. We'll bet the watch against Tass and Masby's ten dollars," Ham declared.

"Law me! Dad will beat our hides if we do that," Domer said. "Gosh, Ham, Dad's watch is worth over a hundred dollars! We can't bet the watch, and that's final. That would be like giving a fortune for a feather."

"Do you doubt that Ol' Red Ballard will win the contest?" Ham asked.

"I'm sure that he'll win if we bet money, but just as sure as we stake the watch, he'll choke up and squeak out a half-second croak," Domer replied.

The brothers talked for a long time before an agreement was made to stake the watch on the rooster, with Domer reluctantly agreeing to it in protest.

The morning waned and turned to afternoon. An excruciating heat wave came along as the day's guest.

Ham and Domer walked along the road that wound in a snake-like trace through the beautiful hills of Southwest Virginia. Dust puffed up from the hot road as the two silent boys trudged on their way. The dust slowly filtered back to the road due to the stillness of the air.

Red Ballard rooster-talked as he was constantly kept off balance in his wire cage. His feet thump-thumped against the wooden bottom of his suitcase-like enclosure. He arched his neck and tried to crow in his cramped quarters.

The loud, energetic sounds of a huge crowd carried through the air. The hum of a bevy of voices reached out to Ham and Domer, and judging from the commotion coming from behind the big dome-topped barn, there was a large audience to witness the much-anticipated contest.

"Here come our most worthy opponents from over Coaley Creek way," Masby Wheddle chimed in his high-tenor voice.

"You're so right," Ham agreed.

"Have you brought that fry-chick with you? Or have you chickened out?" Masby asked, jokingly. "Hey, how did you like my joke?" He repeated himself so that everyone present could hear that he had made a funny. "I said that they must have chickened out with their chicken."

The barnyard hummed with activity. A congregation, exceeding two hundred, talked and laughed among themselves. Grown-ups and children alike milled about the arena.

"What does this mean?" Domer asked his bewildered brother.

"Couldn't tell you," came Ham's slow answer.

The din quieted as the two boys approached the large crowd, where they were greeted by a host of thistle-eating grins.

"Here are our most worthy competitors," Tass Wheddle said, bowing and presenting Ham and Domer Sedder to the huge throng of spectators.

"Who put out all the advertisement?" Domer asked, slapping Tass Wheddle on the back.

"News travels fast," Tass replied, returning the greeting by grabbing Domer by the shoulder. He gave his friend a playful shake.

"With a crowd like this on hand, Ol' Red Ballard might not crow his best," Domer said seriously. "I couldn't come up with the ten dollars for the bet, but this watch of Dad's is worth much more than ten dollars. Would you chance ten dollars against it?"

"Sly Muncy probably won't, either," Tass agreed, referring to a gray rooster in a banana crate against the barn wall. "Let me have a look at that watch. I'll have to give it some consideration before betting on a used ticker." He looked at the watch with his mouth open and readily agreed to bet with his friend.

"Do you know what?" Masby chimed, joining the huddle of boys. "There's a newspaper reporter from town out here amongst the crowd. He's asking questions, and I've been trying to avoid him so I won't have to give him any answers about our contest."

"We don't want this in the newspaper!" Domer exclaimed. "Dad takes the local paper. He'll read about this and give us the thrashing of our lives for borrowing his watch with out his consent."

"We have to do something. We can't evade him all day," Ham insisted. "We decided to have the contest, so I guess we'll have to cooperate with the news media."

"Who told a news reporter about our contest?" Domer wanted to know, directing the question to Tass.

"I don't know, but I have a pretty good idea, though," Tass alleged, nodding his head toward Masby and Ham.

"Let's give him his interview," Ham quipped. "Maybe we might earn national fame—might even get a chance to go to the Olympics."

"Bull!" Domer said in disgust. "Listen to the dreamer. You dreamed up the contest. Now you eye a spotlight in the world. A stopwatch and ten dollars won't get you to the Olympics. They don't have such as a rooster crowin' contest in the Olympics."

"They could if they wanted to," Ham blared.

"That's made up of physical abilities of people—not a rooster crowing," Domer insisted.

"I thought it was a good idea, although it didn't last long," Ham laughed. He ran through the milling crowd, with Masby right behind him, shouting, "Mr. Newspaper Reporter, where are you?"

A comfortably dressed man announced himself in introduction. "I'm Roebo Tuttle, a reporter for the local paper," the stranger said, extending a soft hand to the two youngsters. "Pleased to meet you."

"Just as pleased to meet you, too," Ham greeted. And Masby repeated the greeting as each of the youngsters shook the man's hand.

"I would like to ask a few informal questions if you gentlemen have time," Mr. Tuttle announced, taking a yellow legal pad and sharp pencil from a leather briefcase.

"Anything you wish, sir," Ham said politely, doing his best to be cooperative.

"First of all, give me your names, ages, and addresses," the reporter requested.

"Sure will," Masby Wheddle said with a broad grin that showed a set of strong, even teeth. Then he began to introduce the quartet of contestants. "I'm Masby Wheddle. I'm thirteen, going on fourteen, and this is my brother, Tass. His last name is Wheddle, too, just like mine. He's fifteen, going on sixteen. We live on Blue Domer Creek—right here where we're standing. And. . . ."

"And I'm Ham Sedder," Ham butted in. "I'm thirteen, going on fourteen, too, just like Masby there, and this is my brother, Domer Sedder. He's fifteen, going on sixteen, just like Tass. We're all about the same age and sizes. Me and Domer live over the mountain on Coaley Creek."

"You must be Baggley Sedder's sons," the reporter replied, recognizing the Sedder name. "How did you boys come up with the idea to have a rooster-crowing contest?"

"Big mouth did it," Domer replied.

"Who is that?" the reporter asked.

"Him," Domer grumbled, pointing to Ham. "I hate to cut you short in your interview, but we have to get started." He took his father's watch from his front pocket and asked for silence. As far as he was concerned, the interview was over. The reporter had enough information already to incriminate the brothers. Baggley Sedder would recognize the boys from their names alone—and he should—since they were his sons.

"In order to have our contest, I'll have to ask you all to remain as quiet as possible while the match is under way," Domer began. "We'll use the two-best-out-of-three procedure. We'll time each rooster as he crows. Let's select three impartial judges. Remember to be quiet now. If we have too much of a racket from the crowd, our roosters won't do any serious challenging. Crowing is what we're interested in. So, I ask you again, please remain as quiet and still as possible."

"Great!" Ham screamed, applauding enthusiastically. "Great speech, Domer." His hands smacked together like a beaver's tail striking the still surface of a mountain pond.

"You clown," Domer laughed, slapping his younger brother on the back. "First off," he continued, after the laughter had subsided, "we must select some judges. We want judges that are impartial and don't give a whit about who wins."

"How about Mr. Tuttle?" Masby suggested.

"No, please," the reporter began in protest. "I will have all that I can handle as I write my account of this unusual event. Thanks for considering me, though. It is an honor just to be asked, but I can't judge the contest and write my report, too."

After five minutes of consideration of candidates for judges, an acceptable panel was chosen—since no one else wanted to serve in that capacity.

"All right, folks," Domer continued his role as master of ceremonies for the event, "we've chosen three judges: Ratio Cornfield, Jock Ponders, and Lofe Breading."

The three men smiled as a round of applause echoed about the arena, sparked by the animate Ham Sedder as he clapped with a fury.

"All right, folks, I'll turn it over to Ratio Cornfield," Domer said, bowing to the man.

"Thank you, young man," Ratio Cornfield grunted, clearing his dry throat. "Now, boys, get your roosters. It's time to get started."

Domer Sedder removed his chicken from its cramped quarters and stroked the glossy feathers on its back.

Quietness hovered about the barnyard. Only the hush-hush of an occasional movement, a sniff from someone, or the clearing of a dry throat broke the silence.

Tass Wheddle removed his rooster from its banana-crate cage, while the curious crowd looked on.

When Red Ballard saw the small gray rooster in Tass' hands, he cackled a reminder that he was around, and Sly Muncy cackled an answer right back at Red Ballard.

Ratio Cornfield held the stopwatch ready for the count, if one fowl should decide to challenge the other.

Jock Ponders and Lofe Breading stretched their long necks from each side of Ratio in order to see the face of the watch.

Seconds ticked slowly by as the already-tense crowd grew more apprehensive by the strained waiting.

The tense silence was finally broken as Red Ballard crowed a challenge to the little gray rooster staring quietly back at him.

"Just a fraction over six seconds," Ratio Cornfield said in a loud voice—loud enough for the crowd to hear.

"Oh, boy!" Ham shouted with excitement.

"Quiet, please," Ratio warned, putting his index finger to his lips.

"Sorry," Ham whispered apologetically.

The gray rooster arched his neck and returned the challenge to Red

Ballard.

"Just under six seconds," Ratio informed the contestants.

"Man, that was close!" Domer sighed in relief.

"Oh, you," Tass Wheddle groaned, shaking his clinched fist under his rooster's beak. "Why don't you show us just what you can do?"

Ham was so excited that he could hardly control himself. He was too worked up to be still.

In the second round Red Ballard failed his handlers, giving Tass and Masby Wheddle the opportunity to celebrate.

The third and decisive round came. It brought on a strained silence as the tension grew.

Red Ballard arched his neck and crowed long and loud. "Six and a half seconds!" Ratio exclaimed.

Ham wanted to say something, but he knew that he should remain silent. That was a hard thing for him to do at any time, and at that moment it was even harder.

Sly Muncy crowed shrilly in the stillness. "Six seconds right on the dot. Well, folks, the show is over," Ratio Cornfield announced. "The winner is that big red feller right there." He pointed to Red Ballard.

Ham could no longer control his emotions. He jumped up and down excitedly, laughing as he ran about, slapping the backs of everyone near him.

The crowd applauded the contestants, and at the request of the judges, the roosters were recognized in a long round of applause. Then the judges received recognition for a job well-done, when all they had done was look at the face of a watch while the roosters did all the work.

Ham ran to Ratio Cornfield, the judge who held his father's stopwatch. As he accepted it in his shaking hand, someone in the crowd accidentally bumped his arm and knocked the timepiece from his grasp.

The watch fell to the ground; a rock received the delicate instrument. As it struck the stone, pieces of glass flew in all directions as its crystal was smashed to smithereens.

When Ham picked up the watch, he found that there was no longer a happy tick coming from the interior of what had once been a hard-working little timepiece.

"Ham, you should have been more careful," Domer wailed, taking the watch from his brother's shaking hand. "I know," he continued, "that you were excited. So was I. But now I'm no longer happy about the win." He turned the watch over in his hand. "I hope it doesn't cost more than ten dollars to have it repaired."

"We won, but it will cost us in the long run," Ham lamented, nearing tears, not because of his weak emotions, but because of his undue awkwardness.

The crowd began to disperse, leaving only the contestants and the newspaper reporter.

"I'm sorry that you broke the watch. Here take the ten," Tass Wheddle said, handing the unsteady Ham a ten-dollar bill.

"This little bit of paper is some consolation, but just think of the big limb that Dad has laid up waiting for us when we get home," Ham groaned.

"Maybe your father won't find out about this contest and your breaking his watch before you can have it repaired," the reporter stated, attempting to elevate the spirits of the dejected boys.

"You don't know Dad," Domer replied. "He wouldn't let that watch stop for anything. I doubt if it has stopped once in the last ten years. He winds it as often as each day rolls around. When he goes to wind it tomorrow, he'll find that it's gone."

"We're surely in for it," Ham said, turning to Red Ballard who rooster-talked contentedly. He lifted the cage from its resting place in the shade of the barn. "Let's go take our medicine."

The brothers left the silent reporter and Tass and Masby Wheddle standing in the deserted barnyard.

"We'll have to tell Dad about the accident," Ham broke the silence as the boys walked home.

"I guess so," Domer answered slowly, his mind still hard at work trying to figure a way to amend the misfortune of breaking the watch.

"Let's take the watch down to Warty Broad's jewelry shop and have him fix it. He lives upstairs. We can find him at home today, and maybe he can fix it while we wait for it," Ham suggested.

"That's a good idea," Domer agreed. "Let's give it a try."

They found the little shop and rapped on the upstairs door, waited impatiently for an answer, then explained the reason for their visit as Mr. Broad opened the door and greeted his company.

"No, boys, I can't repair it today," Warty informed the boys. He took the watch, looked it over closely, and shook it to see if he could get it to run. "I'll probably have to order a crystal, and maybe a balance wheel and hair spring. I'm fairly sure that I'll need those parts. There might be other parts damaged, too."

"How long will we have to wait for it?" Ham inquired. "You see, we borrowed it without Dad knowing that he was loaning it to us. He'll expect it to be in the same condition it was in when we borrowed it. He wouldn't loan his watch to anyone—not even the President."

"It will take a week, at least," Warty informed Ham.

"Will ten dollars cover the charges?" Domer asked the little watch tinker, then waited anxiously for an answer.

"I can't say right off, but it'll be in the neighborhood of ten dollars," Warty said, continuing to shake the watch in an effort to make it run.

"Take this money, sir. If there's an extra charge, I'll pay you as soon as I get it," Domer promised, placing the money in the man's hand.

"No! Wait till I complete the repairs before you pay me," Warty protested, refusing the money.

"Take it," Domer insisted. "I might spend it or lose it before you fix that watch, and I definitely need to pay you for fixing it. I've certainly learned something from this little adventure. It doesn't pay to gamble. Dad has told us to never bet on anything."

"I'll let you know when it's ready for you to pick up," Warty told the nervous boys.

"We'll be here every day till you get it repaired," Domer replied. "Come on Ham. Let's go home and hope that Dad won't find out about this."

The boys left the jeweler and plodded down the long stairs.

* * * *

The next few days were slow and nerve-wracking, but the flood of tension from waiting broke loose on Friday with the arrival of the local newspaper, which Baggley Sedder received each week.

"What's this?" Baggley inquired as he scanned the paper's account of the rooster-crowing contest.

"What's what?" Domer asked as he entered the room through the front door. His face was flushed from running in the warmth of the summer day. He held something in his right hand.

Ham grinned all over himself as he saw the little package gripped firmly in his brother's clinched fist.

"This story in the paper says that some Sedder boys and Wheddle boys had a rooster-crowing contest," the father read. "Could my two sons be the Sedder half of that quartet?"

"Yes, Dad," Domer reluctantly admitted.

"And what was the outcome?" Baggley asked.

"Oh, we won the contest," Ham said, getting into the conversation, hoping to give Domer a chance to return the watch to its resting place in the closet.

"What did you win?" Mr. Sedder queried further, pretending to scan other parts of the paper. "Well, I see here that Chalmer Eskers passed away last week."

"Yeah, I heard that, too," Ham said, grasping the opportunity to change the subject.

"Domer, I asked what you won," Baggley stated as Domer neared the closet door. "By the way, what's in that little package in your hand?"

"Oh, just some kidney pills that Mom wanted me to get at the drug-store," Domer answered nervously.

"My watch is in good shape, I hope," Baggley continued, scanning different parts of the paper.

"I hope so," Domer told him. "It should be. You ought to know. When you wound it the last time, was it running then?"

"I didn't wind it the last time," Mr. Sedder remarked. "It wasn't in my pocket. I see here in the paper that a watch was bet against ten dollars, but some unfortunate lad was so nervous over winning that he dropped the watch and broke it. Then it goes on to say here that that same boy fig-ured that it would take all his winnings to cover his losses—meaning his broken watch. Domer, give me a kidney pill, please. My kidneys have been hurtin' a lot lately."

"I'll get you some water so you can take your pill," Ham volunteered.

"Get a big glass," Mr. Sedder directed. "It will take plenty of water to take this pill, but not as much as you boys will need for the dose of medi-cine that I'm fixing to prescribe for you."

"Why didn't you say that you knew that it was us in the contest and that it was your watch that was bet and broken and had to be fixed?" Domer whined.

"I wanted you boys to tell me about it. I surely am disappointed in you," the father said, laying the paper on the coffee table. "You know that I have taught you to always be honest and truthful. I have taught you that lying and stealing are wrong. You lied to me about taking the watch. You stole the watch, you know, even though you thought you were just borrowing it. You gambled, too. I would say that you have been two very bad boys. You can meet me outside." With that assertion he left the room.

"What must I do with these pills—I mean this watch?" Domer asked.

"Put it back where you got it Sunday morning," Baggley said as he descended the steps.

"Look what you got us into," Domer grumbled. "Do you think that Dad would accept an apology and let us off easy this time? He knows that we have learned our lesson, even without this butt busting."

"What do you think?" Ham asked.

"No, he won't," Domer groaned. "I still can't understand why I let you talk me into making a bet on that loud-mouthed chicken. Usually, I'm not swayed easily, but I thought that we had a good chance to make a quick ten dollars, and we would have if you hadn't been so awkward there at the end when you broke the watch. It doesn't pay to gamble, even on a sure thing. I've learned an expensive lesson."

"Yeah, you're right. But anyway, I know now that I have the crowin'est rooster in this part of the country," Ham bragged.

"You and that rooster," Domer said, shoving Ham out the front door.

The Fourth Round

Brother Trankle Cornfield drove his old 1937 Chevrolet pickup truck over the rough mountain road. The vehicle chugged laboriously along in its efforts to reach the top of Rattlesnake Ridge. Fumes filtered through rust holes where the rubber mats were tattered and worn. Gravel, sand, and dried grass covered the floor, leaving an unkempt appearance. The interior of the old vehicle had not received a good cleaning in a long time, even though it was the only form of conveyance the preacher had as he pursued his calling to the ministry. At the top of the mountain, Trankle stopped the truck and got out to survey the peaceful little valley below. From his vantage point, he could see Hen Eggaman's cottage-type abode situated in the middle of a lush meadow.

Hen had built his house near the middle of the field where an abundance of cool, soft, clear water from a mountain spring meandered through its grassy center. Everything was handy for the moonshiner to ply his trade.

The wind stirred the leaves above Brother Trankle as he stood looking down at the peaceful valley. A strand of gray hair tickled his face. He held an old King James Bible in his big hand. "I hope and trust that my efforts are worthwhile. I hope that I do something to change Hen's way of life," the preacher mumbled.

After a moment of silent prayer, Brother Trankle got back in his rattletrap truck and started the descent of the rough mountain road. The gears screamed as he pushed in the worn clutch and released it, causing the gears to grind in an effort to mesh. The automobile was almost worn out but would have to hold together for a few more seasons. The self-proclaimed preacher would have to wait a little longer before he could purchase a newer form of conveyance. Donations at the church were for the upkeep of the church-house. There was no salary for the moderator, as the head of the church was called. The church did not believe in paying the preacher, nor did Brother Trankle, but a little extra money could help him through some trying times. He could use a new truck.

Brother Trankle was on a mission. He saw the need to butt into another man's business, which was unusual for him, but in this case he decided it was necessary and acceptable. He was ready to exert a serious effort to convert this sinner to a new and better way of life. The first round in a bout to rescue a soul from its descent to purgatory was ready to commence.

"Howdy, Hen. How are you this fine morning?" Brother Trankle spoke upon arriving at the moonshiner's house.

"Hey, Trankle!" Hen returned the greeting. "I'm about as fine as the fuzz on a snake's nose. How in the cat hair are you doing on a fine day like this?"

"Well," Brother Trankle began lamely, "I'm just about down in my back since so much of this rheumatiz is going 'round."

"If you feel so bad, what brings you out?" Hen asked, looking straight at his complaining visitor. "I have a cure for your complaints, you know, Trankle. Right here in this jar." He shook the container and watched the liquid bead up on top. "Come in if you can get in. I ain't had time to do much housecleaning. I have more work to do than I can say grace over right at the moment." He kicked an empty box out of his way. "I've got orders to fill, galore. What did you say was the reason for your surprise visit? Want a drink?" he asked, offering the bottle to the preacher.

"No, I don't want a drink. I came over here to try to change your way of life," Brother Trankle began. "I want to help save your soul and stop you from ruining your life, along with the many others that swill your rotten liquor."

"If it wasn't for my efforts to make a good stimulating drink, there would be a bunch of stiff, sore, sick people hobbling around in their efforts to stay on the go," Hen smiled. "Better take a big swig of this toad juice. Might help you, you know."

"Hen," Brother Trankle spoke soberly, "you know that I wouldn't touch a drap of that stuff. You know that I'm a child of God. Why don't you change your ways and become a good Christian. You could be a good man like me."

"What makes you think that I ain't already as good as you?" Hen asked.

"You ain't accepted Christ is the reason why you ain't a good person," Brother Trankle stammered. "You're living the life of a heathen, Hen."

"That's your opinion, and you know what I think of opinions," Hen said, emptying a bag of meal into a huge barrel to be mixed with water, sugar, and yeast to ferment.

"Why don't you give it a try, Hen? Would you?" Brother Trankle pleaded. "I'll kneel with you and help you pray away your sins. We'll ask Him to help you quit sinning. Then we can tear up this old devil's handiwork and get rid of that liquid sin."

"I'll just be dabbered if you will!" Hen blurted out. "I wouldn't pour one drap of my precious brew out. I'm not gonna give the fishworms a good time by pouring it on them." He lifted the container of liquor and took a drink, smacking his lips.

"I'm just trying to help you to see your faults," Brother Trankle lamented.

"Trankle, ol' buddy, do you see your faults, or do you have faults? And about that religion deal of yours—you can throw it in the creek. No, don't do that. It might contaminate my drink. I know what you can do, though. You can take it and stuff it up that old holler tree over there. Look out the window there and you can see it." Hen pointed toward a hollow white oak tree that stood near the creek. "I've been aiming to cut that tree down, but now I've found a good use for it. It should house all the religion that's needed around here."

"I didn't say anything about religion, Hen," Brother Trankle retorted. "I'm talking about salvation. Anyone can have religion, but only the chosen few can have salvation. There's a big difference in the two. One of these days, I hope, you'll see what I'm trying to do for you."

"I'll wait for that day to listen. Now, if you'll excuse me, I have some urgent work to attend to," Hen said sternly. "Good-bye, preacher."

"Let me help you?" Brother Trankle pleaded.

"Good-bye preacher," Hen repeated.

"Let me help save you?" Brother Trankle offered. "You need help more than you can imagine. I can't save you by myself, Hen. Only God can save you, and that is between you and Him, but I can pray with you and help all I can. Maybe I can get one of your feet in the door."

"Good-bye, Trankle. You're wasting your time, and mine, too," Hen declared, stirring the contents in the barrel.

Seeing that his efforts were not reaching the sinner, the preacher bid the moonshiner good-bye. "S'long," he said in parting. "Come and see me."

"Yeah, I'll do that sometime; when I can't handle the old man from below by myself. You can come back, but next time leave that busted religion at home!" Hen stormed.

Brother Trankle drove up the mountain. At the top of the grade he got out and sat on a big moss-covered rock to think. He read a few verses from his Bible and prayed, asking God to send the law into the peaceful valley to stop Hen's dishonest business. After the prayer he descended the steep mountain. At the bottom of the precipice, he parked his dilapidated truck by a fence, took a hoe from a dogwood sapling, and began to hoe the long rows of tobacco plants.

* * * *

A week passed before the preacher was ready to continue the bout with Hen. Even though Hen had won the first round, Brother Trankle would not give up so easily.

Smoke climbed into the sky, indicating that Hen was plying his trade. He wasn't cooking dinner at two o'clock in the afternoon, Trankle reasoned. Though he dreaded the second round, he would face it with determination—win or lose. He arrived at the little distillery shack and peeked through the wide-open window.

Hen Eggaman sat on a keg, his head and shoulders resting against the rough wall. A half-empty jug sat by his feet.

Brother Trankle shook his head and went around to the front of the building. Tears came to the corners of his eyes as he said to himself, "Poor feller, he ain't hurting anybody else—just himself. He don't realize just how foolish he is. Making and drinking that stuff is no pretty sight." He went inside. "Wake up, Hen. You're gonna let your 'shine scorch, and I know that you don't like scorched 'shine," he said.

"Well, I'll be dabbered! Here's the preacher back again," Hen yawned, rubbing the sleep from his eyes. He stretched all over. "Still wanting to tear up my 'still and pour out my good stuff. No, Brother Trankle, you'll never get to do that. As for that religion, you. . . ."

"I know what I can do. I can take my religion and stuff it up that old tree over there," Brother Trankle interrupted. "Is that what you want? Hen, you just won't face reality. You know if you were to die right now, you'd be in the hot spot before daybreak tomorrow morning, and that would be a big nosedive straight down."

"Why don't you quit your yammering?" Hen stated, puttering about the room, trying to ignore the preacher. "I'd be the one going down on my nose, not you."

"Hen, let me read to you what it says about taking of strong drink," Brother Trankle said, taking his well-worn Bible from his overalls pocket.

Hen calmly reached over, lifted the Bible from the preacher's big hand, and threw it into the roaring fire in the furnace. "Just leave it where it is," he warned as Brother Trankle attempted to pluck the book from the furnace, using a stick of firewood.

Brother Trankle began to tremble. That Bible had been in the family for a hundred years. It was given to him by his father. His father had received it from his father. Parting with it in such a manner was more than he could bear. With tears blinding his way, he stumbled from the room and ran headlong up the rough path toward home. "The devil will surely get you, Hen Eggaman, and I want to see that!" Trankle cried. He could hardly see where he was going.

"Don't worry your pretty noggin' so much, Trankle," Hen called to the preacher. "Hey, you forgot your truck!"

Brother Trankle retraced his steps and raced out of the yard, slinging gravels against the building as he left. He had lost another round of the fight, but he was determined to fight on. Maybe someday he would strike a good punch that would enable him to carry through with his plan of attack on the sinner. He knew that he should be patient, one virtue that he had thus far been blessed with, but when working with a character like Hen Eggaman, his patience could easily be torn apart.

* * * *

Another week passed before the battle was resumed. Again Brother Trankle looked down on the peaceful little valley. The warm July morning air stirred the leaves on a hickory tree above the preacher. Birds sang in the trees on the high ridge. Insects chattered and buzzed, while buzzards sailed smoothly along on the warm air currents radiating upward from the hot earth. No smoke rose from the chimney of the little building in the valley. "Wonder what's wrong with Hen. Probably drunk again," Brother Trankle thought aloud.

The third round was coming up. Who would be the winner? Would it last twelve rounds like a boxing match?

Brother Trankle had done a lot of meditating and thinking during the past week. Of the many thoughts he had had, one in particular began to bump against the gray matter of his brain. He needed a new truck and spending money in order to reach out to more people in his ministry. He had noticed the fine churches in town, and the fine automobiles sitting in the parking lots, especially the big sedans parked in front of the parsonages of the preacher-paying churches. Maybe he could reach more people if he had a new automobile. The man had been doing some serious thinking, but the answer to his dilemma still eluded him. If only he could have an outside income, then maybe he could reach a different plane; reach out and grasp something that would put him in a respectable conjunction with other preachers who were filling their churches to the bursting point. His simple approach was not the way to reach an ever-changing world. Maybe he should change with the times, but how could he? His doctrine was a strong doctrine, with no deviations; word for word in the Bible; a fundamentalist through and through. If the scribes wrote the Word through spiritual dictation, then each word was put in there for a purpose. It should be taken as Bible, with no changing to satisfy someone's want to change.

"When I finish my appointment with Hen Eggaman," Brother Trankle mused, "I'll look at my calling with a different perspective. Maybe then I can get a hold of a little money to further my ministry in a more positive way. If I can't reach out one way, I'll reach out in another way—whatever that way may be. But I'll have to take care of first problems first."

The preacher drifted his truck down the mountain in order to save gas. The worn brake shoes cried unmercifully as they tried to grip the spinning outer drums. Metal against metal had little effect in slowing the vehicle. The speed gradually increased, causing two wheels of the truck to rise off the ground as it took the stiff curves at breakneck speed.

Brother Trankle's mind wasn't with his efforts to keep the old truck in the road. He went through the motions of steering in a trance-like state. The wild ride ended as he wheeled the vehicle into the driveway to Hen's house. The brakes stopped their crying as he lifted his heavy foot off the brake pedal.

A silence greeted the preacher as he slowly got out of the truck. He wrinkled his nose, disgusted with the odor reeking the entire yard. The wind whipped the stench to a radius of a hundred yards into the trees and meadow. How could a man stay in the same building with the odor of the fermenting barrels and the remains of a run poured into a trough, tilted at an angle to let the slop flow outside.

Hen Eggaman lay on the bed—asleep.

Brother Trankle poked the sleeping figure. "Wake up, Hen," he ordered. "You're sleeping away the biggest part of the day. Look at the sun—striaght overhead—and you're sleeping like a crock of hominy."

"I'm taking a holiday break," Hen groaned, stretching the sleep away.

"How come you're taking a holiday today?" Brother Trankle queried.

"Don't you know what day of the month today is?" Hen asked.

"It's the fourth. Why, I keep up with the calendar, but what's so special about the fourth?" Brother Trankle wanted to know.

"The fourth is a legal holiday." Hen stated. "It's the Fourth of July."

"I remember it just as well as you do. I reckon it just skipped my mind, though, since I'm so troubled and worried these days, and on account of you," Brother Trankle snapped. "Have you thought about the things I've been trying to warn you about here lately?" he asked, changing the subject. He dreaded to hear the answer.

"Well," Hen began as he straightened up, his weasel-like face growing into a short smile—a wicked smile, "I just thought about them while you were in sight. But, when you disappeared amongst the trees on the hill up there, they left me. The other night they were brought to my mind. I had a horrible nightmare. It bothered me a day or so, but I'm all right now."

"What kind of dream did you have, Hen?" Brother Trankle asked, his curiosity rising. "Maybe I can help you to understand it."

"Now, don't try to be one of those Bible prophets who did all the miracles and foreseeings for the sinning world," Hen stated. "Trankle, I'm getting fed up—up to here." He pointed toward his Adam's apple with his index finger. "Now, you've been here moaning about me being a sinner, and so on. I'm getting mighty tired of your blabbering around about what a good man you are and how mean and wicked I am."

"I'm just trying to help a lost soul find the right road to walk," Brother Trankle spoke solemnly.

"Since you would like to hear my dream," Hen began, "and now that I'm taking a day off, I'll relate it to you. Drag up a chair and listen to this."

The preacher sat down.

"I guess you remember the day I burnt up your Bible," Hen said.

Brother Trankle slumped in his chair. "I'll allus remember that awful thing that you did," he wailed.

"Well, that night I had this crazy dream," Hen continued. "I could see all kinds of things. I saw Jesus with the cross come out of my 'still furnace, right into the room with me. A bunch of people came in and said that they were gonna nail Him on that cross, and anybody else that stood in their way. Preacher, I saw you holding to His right hand, trying to pull Him out of the grip of the crucifiers. You and Him went out that door and wouldn't even speak to me. I began to cry and asked you and Jesus to come back. You wouldn't. I started getting hotter and hotter. My hands even got hot, and pretty soon I was hot all over, but my right hand the most. Then I woke up all of a sudden. While thrashing 'round in my sleep, my hand fell against the furnace. I have a good blister where I was fried to a turn." He held his hand out for the preacher's inspection. "A man can dream some silly things."

Brother Trankle began his speech slowly. "You mean to sit there and tell me that you didn't even worry about such a dream?"

"Shucks, no! I don't worry about foolish dreams," Hen said flatly. "I just worry about my 'still and making money. Dreams are just your imagination working while you sleep and rest for your work the next day. You don't work, though. You just shout and holler and sweat a lot while you preach to your congregation of goofs like me. Not many people will gather around to hear me beller my fool head off."

"Hen, you should take heed to your dream," Brother Trankle warned. "You drink that old whiskey all the time. It's a caution that you ain't dead. You probably stay broke all the time, too."

"Trankle, let me tell you a little secret," Hen said. "I have better than twenty thousand dollars in the bank. Gettin' it wasn't too hard. I just have to be quiet and sly with my trips to town and back, and watch out who I do business with. There's no reason for me to tell you this, but I thought I'd tell you anyway, since you think I'm broke all the time."

"I'd never have thought it, the way you drink so much," Brother Trankle spoke in awe.

"Well, I have," Hen stated. "You could be in the same shape, if you would listen to me instead of wanting everybody else to listen to your hollering and squawking. You could be making more in a month with me than you could make in a whole year at the rate of your income. I make some good money. It ain't honest, but I'm doing no more wrong than you are."

"How's that?" Brother Trankle asked, showing surprise with the blunt accusation.

"Well, you raise 'backer," Hen began. "The people chew, dip, and smoke it. Doctors say that 'backer is harmful to the body—causes cancer of the lungs and mouth. You say that my product is harmful. I suppose it is. But that doesn't make it right for you to raise your 'backer and hurt people, and me wrong for making 'shine and distributing it about the country amongst my customers."

Hen had some good points that grabbed the preacher where it hurt. Those points made a temptation rise in the preacher's mind, but the determination to show his point of right and wrong to Hen caused him to fight the enticement from his thoughts.

"I'd be willing to let bygones be bygones and take you in as a partner," Hen offered. "I could use a little help with my work. I can move every drap I can make. The market is wide-open. Although the law is snooping around to close me down, I have a booming business, and the demand is more than I can keep up with. I need some help."

The preacher fought with a rising temptation as his mind wandered back to his problem: he needed a new truck! There was no way for him to earn enough money to buy a truck. Maybe he could get the money from Hen, in the form of a loan, of course. "No, I can't!" he said aloud to his conscience. His wandering mind had almost led him to the breaking point, to the point where he would be of no use to God, man, or even to himself.

"No, you can't what?" Hen wanted to know.

"Just thinking, I guess," Brother Trankle replied, rubbing his foot on the floor.

"Are you thinking about my proposal?" Hen asked the nervous preacher.

"I'd better be going, Hen," Brother Trankle said, hurriedly leaving the room.

"Think it over, preacher," Hen called after the confused minister.

* * * *

Two days of worry and torment accompanied Brother Trankle. He could not forget his last visit with Hen. The need for a new truck grew until it was demanding in his mind, almost a necessity. *Almost* a necessity? It *was* a necessity, but he couldn't accept Hen's offer to join him in his dishonest business. He asked God to forgive him for even considering the wicked idea. He could not get a justifiable answer from God. Had he gone too far already? He would talk to Hen on the matter. He had tried to change Hen's sinning ways. Now, he would have to go to Hen for help. He wanted Hen to shame him for stooping so low, for thinking of doing something wrong. Hen would just laugh. He wouldn't care if Brother Trankle should break over. There would be no pity from that man.

Brother Trankle parked his truck in the driveway and entered the house without knocking. He had been to see Hen so often that there was no use to knock before entering.

"Howdy, Trankle," Hen greeted the minister.

"Howdy, Hen," Brother Trankle returned the salutation.

"Been 'specting you. My nose has been itching all morning," Hen said, without looking up from his work. "'Spected you before now, though. Where've you been so long, and what is on your ever-loving mind? More preaching, I suppose."

"Not this time," Brother Trankle replied shyly. He did not feel uncomfortable while in the presence of Hen and his work.

"You can see that I'm covered up this morning, so state your business and scram before I lose my temper and chuck you out on your thick head," Hen threatened. "I'm expecting company this morning, and I sure don't want you to preach to them. I have to move some merchandise."

"I came over to see if I could borrow some money," Brother Trankle began lamely. "I need a new truck so I can reach more people in my ministry."

"Forget about borrowing money from me, Trankle," Hen stated flatly. "I wouldn't loan money to my brother. I'll let you buy in as a partner, as I offered before. No loans, though. How much money do you have with you?"

"Why do you ask that?" Brother Trankle wanted to know.

"How much do you have?" Hen continued.

Brother Trankle took a wrinkled, draw-topped purse from his pocket, opened it, and shook out a small roll of bills. "I have twenty-seven dollars," he reported. As he laid the last one-dollar bill on the table, Hen began to speak in an unknown tongue.

"Let me tell you what I'll do," Hen began. "I'll let you buy into my business with that pile of money."

Brother Trankle had already returned the money to the leather pouch.

He tied the strings as he pursed his lips in a whistling pucker, thinking about Hen's proposition. Confusion stepped into the picture. What should he do?

Hen helped the preacher make a decision by saying, "This load will net nearly a thousand dollars. That's a big sum of money, the way I look at it. You could have half of this run just as a partnership gift from me. That five hundred dollars will make a down payment on a new truck. What do you say? The offer might not last long."

"It sounds tempting, but I just can't buy in," Brother Trankle replied.

"Suit yourself," Hen said. He continued. "You can be my silent partner. You can help buy all the stuff that we need. I'll make it into produce. I might need a little help once in a while, but I can hire someone to help me—at your expense, of course."

"If you can make me a silent partner, I might go along with you. But, if you intend to mention my name to anyone who might know me, the partnership will be liquidated. Is that clear?" Brother Trankle asked, his voice shaking. He wanted it understood that his name was not to be mentioned to anyone. "Brother Toby Hood's wife runs that cafe in town. She sells beer and stuff like that, so I can sell a little 'shine—as a silent partner, of course—and it won't be any worse than what Brother Toby and his wife's doing."

"You're right there, Trankle," Hen agreed, a broad smile cracking his face.

Brother Trankle opened the wrinkled purse and removed the wad of bills. He handed the money to Hen Eggaman, demanding a promise to keep his name a secret before the money changed hands.

"Rush Lightfoot will be here sometime tomorrow to get a load. You're going to get a big payday the second day in the business. Don't worry about Rush. He's a reliable feller," Hen said.

"I've never heard of Rush Lightfoot. Does he live around here?" Brother Trankle wanted to know.

"He goes around and contracts a load from each of the local producers, then goes back and makes arrangements for delivery and payment," Hen explained. "I've found him to be a reliable person. He's done right by me. He slips me a few extra dollars now and then. That helps buy more ingredients. You'll like him a lot. He might slip you some extra money once in a while."

"He's not supposed to know that I'm part of the operation," Brother

Trankle replied, concern showing in his wrinkled face.

"It won't matter if he knows. He ain't from around here," Hen stated. "Our partnership won't matter a whit to him. He wouldn't care one way or t'other. Relax, man! You're gonna make it all right. Be here bright and early in the morning. I'll divvy up your part of the take, and then you can commence to shop for a new truck."

"Will anybody see me when I come over?" Brother Trankle asked. "I don't want to be recognized. I have a flock to feed, you know. If they were to find out that I am dilly-dallying in something like this, I would lose all their attention. They would most likely church me—throw me out of the church. I can't take a big chance like that."

"They don't pay you anything to preach to them. So what right do they have to dictate to you what you should do or not do?" Hen asked.

"Well, they don't have anything to say about how I run my affairs outside the church," Brother Trankle acknowledged. "But they can church me if they find out about my shady side of the new page in my life. Are you sure I'll be undetected as your silent partner?"

"Nobody'll know that you have anything to do with the operation. Even if they did, it would be none of their business," Hen assured his new partner.

"Well, that's good," Brother Trankle uttered. "I'll see you in the morning."

With Hen's assurance that he would remain a secret partner, the preacher left.

* * * *

"I hope you ain't here for the fourth round in our battle for conversion. If you are, it's the final round of our battle, Brother Trankle," Hen said as the preacher entered the room. "I'm ready to quit this business and dedicate myself to the work of the Lord."

"Man, what are you talking about?" Brother Trankle stammered. "What do you mean about quitting? Wait just one minute! I just bought into your business and I want to reap some rewards from it."

"No, Brother Trankle, I can see your ploy by agreeing to join me in my sinnin'," Hen said. "You knew that I would change when I saw how earnest you were in trying to convert me to a Christian way of life. Now I see just what you were getting at. You wanted me to think that you would stoop to my level to change me."

"No, Hen, I didn't do it that way," Brother Trankle moaned. "I really need that truck. I've got to do something. I don't want to lose my chance to get something new to drive. I've already lost my dignity by agreeing to enter your way of life. I sure don't want to lose everything else."

"Brother Trankle, I had that same dream again last night," Hen stated. "It was even worse this time. I have to stop this way of life. I was up all night—with no sleep at all. I wanted to give you the pleasure of taking an axe and hacking that boiler and thumping keg into smithereens. You can bash the working barrels apart and watch the fermenting mash run out of here. Here's the axe. Start chopping." He offered the axe to the bewildered preacher.

"Wait, Hen. We had an agreement. We're partners in this deal," Brother Trankle said, refusing to take the axe. "Let's sit down and talk about this. You just had a dream—anybody can dream—but that doesn't mean that you have to pay heed to it. Dreams are just the mind imagining things while you're flat on your back all sacked out snoozing. I know that you aren't going to pay attention to a dream."

The men heard an automobile as it descended the winding mountainous road. The drone of the engine grew louder as the car came nearer.

Brother Trankle moved nervously about the room like a caged fox. He wanted to run, but he didn't know which direction to take. The only exit was through the door, or maybe the window. He would be seen if he took either exit. He was trapped with no way out, and it was too late to flee. He would have to face whatever occurred.

"You stay in here," Hen cautioned as he prepared to leave the building. "I'll get rid of them. Then we can commence to tear up this devil's handiwork."

"Let's sell them the brew. Then we can tear up the 'still if you're crazy enough to pour a fortune down a crawdad hole," Brother Trankle wailed, protesting his friends decision to destroy the whisky.

"No, Brother Trankle, I'm gonna wipe the slate clean and then start all over again—on the right path this time." Hen said. "You sure are a persuasive preacher. You just won't give up when you get on the scent of a sinner. You hang in there like a good foxhound. I tell you flat; the acting you did when you wanted to buy into my business was the thing that showed me that you were earnest about caring for my soul. I can never repay you for what you did for me, if I live to be a hundred years old."

"I wasn't acting about needing money," Brother Trankle said. "I really need money, and you should sell what you've already made. You've paid for the ingredients, so you should get your money back. I've got twenty-seven dollars invested, and I would like to see some interest on that investment."

"You have to be a very dedicated preacher to act that well," Hen said. "I certainly admire you for your faith and dedication for the Lord's cause."

The automobile stopped outside and a man got out. "Hello, in there!" he called from the yard.

"You stay in here, Brother Trankle," Hen whispered. "Howdy, strangers," he spoke, stepping through the open door.

"Sell them the brew, Hen. Please sell them the brew," Brother Trankle begged. "Just for me, Hen!" he whispered through the open door.

"What can I do for you this fine morning?" Hen asked, descending the steps.

A well-dressed man and an ill-clad local stood at the gate in the paling fence.

"Hen Eggaman?" the stranger spoke, studying the bewildered face of his host.

"Yes, I'm Hen Eggman, but I don't know you," Hen replied, cautiously approaching the gate. "I know your friend there, though."

"Todd Ratio here," the stranger said, extending his hand in greeting. "Rush Lightfoot was under the weather and couldn't be here, so I was called in to fill his job today. Do you have everything ready?"

"What do you mean by that?" Hen questioned, becoming more cautious. The stranger did not look like the type of runner he had always done business with. He had no intentions of selling his last batch of brew to a stranger. He had no intentions of selling it, period.

"Boots will load up while we take care of the financial end of the deal," Todd Ratio said, motioning for the derelict to carry out his command.

"You don't understand, sir," Hen groaned, "I have nothing for him to load up."

"We'll just look inside," Ratio snapped, reaching for the gate.

"You can't go into my house, sir," Hen protested as he held the gate latch. "No one goes into my house without an invitation, and I ain't inviting you in."

"We'll go in," the stranger vowed, producing an officer's badge, waving his hand in a gesturing motion.

Several uniform-clad officers emerged from the woods behind the house.

"Mister, I ain't in the business any longer," Hen declared. "You see, I just got religion with Preacher Trankle Cornfield. He's in the house waiting for you all to leave so we can cut up my 'still and pour out all the devil's juices on the ground. If you'll leave us alone, we can get on with our chore, and you won't have to worry about me anymore. I tell you, I just got religion, sir!"

"Yeah, and Ol' Coaley just gave birth to his first litter of pups, too," the officer laughed. "Come on men," he ordered. "Mr. Eggaman, I have all the legal papers I need to search your property. Open the gate."

Brother Trankle Cornfield paced nervously about the room like a caged animal. When he heard the officer's order to search the building, he raised his eyes toward the ceiling and asked rather lamely, "Will you forgive me Lord? Sorry I let You down." Tears welled up in his eyes, overflowed, and streamed down his face. He sat down to wait for the officers to enter the building.